Buffy the Vampire Slayer

The Script Book

Season Two, Volume Three

Simon Pulse

New York   London   Toronto   Sydney   Singapore

Historian's Note: These teleplays represent the original shooting scripts for each episode; thus we have preserved any typos and misattributions. The scripts may include dialogue or even full scenes that were not in the final broadcast version of the show because they were cut due to length. Also, there may be elements in the broadcast that were added at a later date.

First Simon Pulse edition November 2002

SIMON PULSE
An imprint of Simon & Schuster
Children's Publishing Division
1230 Avenue of the Americas
New York, NY 10020

Printed in the United States of America
10 9 8 7 6 5 4 3 2 1

Library of Congress Control Number 2002110983

ISBN 0-689-85491-9

BUFFY THE VAMPIRE SLAYER

"Surprise"

Written By

Mari Noxon

Directed By

Michael Lange

<u>SHOOTING SCRIPT</u>

November 17, 1997 (WHITE)

BUFFY THE VAMPIRE SLAYER

"Surprise"

CAST LIST

BUFFY SUMMERS........................... Sarah Michelle Gellar
XANDER HARRIS........................... Nicholas Brendon
RUPERT GILES........................... Anthony S. Head
WILLOW ROSENBERG....................... Alyson Hannigan
CORDELIA CHASE........................ Charisma Carpenter
ANGEL................................. David Boreanaz

JOYCE SUMMERS.........................*Kristine Sutherland
JENNY CALENDAR........................*Robia La Morte
SPIKE.................................*James Marsters
DRUSILLA..............................*Juliet Landau
OZ....................................*Seth Green
DALTON................................*Eric Saiet
HARMONY...............................
GYPSY MAN.............................*Vincent Schiavelli
THE JUDGE.............................*Brian Thompson

BUFFY THE VAMPIRE SLAYER

"Surprise"

SET LIST

INTERIORS

SUNNYDALE HIGH SCHOOL
    HALL
    LIBRARY
        GILES' OFFICE
    LOUNGE
    MS. CALENDAR'S CLASSROOM
BUFFY'S HOUSE
    BUFFY'S BEDROOM
    HALLWAY
    KITCHEN
THE BRONZE
ANGEL'S APARTMENT
    HALL OUTSIDE ANGEL'S APARTMENT
FACTORY
CALENDAR'S CAR
*GILES' CAR

EXTERIORS

SUNNYDALE HIGH SCHOOL
CALENDAR'S CAR
THE BRONZE
    ALLEY BEHIND BRONZE
LOADING DOCK
    WATER
SHIP YARD
SEWER TUNNEL
STREET

"Surprise"

TEASER

1   INT.   BUFFY'S BEDROOM - NIGHT   1

     It's late. All is dark and peaceful. BUFFY stirs in her
     sleep, wakes. Reaches for a glass of water on her night
     stand, finds it empty. A beat. She climbs out of bed-

2   INT. HALLWAY - NIGHT   2

     Still half-asleep, Buffy pads down the hallway. From the
     shadows behind her emerges DRUSILLA, ripe, carnivorous -
     blood staining her mouth. A truly horrifying sight.

     Dru stalks Buffy - is a heartbeat away from grabbing her when
     Buffy senses something and turns.

     There is nothing there. Buffy shrugs it off, moves to the
     bathroom door. She opens it and enters-

3   INT. THE BRONZE - NIGHT   3

     Buffy wanders in, still in her pajamas. The MUSIC is
     haunting, otherworldly-

     WILLOW is at a table, having coffee with a MONKEY - who wears
     a little hat and a vest. She turns and waves. Buffy,
     puzzled, waves back.

     Buffy turns and sees JOYCE, who is drinking coffee out of a
     large cup and saucer. Joyce looks concerned - addresses
     Buffy.

                         JOYCE
               Do you really think you're ready,
               Buffy?

                         BUFFY
               What?

     CLOSE ON JOYCE'S HANDS

     As the saucer slips from her grasp. The plate falls to the
     ground and shatters.

     ON BUFFY

     Who looks from the broken plate back to her mother - but
     JOYCE IS GONE.

                                                          CONTINUED

3 CONTINUED: 3

Buffy turns again, wanders to the dance floor - which is
alive with sexual energy. Couples writhe sensuously to the
music - totally entwined, into each other - oblivious to her.

The crowd parts and Buffy sees ANGEL on the other side of the
dance floor. They meet eyes - smile. Through all the
oddness - it is a moment of true connection, love. They move
toward each other.

Just as Buffy is about to reach Angel, DRUSILLA appears again
behind him. Dru STAKES ANGEL in the back - so swiftly and
suddenly that Buffy can't act in time to save him.

                    BUFFY (cont'd)
          Angel!

Buffy reaches for him.

CLOSE ON THEIR HANDS

Buffy's hand touches Angel's - AND IT CRUMBLES TO ASH.

ON BUFFY AND ANGEL

She looks up at ANGEL - makes a moment of desperate eye
contact before he EXPLODES INTO DUST. Now DRUSILLA is fully
revealed behind him - leering. She addresses Buffy,
relishing every moment of her suffering.

                    DRUSILLA
          Happy Birthday, Buffy.

                                        SMASH CUT TO:

4 INT. BUFFY'S BEDROOM - NIGHT   4

Buffy BOLTS up from her bed, waking in horror from her DREAM.
She's panicked, sweating...

                                        BLACK OUT.

                    END OF TEASER

ACT ONE

5 INT. HALLWAY OUTSIDE ANGEL'S APARTMENT - DAY   5

Buffy knocks at Angel's door. A little tentative.

                    BUFFY
          Angel?

A beat - then, muffled-

                    ANGEL (O.C.)

          Hold on...

He opens the door. Just out of bed. Nicely rumpled.

                    ANGEL
          Hey...   Everything okay?

They move inside.

6 INT. ANGEL'S APARTMENT - DAY   6

The shades are drawn. It's dark as a tomb. Good thing, too.

                    BUFFY
          That's what I was going to ask you.
          You're okay, right?

                    ANGEL
          Sure. I'm fine. What's up?

Buffy moves into his arms, relieved. Angel's happy to hold
her, if a bit confused.

                    BUFFY
          I had this dream. Drusilla was
          alive. It was awful-

                    ANGEL
          What happened?

                    BUFFY
          She killed you. Right in front of
          me. I saw the whole thing.

Angel strokes her, trying to soothe.

                    ANGEL
          It was just a dream. It wasn't real.

                                              CONTINUED

6 CONTINUED: 6

                         BUFFY
               But it felt so real.

                         ANGEL
               It wasn't. Here I am.

Buffy moves away from him now, her anxiety mounting.

                         BUFFY
               This happened before, Angel. That
               dream I had about the Master... It
               came true.

                         ANGEL
               Still, not every dream you have comes
               true. I mean, what else did you
               dream last night? Can you remember?

Buffy thinks, then-

                         BUFFY
               That... Giles and I opened an office
               supply warehouse in Las Vegas.

                         ANGEL
               You see my point.

                         BUFFY
               Yeah. But, I mean, what if Drusilla
               is alive? We never saw her body.

                         ANGEL
               She's not. But even if she was -
               we'd deal.

He moves to her. Draws her back into his arms.

                         BUFFY
               But, what if-

Angel silences her with a kiss. Tense at first, Buffy
relaxes into it. The intensity grows fast. Finally-

                         ANGEL
               What if what?

                         BUFFY
               Sorry. Were we talking?

They kiss some more. The bed in the corner entices. They
both feel it - glance there - but don't go there.

                                                      CONTINUED

> BUFFY (cont'd)
> I... have to get to school.

> ANGEL
> I know.

And they kiss some more.

> BUFFY
> God. You feel-

> ANGEL
> You have to go to school...

Still kissing, Angel picks her up and moves her to the front door. Now they kiss against the door. Finally pull back.

> BUFFY
> Alright. This is me.

Buffy opens the door, but pauses for one last kiss. Then-

> ANGEL
> You still haven't told me what you
> want for your birthday.

> BUFFY
> Surprise me.

> ANGEL
> Okay. I will...

They smile. Neither one wants to end the moment.

> BUFFY
> This was nice. I like you first
> thing in the morning-

> ANGEL
> It's bed time for me.

> BUFFY
> Then I like you at bed time.

She realizes how that sounds. Stammers-

> BUFFY (cont'd)
> I mean... You - know what I mean...

> ANGEL
> I think so.
>   (then)
> What do you mean?

6 CONTINUED: (3)   6

                    BUFFY
          That I... I like seeing you And
          the part at the end of the night when
          we say goodbye, it's... getting
          harder.

Buffy waits for an agonizing beat before he responds.   Then-

                    ANGEL
          Yeah. It is.

They just look at each other. Afraid to say any more.

                                        PRELAP:

                    WILLOW (V.O.)
          "I like you at bed time?" You
          actually said that?

7 EXT. SUNNYDALE HIGH - DAY   7

   Buffy and Willow are walking toward school together.

                    BUFFY
          I know. I know.

                    WILLOW
          Man. That's - I don't know, that's
          moxie or something!

                    BUFFY
          Totally unplanned. It just came out.

                    WILLOW
          And he was into it? He wants to see
          you at bed time, too?

Buffy stops walking. Suddenly feeling the weight of this.

                    BUFFY
          Yeah. I think he does. I mean, he's
          cool about it-

                    WILLOW
          Of course he is. Cause' he's cool.
          He would never, you know-

                    BUFFY
          Push.

                    WILLOW
          Right. He's not the type.

                                        CONTINUED

7 CONTINUED: 7

                    BUFFY
          Willow. What am I going to do?

                    WILLOW
          What do you want to do?

                    BUFFY
          Well... Want isn't always the right
          thing... To do, I mean. To act on
          want can be wrong.

                    WILLOW
          True.

                    BUFFY
          But, to not act on want. You could
          watch your whole life pass you by-

                    WILLOW
          Carpe diem. You told me that once.

                    BUFFY
          Seize the fish?

                    WILLOW
          Not carp. Carpe. It means seize the
          day.

                    BUFFY
          Oh. Right.
               (a long beat)
          I think we're going to... seize it,
          Will. Sooner or later. Once you get
          to a certain point - seizing is sort
          of inevitable.

This sinks in. They start to walk again - slowly.

                    WILLOW
          Wow.

                    BUFFY
          Yeah.

                    WILLOW
          Wow...

Buffy notices OZ, guitar in hand, walking ahead.

                    BUFFY
          Ooh, speaking of wow potential,
          there's Oz. What are we thinking?
          Any sparkage there?

                                                      CONTINUED

> WILLOW
> (glowing a bit)
> He's nice. I like his hands.

> BUFFY
> Ooh, fixation on insignificant
> detail. Definite crush sign.

> WILLOW
> I don't know, though. I mean, he is
> a senior...

> BUFFY
> You think he's too old cuz he's a
> senior? Please. My boyfriend had a
> bicentennial.

> WILLOW
> That's true, I guess... I just...

> BUFFY
> You can't spend the rest of your life
> waiting for Xander to wake up and
> smell the hottie. Make a move. Do
> the talking thing.

> WILLOW
> What if the talking thing becomes the
> awkward silence thing?

> BUFFY
> You won't know unless you try. Come
> on, Will - seize the fish!

Buffy smiles, moves on ahead. Leaving Willow to her task.

ON BUFFY

As she passes on OLD, DARK-SKINNED MAN who lurks near the
school. His dress has a slightly ETHNIC flair. He watches
her enter the building, then moves off - unnoticed.

ON WILLOW AND OZ

Will gathers her courage as she catches up with OZ. He's
pleased to see her. In his Oz-ian way.

> WILLOW
> Hey.

> OZ
> Hey.

7 CONTINUED: (3)   7

                         WILLOW
                    (re: guitar case)
               Do you have a... a gig tonight?

                         OZ
               Practice. The band's kind of moving
               towards this new sound where we suck.
               So, practice.

                         WILLOW
               I think you guys sound good.
                    (shyly)
               I bet you've got a lot of groupies.

                         OZ
               It happens. But I'm living groupie-
               free nowadays. I'm clean.

                         WILLOW
               Oh.

                         OZ
               I'm gonna ask you if you wanna go out
               tomorrow night. I'm actually kind of
               nervous about it. It's interesting.

                         WILLOW
               Oh. Well, if it helps at all, I'm
               gonna say yes.

                         OZ
               It helps. It adds a comfort zone.
               You wanna go out tomorrow night?

                         WILLOW
                    (remembers)
               I can't!

                         OZ
               I like that you're unpredictable.

                         WILLOW
               It's Buffy's birthday and we're
               throwing her a surprise party.

                         OZ
               That's okay.

                         WILLOW
               But, you could come. If you wanted.

                         OZ
               Don't wanna crash...

                                             CONTINUED

7 CONTINUED: (4)   7

> WILLOW
> No, that's fine. You could be my...
> date.

> OZ
> All right. I'm in.

He takes off, Willow standing in place, a little shocked.

> WILLOW
> I said date...

8 INT. SCHOOL HALLWAY - DAY   8

COREDELIA's at her locker. XANDER hangs around, trying to
look like he's not hanging around.

> XANDER
> So, Buffy's party. Manana.

> CORDELIA
> Right. Just because she's "miss save
> the world" we have to make a big
> deal. I have to cook and everything.

> XANDER
> You're cooking?

> CORDELIA
> I'm chips and dips girl.

> XANDER
> Horrors. All that opening and
> stirring.

> CORDELIA
> And shopping and carrying.

> XANDER
> You should have a person who does
> such things for you.

> COREDELIA
> That's what I've been saying to my
> father. But does he listen?

Xander leans in. They talk in hushed tones.

> XANDER
> So, you're going. I'm going. Should
> we - you know - go?

                                                        CONTINUED

8 CONTINUED: 8

A long beat.

                         CORDELIA
               Why?

                         XANDER
               I don't know... This thing. With
               us? Despite our better judgement -
               it keeps happening. Maybe we should
               just admit that we're dating-

                         COREDLIA
               Groping in a broom closet is not
               dating. You don't call it a date
               until the guy spends money.

                         XANDER
               Fine. I'll spend - then we'll grope.
               Whatever. It's just some kind of
               whacked that we feel we have to hide
               from all our friends-

                         CORDELIA
               Well, of course you want to tell
               everybody. You have nothing to be
               ashamed of. I, on the other hand,
               have everything to be ashamed of-

                         XANDER
               Know what? 'Nuff said. Forget it.
               Must have been my multiple
               personality guy talking. I call him
               Idiot Jed, Glutton for Punishment-

He moves off. Cordelia closes her locker, catches up to him.

                         CORDELIA
               Let me... Think about it. Can I
               pick out your clothes?

                         XANDER
               For the party?

                         CORDELIA
               For pretty much... every day.

She walks off. Xander watches her, chagrined, then sees
GILES in the-

9 INT. SCHOOL LOUNGE - DAY   9

Xander moves to him.

                                                        CONTINUED

9 CONTINUED: 9

> GILES
> Good morning. I trust that
> everything is in order for the party.

> XANDER
> Absolutely. Ready to get down, you
> funky party weasel?

Giles sees BUFFY and MS. CALENDAR approaching.

> GILES
> Ah. Here comes Buffy. Remember -
> discretion is the better part of
> valor...

> XANDER
> You could have just gone - "shhhh."
> Are all you Brits such drama queens?

Giles would respond, but Buffy and Ms. Calendar have now
joined them. Xander turns to Buffy-

> XANDER (cont'd)
> Buffy! I feel a pre-birthday
> spanking coming on-

Buffy gives Xander a look that would melt steel.

> JENNY
> I'd - curb that impulse, Xander.

> XANDER
> Check. Cancel spanking.

> GILES
> What's the matter, Buffy? You look
> fatigued.

> BUFFY
> Rough night. I had a dream that
> Drusilia was alive - and she killed
> Angel. It really spun me. I even
> went by Angel's on the way to school
> to make sure he was okay-

> XANDER
> There's a line I haven't tried. "I
> just dropped by to see if you're
> dead." It says caring. Concerned.
> Smootchies guaranteed.

>   BUFFY
>   Please. I didn't go over there for
>   smootchies-
>   (then)
>   Well. When I found out he was okay
>   I was relieved, and so, naturally...
>   (then)
>   Someone stop me.

>   JENNY
>   (obliging)
>   So, Angel's alright?

>   BUFFY
>   Yeah, but... I've just got this bad
>   feeling. This wasn't a normal dream.

>   GILES
>   You feel it was more of a portent?

>   BUFFY
>   I don't know. I don't want to start
>   a big freak-out over nothing-

>   GILES
>   Still. We should be on alert. If
>   Drusilla is alive then we may be
>   facing a cataclysmic state of affairs-

>   XANDER
>   (to Giles)
>   Again. So many words. Can't you
>   just say we'd be in trouble?

>   GILES
>   Go to class, Xander.

>   XANDER
>   Gone.

He starts to move away. Stops.

>   XANDER (cont'd)
>   Notice the economy of phrasing.
>   "Gone." It's simple. Direct.

And he's off.

>   BUFFY
>   I guess I should get gone, too.

9 CONTINUED: (3)   9

                          GILES
              Don't worry yourself unduly, Buffy.
              This could be nothing.

                          BUFFY
              I know. I should keep my slayer cool
              and all, but, it's Angel. Which
              automatically equals maxi-wig.

And she heads to class. Calendar and Giles watch her go -
then move down the hall toward the library. Giles'
expression now betrays the fact that he is more concerned
than he let on.

                          JENNY
              What? You really think Buffy's
              having premonitions?

                          GILES
              It's possible-

10 INT. LIBRARY - DAY   10

Calendar and Giles enter - continuing their talk.

                          JENNY
              I guess it makes sense. I mean, all
              of Buffy's senses are heightened.
              Why should her intuition be different?

                          GILES
              Precisely. It's not unheard of for
              the Slayer to start having prophetic
              dreams and visions as she approaches
              adulthood-

                          JENNY
              Adulthood? Buffy's seventeen
              tomorrow, Giles. Don't rush her.

                          GILES
              I'm not the one rushing her. While
              I'm loathe to say it, the fact is -
              the Slayer rarely lives into her
              mid-twenties. It follows that she'd
              exhibit sign of maturity early on.
              Her whole life-cycle is accelerated.

                                                        CONTINUED

10 CONTINUED: 10

                         JENNY
              Still, you should be careful about
              treating her like a grown-up.
              Like - this thing with Angel. Have
              you even talked to her about it?

                         GILES
              I - I suppose I try not to pry.

                         JENNY
              Maybe you should, a little. The way
              she talks - it's clear she has
              intense feelings for him-

                         GILES
              Well, yes. They're friends-

                         JENNY
              They're more than friends and you
              know it.

A beat as this sinks in.

                         GILES
              I'm not her father, Jenny.

                         JENNY
              She looks up to you. She'll never
              actually say that, but she does. And
              I just think, at her age, it's easy
              to get in over your head. She could
              make some bad choices here. Trust me
              on this one.

                         GILES
              I'll keep an eye to it. Right now
              I'm worried enough trying to think of
              the right birthday present.

11 INT. FACTORY - NIGHT   11

    CLOSE ON: A LARGE AND ORNATE CAST IRON BOX.

    DALTON, the vampire transcriber, arrives at the door under
    the balcony laden down with the box. It is rectangle shaped,
    but has an odd peg and groove device at one end - as though
    it is meant to fit with another piece.

                         DALTON
              I have your package.

    A voice emerges from the shadows.

                                                          CONTINUED

11 CONTINUED: 11

> SPIKE (O.C.)
> Just put it on the table. Near the
> other gifts.

Dalton moves away as SPIKE ROLLS out of a dark corner of the
factory. He's in a WHEELCHAIR, disabled from the accident at
the church - deathly pale and scarred from burns.

> SPIKE
> Are you dead set on this, pet?
> Wouldn't you rather have your party
> in Vienna?

Now we REVEAL DRUSILLA, brimming with vitality, who pushes
Spike into the main room of the factory for a PARTY. It is
being decorated by two VAMPS. Creepy Drusilla style, natch.
Two boxes similar in look but different sizes are on the
table. Dalton adds his to the pile.

> DRUSILLA
> (pouty)
> But - the invitations are sent.

Spike knows this is true - although he doesn't like it.

> SPIKE
> It's just, I've had it with this
> place. Nothing goes off the way it's
> supposed to-

> DRUSILLA
> -until my celebration. My gatherings
> are always perfect. Remember Spain?
> The bulls?

> SPIKE
> I remember, sweet. But Sunnydale is
> friggin' cursed for us. Angel and
> the Slayer see to that.

> DRUSILLA
> Shhhh. I have good games for
> everyone. You'll see.

She sees some flowers woven about two of the chairs. Stops,
suddenly shaking.

> DRUSILLA (cont'd)
> These flowers are wrong. They're all
> wrong - I can't abide them!

                                                       CONTINTUED

11 CONTINUED: (2)   11

She screams with genuine horror and tears them off the
chairs - then stops, as suddenly as she begun. Spike looks
wearily at the two vamps.

                    SPIKE
          Let's try something different with
          the flowers, then.

                    DRUSILLA
                (suddenly excited)
          Can I open one? Can I? Can I?

                    SPIKE
          Just a peek, love. They're for the
          party.

She goes to the boxes.

POV FROM BOX

We see Dru open it, look inside with rapturous glee.

                    SPIKE (cont'd)
          You like it, baby?

                    DRUSILLA
          Oh, it reaks of death. This will be
          the best party ever.

                    SPIKE
          Why's that?

                    DRUSILLA
          Because it will be the last.

She SLAMS the box closed.

                                        BLACK OUT.

                    END OF ACT ONE

ACT TWO

12 INT. BUFFY'S HOUSE - KITCHEN - DAY   12

It's morning and Joyce is clearing plates from the breakfast
table while Buffy gets ready to leave for school. There is
an open birthday card near Buffy's place.

                    JOYCE
          Mall trip for your birthday on
          Saturday. Don't forget.

                    BUFFY
          Space on a mom-sponsored shopping
          opportunity? Not likely.

                    JOYCE
          So, does seventeen feel any different
          than sixteen?

                    BUFFY
          Funny you should ask - I actually
          woke up feeling more mature,
          responsible and level-headed.

                    JOYCE
               (suspicious)
          Really? That's uncanny.

                    BUFFY
          And yet, true. I now possess the
          qualities one looks for in a licensed
          driver.

                    JOYCE
          Buffy-

                    BUFFY
          You said we could talk about it again
          when I was seventeen.

                    JOYCE
          You've been seventeen for forty-eight
          minutes.

                    BUFFY
          And - ?

                    JOYCE
          First of all - you promised you'd
          stay out of trouble in school.

                                              CONTINUED

12 CONTINUED: 12

                         BUFFY
              I try. You know I do. But Principal
              Snyder has it in for me-

                         JOYCE
              I know. But... You behind the
              wheel. It worries me.

                         BUFFY
              It worries all moms. It's biological
              imperative. But I'm going to drive
              sooner or later, so we might as well
              deal sooner - right?

Joyce turns to her - a plate in her hand. The same exact
pose and expression she had in BUFFY'S DREAM.

                         JOYCE
              Do you really think you're ready,
              Buffy?

CLOSE ON JOYCE'S HANDS

As the plate slips from her grasp - shatters on the floor.

ON BUFFY & JOYCE

Joyce reacts to breaking the plate.

                         JOYCE (cont'd)
              Oh, damn it.

She stoops to pick up the pieces. Buffy just stands there,
power-freaked by the dream deja-vu.

CLOSE ON JOYCE

                         JOYCE (cont'd)
              Grab the broom, would you Buffy?

Nothing. Joyce looks up. Buffy's gone. The back door
SLAMS. Joyce looks after her skittish daughter, baffled.

13 INT. MS. CALENDAR'S CLASSROOM - DAY   13

Calendar enters, loaded down with her bag, books, cup of
coffee, etc. She sets some stuff down near a terminal.
Turns the computer on-

                         GYPSY MAN (O.C.)
              Jenny. Jenny Calendar...

                                                              CONTINUED

13 CONTINUED   13

Calendar spins - sees THE OLD MAN we saw earlier outside the
school. He's standing at her desk, reading her nameplate -
speaks with a DISTINCT YUGOSLAVIAN ACCENT.

A beat as Jenny comprehends his presence in her classroom.

                    JENNY
          You startled me.

                    GYPSY MAN
          You look well. Comfortable.

Jenny becomes increasingly uncomfortable.

                    JENNY
          Yes. I'm fine. I - I know I haven't
          written as much lately. I've been
          busy-

                    GYPSY MAN
          I cannot imagine what is so important
          that you ignore your responsibility
          to your people.

                    JENNY
          I've been working. And...
          distracted. I'm sorry.

                    GYPSY MAN
          The elder woman has been reading
          signs. Something is different.

                    JENNY
          Nothing's changed. The curse still
          holds. He's still tortured by all
          that he's done-

                    GYPSY MAN
          No. The elder woman is never wrong.
          She says his pain is lessening. She
          feels it.

                    JENNY
          There is...

                    GYPSY MAN
          There is - what?

                    JENNY
              (with difficutly)
          A girl.

                                                      CONTINUED

13 CONTINUED: (2)   13

The old man's eyes fill with fire. He cannot believe what he
is hearing.

                    GYPSY MAN
          What? How could you let this happen?

                    JENNY
          I promise you. Angel still suffers.
          And he makes amends for his evil. He
          even saved my life-

                    GYPSY MAN
          So you just forget? That he
          destroyed the most beloved daughter
          of your tribe? That he killed every
          man, woman and child who touched her
          life?
                    (then)
          Vengeance demands that his pain be
          eternal, as ours is. If this - this
          girl - brings him even one minute of
          happiness. That is one minute too
          many.

                    JENNY
          I'm sorry. I thought-

                    GYPSY MAN
          What? That you are Jenny Calendar
          now? You are still Janna, of the
          Kalderash people. A gyspy.

                    JENNY
          I know, Uncle. I know...

                    GYPSY MAN
          Then prove it. Your time for
          watching is past. The girl and
          him - it ends now. No matter what
          you must do, take her from him.

                    JENNY
          I - I will see to it.

                    GYPSY MAN
          Good.

He moves off, exits. Leaving Calendar a total mess.

14 INT. SCHOOL HALLWAY - DAY   14

       Cordy and HARMONY stroll to class. See XANDER and WILLOW
       hanging in the LOUNGE in the BG.

                         CORDELIA
                    (too casual)
               Hello. I'm having, like, a totally
               random thought...
                    (then)
               Xander Harris. Is it just me, or
               does his shirt almost match his pants?

       Harmony looks. Shrugs.

                         HARMONY
               Almost. Why do I care?

                         CORDELIA
               Well. If you look at him a certain
               way - is he vaguely... cute?

       THEIR POV

       As XANDER does some spazzy dance for Willow's amusement.

       RESUME

                         HARMONY
               Oh yeah. I'm hot for spaz boy. Are
               you tripping, Cordelia?

       A beat. Cordelia laughs a little too loud.

                         CORDELIA
               You thought I was serious? Please.
               I was just testing you! Ha.
                    (sighs)
               I'm hot for spaz boy. Good one.

15 INT. SCHOOL LOUNGE - DAY   15

       Xander and Willow are at the snack machine.

                         WILLOW
               So we're all set. I've got all the
               decorations. And I think Cordelia's
               bringing snacks and stuff-

                         XANDER
               Yeah. She said she was. Which was
               thoughtful. Don't you think?
                    (more)

                                                        CONTINUED

> XANDER (cont'd)
> (takes the leap)
> Hey. Cordelia: not as horrible a
> person as we once thought? I mean,
> she's obviously trying to be helpful.

> WILLOW
> True.
> (considers)
> Maybe...

> XANDER
> But, you wouldn't ever, like, be able
> to be friends with her or something.

> WILLOW
> You mean, like hang out and take
> Cosmo tests together?

> XANDER
> I mean - actually elect to be in her
> presence.

> WILLOW
> I don't know. She's better - but
> she's still Cordelia.
> (nods to the hall)
> Just... look.

THEIR POV

CORDELIA and HARMONY are joined by a few other Cordettes.
They all SQUEAL in greeting. Jump up and down.

ON WILLOW AND XANDER.

> WILLOW (cont'd)
> Example: what is the shrieking thing?
> They just saw each other yesterday...
> And now, watch - Cordelia's going to
> model her new outfit-

ON CORDELIA, ET AL

Sure enough - Cordelia spins around, showing off her mini-
dress. More shrieks.

ON WILLOW AND XANDER

> WILLOW (cont'd)
> Note the reaction - like Cordelia
> invented clothes.
> (more)

CONTINUED

> WILLOW (cont'd)
> (then)
> They're not bad people, Xander. It's
> just - we are of two worlds.
> (can't help herself)
> And theirs is bad.

Xander lets this sinks in.

> XANDER
> Right. Of course you're right. What
> was I thinking?

Now OZ approaches. Willow immediately gets shy, happy.

> OZ
> Hey.

> WILLOW
> Hey. So - tonight?

> OZ
> I'm there. Feeling surprise-y.
> (then)
> Can I pick you up?

Xander's watching them, unsure what to make of all this.

> WILLOW
> Yeah. That would be... Here-

She writes it on her pad - tears it off and gives it to Oz.

> OZ
> (pleased)
> I have your address.

> WILLOW
> You do.

> OZ
> Excellent.

He moves off. Xander looks at Willow - a little shocked.

> XANDER
> Is this a date?

> WILLOW
> (distracted)
> Hmmm...?
> (then)
> Yeah. It's a date.

CONTINUED

15 CONTINUED: (3)   15

                    XANDER
          Shouldn't you meet him or something?
          Are you sure you should be giving
          some stranger your address?

                    WILLOW
          He's not just some stranger, Xander.
          He's a friend. He took a bullet for
          me.

                    XANDER
          So? I would've taken a bullet for
          you. Nobody offered me one.

     Off Willow - enjoying Xander's discomfort.

16 INT. LIBRARY - DAY   16

     Buffy and Giles are in mid-conversation. Very intense.

                    BUFFY
          -and then my mom broke the plate. It
          was exactly like I saw it in my
          dream, Giles. Every gesture. Every
          word. Beyond creepy.

                    GILES
          Yes. I'd imagine-

     Now Willow and Xander enter the library. See Buffy.

                    XANDER
          Hey! The woman of the hour.

                    WILLOW
          It's happy birthday Buffy!

     They move to her to give her a hug - but sense her mood.

                    WILLOW (cont'd)
          Not - happy birthday Buffy?

                    GILES
          It's just... A piece of the
          nightmare Buffy had the other night
          actually came to pass.

                    XANDER
          Something happen to Angel?

                                                          CONTINUED

16 CONTINUED: 16

                    BUFFY
          He's fine. For now. But if part of
          what I had a dream about came true-

                    WILLOW
          Then all of it may come true.

                    BUFFY
          And Drusilla might be alive.
                    (then/to Giles)
          In the dream, I couldn't stop her.
          She blind-sided me, Giles. Angel was
          dead before I knew what happened-

                    GILES
          Even if she is alive, we can still
          protect Angel. Dreams are not
          prophecies, Buffy. You dreamt the
          Master had risen, but you stopped it
          from happening.

                    XANDER
          You ground his bones to make your
          bread.

                    BUFFY
          That's true, except for the bread
          part. I guess we're one step ahead.
          But Giles, I'd like to stay that way.

                    GILES
          Absolutely. Let me read up on
          Drusilla, see if she has any
          particular patterns. Why don't you
          meet me here at 7:00? Map out a
          strategy.

                    BUFFY
          Okay. What do I do till then?

                    GILES
          Go to class... do your homework...
          Have supper...

                    BUFFY
          Oh, right. Be _that_ Buffy.

     She grabs her book bag, heads out. The others watch her go.

                    XANDER
          That is _not_ a perky birthday puppy.

                                                          CONTINUED

16 CONTINUED: (2)   16

                    WILLOW
          So much for our surprise party.

                    XANDER
          Man. This slayer gig is 24/7. Can't
          even stop for a little pinata-bashing.

     Bummed, Willow starts to get up, collect her things.

                    WILLOW
          I bought little hats and everything.
          Oh well, I'll tell Cordelia-

                    GILES
          No, you won't. We're having a party
          tonight.

                    XANDER
          It looks like Mr. Caution Man
          talking, but the sound he makes is
          funny.

                    GILES
          Buffy's surprise party is going to go
          exactly as we've planned.
                    (to Willow)
          Except I won't be wearing the little
          hat.

                    XANDER
          He has dignity.

                    WILLOW
          But Buffy and Angel-

                    GILES
          -May well be in danger. As they have
          been before, and, I imagine, will be
          again. One thing I have learned in
          my tenure here on the Hellmouth is
          that there is never a good time to
          relax. But Buffy is only turning 17
          this once. She deserves a party.

                    XANDER
          You're a great man of our time.

                    WILLOW
          And anyway, Angel's coming . So
          she'll be able to protect him <u>and</u>
          have cake.

16 CONTINUED: (3)   16

                          GILES
                Precisely.

17 INT. SCHOOL HALL OUTSIDE LIBRARY - NIGHT   17

    Buffy arrives for her appointment with Giles, heads toward
    the door but IS STARTLED BY CALENDAR - who steps from the
    shadows.

                          JENNY
                Buffy.

                          BUFFY
                God. I didn't see you there.

                          JENNY
                Sorry... Giles wanted me to tell you
                that there's been a change of plans.
                He wants to meet you someplace near
                his house. I guess he had to run
                home and get a book or something-

                          BUFFY
                Yeah, 'cause heaven knows there
                aren't enough books in the library-

                          JENNY
                He's - very thorough.

                          BUFFY
                Which is not to bag. It's kinda
                manly in an obsessive/compulsive
                sorta way, don't you think?

                          JENNY
                I have my car. I can drive, if you
                want...

                          BUFFY
                Okay...

    They move off.

18 INT./EXT. - CALENDAR'S CAR - NIGHT   18

    Calendar drives, appears anxious. Buffy looks out the
    window.

                          BUFFY
                So - where are we headed, anyway?

                                                            CONTINUED

BUFFY THE VAMPIRE SLAYER "Surprise"   (WHITE) 11/17/97   29.

18 CONTINUED: 18

    Calendar doesn't reply.

19 EXT. ALLEY BEHIND THE BRONZE - NIGHT   19

    The car pulls into the dark alley. Slows.

20 INT. CALENDAR'S CAR - NIGHT   20

    Buffy checks out their surroundings - confused.

                    BUFFY
            We're going to the Bronze?

                    JENNY
            I'm not sure. Giles gave me an
            address. I'm just following his
            directions-

    Buffy sees something out the window. Grows alert.

                    BUFFY
            Uh oh.

                    JENNY
            What?

    WHAT BUFFY SEES

21 EXT. LOADING DOCK - NIGHT   21

    Where three suspicious-looking guys are checking around
    furtively as they MOVE ANOTHER RECTANGLE-SHAPED CAST IRON BOX
    from the loading dock to a waiting truck.

22 INT. CALENDAR'S CAR - NIGHT   22

                    BUFFY
            this looks funky. Stop for a sec.

    Calendar slows the car.

                    JENNY
            Buffy - maybe you shouldn't-

                    BUFFY
            Sorry. Sacred duty, yadda, yadda,
            yadda-

    She opens the car door. Steps out. Calendar watches.

                                                        CONTINUED

22 CONTINUED: 22

                              JENNY
                         (to herself)
                    What is this...?

Off Calendar's worried expression.

23 EXT. LOADING DOCK - NIGHT   23

     Buffy sneaks toward the possible crooks. One turns - IT'S
     DALTON - in full Vamp face.   Buffy recognizes him.

                              BUFFY
                    Every time I see you you're stealing
                    something. You should talk to
                    somebody about this klepto issue-

     WHUMP! Buffy is attacked by a HULKING VAMP - she fights him
     off, but is distracted when she HEARS THE TRUCK START. She
     looks and sees that DALTON is now in the back of the truck
     with the box, struggling to close the cargo gate.

     Buffy leaves the hulking vamp and LEAPS for the driver's side
     of the truck - gets the door open and STAKES the vamp behind
     the wheel before he can get the truck in gear.

     Now Buffy moves to the back of the truck to intercept Dalton
     and the box. Dalton knows he's no match for her and RUNS
     OFF, leaving the BOX behind.

     A beat as Buffy catches her breath. Then the HULKING VAMP is
     on her. FITE! (and if we can afford it) FITE! FITE!

24 INT. THE BRONZE - NIGHT   24

     Giles, Willow, Oz, Xander, Cordelia and Angel all huddle in
     the dark. The Bronze is decorated for Buffy's birthday and
     the place is empty except for the gang. Angel looks
     anxiously at the clock on the wall.

                              ANGEL
                    Where is she?

     They hear the sound of some kind of disturbance on the other
     side of the back wall of the Bronze.

                              WILLOW
                    Shhh! I think I hear her coming-

25 EXT. LOADING DOCK - CONTINUOUS - NIGHT   25

    Buffy and the hulking vamp continue to battle. She knocks
    him back - but he's up again in an instant, BODY SLAMMING HER-

26 INT. THE BRONZE - CONTINUOUS - NIGHT   26

    Another beat of quiet as everybody lies in wait. Until-

    BUFFY AND THE HULKING VAMP come CRASHING THROUGH THE WINDOW
    BEHIND THE STAGE AT THE BRONZE! Glass flies everywhere.

    They LAND ON THE STAGE, struggle briefly but BUFFY has the
    upper hand. She STAKES him. Dusto-rama.

    A long, stunned beat. Everyone stares. Then Cordelia POPS
    from behind a couch.

                    CORDELIA
                Surprise!

                    OZ
                That pretty much sums it up.

    ON BUFFY, ANGEL AND GILES

    As they move together.

                    ANGEL
                Buffy, are you okay?

                    GILES
                Yes - what happened?

                    BUFFY
                There were these vamps in the alley.
                And one of Dru's guys was-
                    (stops - notices)
                What's going on?

                    GILES
                    (a bit lamely)
                Surprise party.

                    CORDELIA
                Yeah, happy birthday.

                    BUFFY
                You guys did all this for me? You
                are so sweet!

                    ANGEL
                You're sure you're okay?

                                                        CONTINUED

                         BUFFY
              I'm fine.

ANGLE: OZ

is still staring at the spot where the vampire turned to
dust. Willow approaches him.

                         WILLOW
              Are you okay?

                         OZ
              Yeah. Did everybody else see a guy
              turn into dust?

                         WILLOW
              Uh, sort of...

                         XANDER
              Yep. Vampires are real, lot of 'em
              live in Sunnydale, Willow'll fill you
              in.

                         WILLOW
              I know it's hard to accept at first...

                         OZ
              No, actually, it explains a lot.

MISS CALENDAR comes in the door with the IRON BOX that the
vamps left. She's struggling under its weight.

                         JENNY
              Can somebody give me a hand here?

Angel and Giles move to help her. They put the box down on
a table.

                         JENNY (cont'd)
              Those creeps left this behind.

                         BUFFY
              What is it?

                         GILES
              I have no idea. Can it be opened?

Buffy moves to the box, runs her hands under the lid.

                         BUFFY
              It feels like it has some kind of
              release... There.

26 CONTINUED: (2)   26

    Buffy slowly lifts the lid. Everyone peers into the box. A
    beat as their faces register shock and amazement.

    ANGLE: IN THE BOX

    is a powerful, heavily armored <u>ARM</u>.

    Then the ARM shoots from the box - GRABS BUFFY BY THE NECK.

                             BLACK OUT.

                 END OF ACT TWO

ACT THREE

27 INT. THE BRONZE - NIGHT   27

That live human-looking arm? Very bad. Very much gripping
Buffy's neck.

Angel grabs her, takes hold of the arm. Finally manages to
pry the thing's fingers from Buffy's neck, one by one, and
wrestle it back in the box. He slams the lid shut, locks it.

ANOTHER stunned beat of silence as Buffy gasps for breath.
Then-

                    XANDER
          Clearly - the Hellmouth's answer to
          "what do you get the Slayer who has
          everything?"

                    GILES
          Good heavens, Buffy, are you alright?

Angel is helping Buffy to a chair. She sits.

                    BUFFY
          Man. That thing has major grip-

                    WILLOW
          What - what was that?

                    OZ
               (matter of fact)
          Looked like an arm.

Angel, troubled, gets up and moves to the box. Checks it
over more carefully.

                    ANGEL
          It can't be- She wouldn't...

                    XANDER
          What? The vamp version of "snakes in
          a can?" Or do you care to share?

Buffy reads Angel's expression. Moves to him.

                    BUFFY
          Angel?

                                                    CONTINUED

> ANGEL
> It's a legend. Way before my time.
> Of a demon brought forth to rid the
> earth of the plague of humanity. To
> separate the righteous from the
> wicked... And burn the righteous
> down. They called him the Judge.

This obviously registers with Giles.

> GILES
> The Judge... This is he?

> ANGEL
> Well, not all of him...

> BUFFY
> Uh, still needing backstory here...

> GILES
> He couldn't be killed.

He looks to Angel for confirmation, and continues as Angel
nods:

> GILES (cont'd)
> An army was sent against him. Most
> of them died, but they were finally
> able to dismember him. But not kill
> him.

> ANGEL
> The pieces were scattered - buried in
> every corner of the earth.

> XANDER
> You think they left his heart in San
> Francisco?

Scattered glares.

> OZ
>   (aside to Xander)
> I had that thought too.

> JENNY
> So all these parts are being brought
> here.

> BUFFY
> By Drusilla. The vamps outside were
> Spike's men.

                    ANGEL
          She's just crazy enough to do it.

                    WILLOW
          Do what? Reassemble the Judge?

                    ANGEL
          And bring forth Armageddon.

                    CORDELIA
          Is anyone else gonna have cake?

No takers. She moves to the cake.

                    GILES
          We have to get this out of town.

                    JENNY
          Angel.

                    BUFFY
          What?

                    JENNY
          You've got to do it. You're the only
          one who can protect this thing.

                    BUFFY
          What about me?

                    JENNY
          You're just gonna skip town for a few
          months?

                    BUFFY
          Months?

                    ANGEL
          She's right. I have to take this to
          the remotest region possible.

                    BUFFY
          But that's not months.

                    ANGEL
          I can catch a cargo ship to Asia,
          maybe trek to Nepal...

                    BUFFY
               (to Angel)
          You know - those wacky, newfangled
          flying machines are much safer than
          they used to be...

                    ANGEL
I can't fly. There's no sure way to
guard against the daylight.
       (then)
I don't like this any more than you
do, Buffy. But there's no other way.

                    BUFFY
When?

                    ANGEL
Tonight. As soon as possible.

                    BUFFY
       (pathetic)
But - it's my birthday.

Calendar moves to Buffy - puts a hand on her shoulder.

                    JENNY
I'll drive you to the docks.

Buffy and Angel meet eyes. Buffy knows he has to go - but
she's desparate for him not to.

Everyone stands silently amid the festive decorations. This
was not the way it was supposed to happen.

28 INT. FACTORY - NIGHT

The vampire DALTON stands QUAKING with fear before Drusilla,
who is seriously unhappy. Spike is in his chair nearby.

                  DRUSILLA
You <u>lost</u> it? You lost my present?

                    DALTON
I know... I'm sorry-

                    SPIKE
Bad turn, man. She can't have her
fun without the box.

                    DALTON
The Slayer, she came out of nowhere.
I - I didn't even see her-

Drusilla moves to DALTON - snakes one hand around his neck.
With the other, she lifts Dalton's glasses from his face and
drops them to the floor. Steps on them.

CONTINUED

28 CONTINUED: 28

                          DRUSILLA
                        (sweetly)
                    Make a wish.

                          DALTON
                    What?

She points HER RAZOR SHARP FINGER NAILS at his EYES. Pulls
back, about to strike. Dalton cowers.

                          DRUSILLA
                    I'm going to blow out the candles-

                          SPIKE
                        (casually)
                    Dru, sweet. You might give him a
                    chance to find your lost treasure.
                    He's a wanker, but he's the only one
                    we've got with half a brain. If he
                    fails - you can eat his eyes out of
                    the sockets for all I care.

Dru hesitates.

                          DALTON
                    I'll get it. Please. I swear-

Dru considers. Then slowly lowers her hand. She picks
DATLON'S TWISTED, SHATTERED GLASSES off the floor - places
them on his nose. Potemkin style.

                          DRUSILLA
                        (sweet again)
                    Hurry back, then.

Off Dalton. He doesn't like these reindeer games.

29 EXT. DOCKS - NIGHT   29

Angel, who holds the IRON BOX, and Buffy move furtively down
the docks toward a large CARGO ship. They stop when they are
still some distance away. Angel sets the box down.

                          ANGEL
                    I should go the rest of the way alone.

                          BUFFY
                    Okay...

Buffy tries to smile, be the brave little soldier. Can't.

                                                          CONTINUED

                          ANGEL
               I'll be back.

Buffy nods - unconvinced.

                          ANGEL (cont'd)
               I will.

                          BUFFY
               When? Six months? A year? Who
               knows how long it will take. Or if
               we'll even-

                          ANGEL
               If we'll even - what?

                          BUFFY
               Just, if you haven't noticed, someone
               pretty much always wants us dead.

                          ANGEL
               Don't say that. We'll be fine.

                          BUFFY
               But we don't know.

                          ANGEL
               We can't know, Buffy. Nobody can.
               That's just the deal.

A pained beat. Then-

                          ANGEL (cont'd)
               I... have something for you. For
               your birthday. I was going to give
               it to you earlier, but...

He pulls a small box from his coat. Hands it to her.

CLOSE ON THE BOX

As Buffy opens it. Inside is a SILVER RING WITH TWO HANDS
HOLDING A HEART ENGRAVED ON IT.

ON BUFFY

                          BUFFY
               It's beautiful.

                          ANGEL
               My people... Before I was changed,
               they exchanged this as a sign of
               devotion.
                          (more)

                                                        CONTINUE

                      ANGEL (cont'd)
                  (then)
        It's a Claddagh ring. The hands
        represent friendship, the crown
        represents loyalty. The heart, well,
        you know... Wear it with the heart
        pointing toward you, it means you
        belong to somebody-

Buffy just looks at him. He lifts his own hand. He is
wearing a ring like the one he gave her. Heart turned in.

                      ANGEL (cont'd)
        Like this.

Buffy's trying hard not to lose it.

                      BUFFY
        Angel-

                      ANGEL
        Put it on.

She does. Heart pointing in. Looks at it. Then at him.

                      BUFFY
        I don't want to do this.

                      ANGEL
        Me either.

                      BUFFY
                  (small)
        So - don't go.

They both know he has to. He takes her into his arms and
they kiss. The potentially <u>last</u> kiss kind of kiss. Then-

                      ANGEL
        Buffy... I-

BOOM!!

He never gets to finish because DALTON AND TWO OTHER VAMPIRES
suddenly leap on them from a CARGO NET THAT HANGS ABOVE THEIR
HEADS.

Vamp #1 takes on ANGEL, while #2 knocks BUFFY to the ground.
Dalton makes a bee-line for the BOX.

                      BUFFY
                  (seeing Dalton)
        Angel! The box!

                                        CONTINUED

29 CONTINUED: (3)   29

Angel beats vamp #1 off him - at least for the moment - and TACKLES DALTON. The box falls from Dalton's hands.

While Dalton and Angel struggle, Buffy is engaged with Vamp #2. They fight fiercely, but Vamp #2 manages to knock Buffy into a THICK WOOD PYLON. Buffy hits her head hard, is momentarily stunned. Vamp #2 then SIDEKICKS her legs out from under her, sending her sprawling OFF THE EDGE OF THE DOCK and INTO THE WATER.

Angel hears the SPLASH just as VAMP #1 grabs the IRON BOX. Angel turns to look for Buffy-

                    ANGEL
               Buffy!?

She's gone. In the soup. Angel sees Vamp #1 making off with the box - but he has no choice. He drops Dalton and DIVES OFF THE DOCK TO BUFFY'S RESCUE. Dalton runs off.

30 EXT. WATER - CONTINUOUS - NIGHT   30

Angel fishes a dazed Buffy out of the water (we see this from the back at a good distance, if you know what I mean).

31 INT. LIBRARY - NIGHT   31

Giles, Willow and Xander are gathered - waiting for Buffy and Calendar to return. There are a number of books open on the table. Giles checks his watch.

                    GILES
               They should be back by now...

                    WILLOW
               Maybe Buffy needed a few minutes to
               pull herself together.
                    (then)
               Poor Buffy. On her birthday and
               everything.

                    XANDER
               It's sad. Granted. But let's look
               at the up-side for a moment. I mean,
               what kind of future could she have
               really had with him? Working two
               jobs. Denny's waitress by day,
               Slayer by night. Angel's always in
               front of the tube, with a big ole'
               blood belly...
                    (more)

                                                    CONTINUED

31 CONTINUED: 31

                         XANDER (cont'd)
          And he's dreaming of the glory days
          when Buffy still thought the whole
          creatures of the night routine was a
          big turn-on...

                         WILLOW
          You've thought way too much about
          this-

                         XANDER
          That's just the beginning. You want
          to hear the part where I fly into
          town in my private jet and take Buffy
          out for prime rib?

     Xander does not see Buffy - who enters in a new outfit.

                         WILLOW
          Xander-

                         XANDER
          And she cries?

                         GILES
          What happened?

                         BUFFY
          Dru's guys ambushed us. They got the
          box.

                         GILES
          Where's Jenny?

                         BUFFY
          She took Angel to his apartment to
          get clothes. I had some here.

                         XANDER
          And we were needing clothes
          because....

                         BUFFY
          We got wet. Giles, what do we know?

                         GILES
          The more I study the Judge, the less
          I like him. His touch can literally
          burn the humanity out of you. A true
          creature of evil can survive the
          process. No human ever has.

                                             CONTINUED

31 CONTINUED: (2)   31

                    XANDER
            So what's the problem? We send Cordy
            to fight this guy and we go for pizza.

                    BUFFY
            Can he be stopped? Without an army?

                    GILES
              (reads)
            "No weapon forged can kill him." Not
            very encouraging. But if we can keep
            them from assembling him...

                    BUFFY
            We need to find his weak spots. And
            we need to figure out where they'd be
            keeping him.

                    GILES
            This could take time.

                    WILLOW
            We better do a round robin. Xander,
            you go first.

                    BUFFY
            Good call.

Xander moves to the phone.

                    GILES
            Round robin?

                    WILLOW
            Everybody calls everybody's mom and
            tells them they're at everybody
            else's house.

                    BUFFY
            Thus freeing us up for world savage.

                    WILLOW
            And all-night keggers.
              (off looks)
            What, only Xander gets to make dumb
            jokes?

        ANGLE: XANDER

        on the phone.

                                                          CONTINUED

31 CONTINUED: (3)   31

> XANDER
> Hey, mom. Listen, Willow and I are
> studying, I'm gonna stay over here...
> uh huh...

                                        DISSOLVE TO:

32 INT. LIBRARY - NIGHT - LATER   32

The clock reads 2:00 am. Willow and Xander are at the table,
looking through books and research material. Calendar is
absorbed in work at the computer.

> XANDER
> (tired)
> I think I read this already...

> WILLOW
> I can't get over how cool Oz was
> about all this.

> XANDER
> Gee, I'm over it.

> WILLOW
> You're just jealous cuz you didn't
> have a date for the party.

> XANDER
> No, I sure didn't...

Giles moves with Angel from the stacks to his office - stops.

WHAT HE SEES

BUFFY, asleep at his desk.

ON GILES

Who looks at her kindly, backs away.

> GILES
> It seems Buffy needed some rest.

> ANGEL
> Yeah. She hasn't been sleeping well.
> You know, tossing and turning-

Willow, Xander and Calendar look at him, suspicious.

> ANGEL (cont'd)
> She told me. Because of her dreams.

33 INT. GILES' OFFICE - CONTINUOUS - NIGHT   33

    WE MOVE IN CLOSE ON BUFFY,

    Who, indeed, sleeps fitfully.

34 INT. FACTORY - NIGHT - BUFFY'S DREAM   34

    Buffy, dressed for a party in a SLEEK BLACK DRESS, moves
    through THE FACTORY, which especially dark and spooky. Black
    and tattered party decorations hang down from the ceiling.
    Buffy has to push them aside as she moves forward.

    Ahead of her, a female figure darts among the streamers.
    Buffy follows her-

                         BUFFY
                 Hello? Who is that?

    The figure turns. It's MS. CALENDAR, who promptly ducks back
    into the shadows. Buffy reacts, confused.

    Now Buffy TURNS, sees ALL THE CAST IRON BOXES in a circle.
    She moves to them - reaches for one - but is stopped by
    DRUSILLA'S VOICE.

                         DRUSILLA (O.C.)
                 Now, now. Hands off my presents.

    Buffy looks up. Drusilla, wearing the SAME DRESS that Buffy
    has on, stands with ANGEL IN HER GRIP, holding a GLEAMING
    KNIFE TO HIS THROAT. She starts to draw it across his neck.

    CLOSE ON BUFFY

                         BUFFY
             No!

    Now Buffy looks around, horrified. Angel and Drusilla have
    suddenly vanished.

                         ANGEL (O.C.)
                 Buffy?

35 INT. GILES' OFFICE - CONTINUOUS - NIGHT   35

    Buffy's EYES snap open. Angel is standing over her, gently
    shaking her shoulder.

                         BUFFY
                 No! Angel!-

                                                          CONTINUED

35 CONTINUED: 35

                          ANGEL
                It's okay...

Buffy, not quite out of the dream world, moves into his arms,
shaking and terrified.

                          ANGEL (cont'd)
                I'm here. I'm right here.

CLOSE ON BUFFY

Wide-eyed and full of fear.

36 INT. FACTORY - NIGHT   36

CLOSE ON

Another pair of FEMALE EYES. Wide-eyed in a different way -
with excitement.

WIDEN TO REVEAL

Drusilla, in the DRESS FROM BUFFY'S DREAM.

                          DRUSILLA
                More music!

She clasps her hands with delight as we continue to widen,
until we see HER PARTY IN FULL SWING. There are a number of
VAMPS dressed to the nines - drinking, reveling. Spike rolls
up to Drusilla - he has a SMALL, HEAD-SHAPED CAST IRON BOX in
his hands.

                          SPIKE
                Look what I have for you, ducks-

                          DRUSILLA
                Ah! The best is saved for last.

Drusilla takes the box from Spike.

WE FOLLOW DRUSILLA

As she moves around a corner. We see for the first time that
the rest of the IRON BOXES have all been assembled. They fit
together perfectly - creating the form of a LARGE MAN.

Drusilla moves to a foot stool, PLACES THE LAST BOX. As soon
as the box is attached - A SURGE OF ENERGY SURROUNDS THE
BOXES. It continues for a moment, then abates. Now the
boxes ALL OPEN AT ONCE, revealing THE JUDGE.

                                                        CONTINUED

36 CONTINUED: 36

He's enormous, dressed in black armor. His skin is sickly
pale BLUE. There is something primordial about him - not
quite fully formed. His eyes open - revealing SOLID BLACK.
No iris. No light. He is horrible. Terrifying.

CLOSE ON

Drusilla - thrilled. She grabs Spike's hand.

                    DRUSILLA (cont'd)
          He's perfect, my darling...
                    (darkly)
          Just what I wanted.

                                        BLACK OUT.

                    END OF ACT THREE

ACT FOUR

37 INT. FACTORY - NIGHT   37

CLOSE ON THE JUDGE

And he takes his first, LUMBERING steps out of the BOX. His
aura is that of deadly indifference. He is a killing thing,
not good or evil.

ON DRUSILLA AND SPIKE

Drusilla starts to move forward, but SPIKE holds her back.

> SPIKE
> I'd let our guest make the first
> move, precious.

Drusilla pauses. The JUDGE TURNS TO THEM.

> THE JUDGE
> You...

A beat. He takes another step. STARTS TO LIFT HIS HAND TO
THEM. Spike immediately rolls forward - getting in his face.
Well, sort of...

> SPIKE
> Ho! Ho! What's that, mate?

> THE JUDGE
> You two stink of humanity. You share
> affection. Jealousy...

> SPIKE
> Yeah, what of it? Do I have to
> remind you that we're the ones that
> brought you here?

> THE JUDGE
> I have no alliances.

> SPIKE
> Right then. You want to go back in
> the little boxes?

A long beat as the Judge considers this. Then-

> THE JUDGE
> You may live. You will help me serve
> my purpose.

CONTINUED

37 CONTINUED: 37

                         SPIKE
                        (grins)
               Works for me.

Drusilla moves to the Judge, points to the assembled PARTY
GUESTS, who have gathered to watch.

                         DRUSILLA
               Would you like a party favor?

The judge nods. Scans the crowd. His eyes land on DALTON.

CLOSE ON DALTON

Getting the drift. Uh oh.

THE JUDGE

Points to Dalton.   *

                         THE JUDGE
               This one - is full of feeling.
                        (disgusted)
               He reads.

The Judge nods to a VAMP MINION.   *

                         THE JUDGE (cont'd)   *
               Bring him to me.   *

                         SPIKE   *
               What's with the bringing, mate? I   *
               thought you could just... zap people.   *

                         THE JUDGE   *
               My full strength will return, in   *
               time. Until then - I need contact.   *

Dalton is brought before him, pleading. But THE JUDGE raises   *
his hand to his chest.   *

                         THE JUDGE (cont'd)
               Silence...

Dalton begins to SHAKE AND SMOULDER. Then the JUDGE'S HAND
GOES TO HIS CHEST. Dalton's flesh BLACKENS and CRUMBLES.
Finally, FLAMES shoot from his eye sockets and he falls into
a burned-out heap.

A stunned beat as all gathered take in this hideous sight.
Then Drusilla STARTS TO CLAP and jump like a small child.

                                                          CONTINUED

37 CONTINUED: (2)   37

                         DRUSILLA
                Do it again! Do it again!

38 INT. LIBRARY - NIGHT   38

    Buffy comes out of the office, Angel on her heels. She
    starts gathering her weapons, etc. Giles, Calendar, Willow
    and Xander react to her urgency.

                         GILES
                Buffy? Are you alright?

                         ANGEL
                She had another dream-

                                                            CONTINUED

38 CONTINUED: 38

                         BUFFY
         I think I know where Drusilla and
         Spike are-

                         GILES
         Very good. However, you need a plan.
         I know you're concerned, Buffy, but
         you can't just go off half-cocked-

                         BUFFY
         We have a plan. Angel and I go to
         the factory to do recon. See how far
         they've gotten assembling the Judge.
         You guys fan out and check places the
         boxes may be coming into town. Ship
         yards, the airport... We have to
         stop them from getting all the boxes
         in one place-

                         GILES
                    (nonplussed)
         Yes, well... That's quite a good
         plan, actually.

                         BUFFY
         This thing is nasty and it's real,
         Giles. We don't have time to wait
         for it to come get us.

    She heads out the door. Angel follows her. A beat while
    everyone reacts to General Buffy.

39 INT. FACTORY - NIGHT   39

    Buffy and Angel steal in through a dark doorway on the
    balcony. They keep out of sight, talk quietly.

                         BUFFY
         Angel. Maybe I should go in alone.
         I mean, if my dreams are so true-

                         ANGEL
                    (firmly)
         I'm not letting you go by yourself.

    Buffy knows she can't fight him on this.

                         BUFFY
         Okay - what do we do if the Judge is
         already put together?

                                                              CONTINUED

39 CONTINUED: 39

                         ANGEL
          I'll deal with it. You keep your
          distance.

Buffy looks at him. Blinks.

                         BUFFY
          We're going to have to get over this
          virtuous thing or we're dead meat.

                         ANGEL
               (she's right)
          If he's assembled, we retreat.
          Together. Get the others and make a
          battle plan.

                         BUFFY
          Deal.

They creep along the UPPER DECK AREA of the factory. Peer
over the edge.

WHAT THEY SEE

The PARTY CONTINUES BELOW, more macabre than ever. Spike,
Drusilla and the Judge aren't in sight.

ON BUFFY AND ANGEL

                         BUFFY (cont'd)
               (whispering)
          I saw this. The party...

Angel nods - then grows alarmed, seeing something downstairs.
Buffy follows his gaze to-

THE JUDGE -

Who strides across the room with Spike and Drusilla. He
seems to SENSE something. Stops.

                         DRUSILLA
          What? What is it?

The Judge doesn't reply. Just starts scanning the room.
Then looks UP.

ON ANGEL AND BUFFY

Angel grabs Buffy - speaks in an urgent, hushed tone.

                         ANGEL
          We have to get out of here-

                                                    CONTINUED

39 CONTINUED: (2)   39

    They move quickly toward the WINDOW THEY CAME IN, but find
    TWO VAMP MINIONS have come up the back way. Another TWO
    BLOCK the only other escape route.

    Off BUFFY AND ANGEL, caught.

40 INT. FACTORY - MOMENTS LATER - NIGHT   40

    Buffy and Angel are BROUGHT BEFORE THE JUDGE by the minions.
    Spike and Dru are digging it, big time.

                    SPIKE
            Well, well. Look what we have
            here - crashers.

                    BUFFY
            I'm sure our invitations just got
            lost in the mail-

    Drusilla moves to Buffy - examining her closely. Runs a
    finger along her cheek. Buffy holds her ground, defiant.

                    DRUSILLA
            It's delicious. I only dreamed you'd
            come.

    Angel tries to shake off the minions restraining him.

                    ANGEL
            Leave her alone-

                    SPIKE
                (to Angel/wry)
            Yeah, that'll work. Now say pretty
            please-

    Now the JUDGE STEPS FORWARD. Sets his sights on BUFFY.

                    THE JUDGE
            The girl.

                    DRUSILLA
            Chilling, isn't it? She's so full of
            good intention.

    The Judge starts to MOVE TOWARD HER. But ANGEL BREAKS FREE
    from his captives - moves in front of her.

                    ANGEL
            Take me. Take me instead of her.

                                                        CONTINUED

40 CONTINUED: 40

The JUDGE is almost on top of him. Angel starts to shake -
just like Dalton did.

                    SPIKE
        You're not clear on the concept, pal.
        There is no "instead". Just <u>first</u>
        and <u>second</u>-

                    DRUSILLA
        And if you go first - you don't get
        to watch the slayer die.

She motions to the minions, who move in on ANGEL again, drag
him away from the Judge.

Now THE JUDGE MOVES TO BUFFY, who struggles against the vamps
holding her. She manages to KICK the Judge.

                    ANGEL
      No, Buffy - don't touch him!

Sure enough - Buffy starts to TREMBLE UNCONTROLLABLY.

CLOSE ON ANGEL

Who sees THE CLUSTER OF TELEVISIONS HANGING OVER THE JUDGE
and the CHAIN THAT HOLDS IT UP.

ON BUFFY

Getting weaker. She's moments away from the brun.

ON ANGEL

Who SUMMONS ALL HIS STRENGTH, knocks the vampires off him and
dives for the chain that holds the televisions.

Before the vamps can get to him, he YANKS THE CHAIN FROM THE
GROUND-

ON THE JUDGE

As he reacts to the GROANING LOAD ABOVE HIS HEAD. He manages
to JUMP CLEAR as the thing FALLS, and CRASHES THROUGH THE
FLOOR! The hole it opens reveals A SEWER TUNNEL that runs
under the FACTORY FLOOR.

Buffy takes advantage of the confusion that follows this
spectacle, breaks free from the vamps and runs to ANGEL.

                    BUFFY
      This way-

CONTINUED

40 CONTINUED: (2)   40

     She moves to HOLE in the floor and they LEAP IN. Drusilla
     sees them, calls to her minions-

                         DRUSILLA
               Stop them!

41 INT. SEWER TUNNEL - NIGHT   41

     Angel and Buffy run down a tunnel with a pair of minions not
     far behind. It's RAINING, so the tunnels are especially DAMP
     and hard to negotiate.

     They turn a corner, duck into a dark alcove. The MINIONS RUN
     PAST - not seeing them in their hiding place.

42 EXT. STREET NEAR ANGEL'S APARTMENT - NIGHT   42

     The rain continues as Buffy and Angel cautiously emerge from
     the sewers.

                         BUFFY
               I think we lost them-

     Angel looks at Buffy - shaky, exhausted, soaking wet again.
     Her shirt is ripped in the back and she has a bloody cut.

                         ANGEL
               Come on. You need to get inside.

     She nods. He leads her off.

43 EXT. SHIP YARD - NIGHT   43

     Giles and Calendar return from A SHIPPING OFFICE, get in his   *
     car.

                         JENNY
               Well that was a big zero. No box, no
               vamps.

A44 INT. GILES' CAR - CONTINUOUS - NIGHT   A44   *

                         GILES
               Perhaps you ought to go home and get
               some sleep. I'll continue from here.

                         JENNY
               Like I could sleep, Giles.

                                                              CONTINUED

A44 CONTINUED: A44

> GILES
> Yes, I feel rather restless myself.
> Buffy and Angel can handle
> themselves, of course, but...

> JENNY
> I know. I'm worried too.

Giles nods. Calendar takes his hand, tries on a smile to
cover her mounting guilt.   *

44   INT. ANGEL'S APARTMENT - NIGHT   44

Buffy and Angel enter his apartment. He turns on a few
lights.

> ANGEL
> You're shaking like a leaf.

> BUFFY
> Cold.

> ANGEL
> Let me get you something.

He goes to his wardrobe. She moves about a little aimlessly,
the way a person does on somebody else's turf. He comes back
with a SHIRT and some SWEATS, leads her to bed.

> ANGEL (cont'd)
> Put these on and get under the
> covers. Just warm up.

She nods, waits. He gets it - turns his back to her.

> ANGEL (cont'd)
> Sorry.

Buffy starts to take off her shirt - winces with pain.

> ANGEL (cont'd)
> What?

> BUFFY
> I - I got cut or something on my back.

> ANGEL
> Can I... Let me see.

> BUFFY
> Okay.

CONTINUED

44 CONTINUED   44

He turns back. Buffy's holding her unbuttoned shirt around
her. Angel moves to the bed. Sits on the edge, gently moves
her shirt off her shoulder so he can see her injury. He
touches her back - looks at the wound, which is small.

                    ANGEL
          It's already closed. You're fine.

A beat. She's still turned away from him. They are both
obviously affected by being this close. This vulnerable.
She leans back into him. His arms go around her. He
breathes her in...

                    BUFFY
          You almost went away today-

                    ANGEL
          We both did.

He holds her tighter. For an intoxicating beat.

                    BUFFY
          Angel. I feel like - If I lost you...
               (then)
          But you're right. We can't be sure.
          About anything-

                    ANGEL
          Shhhhh. I-

She turns. They are face to face.

                    BUFFY
          You - what?

A long moment. Angel finally says exactly what's been on his
mind for some time.

                    ANGEL
          I love you.
               (pained)
          I try not to, but I can't stop-

                    BUFFY
          Me too. I can't either.

They kiss. A kiss that is the beginning of something much
bigger and they both know it. Angel stops - pulls away.

                    ANGEL
          Buffy. Maybe we shouldn't-

                                                      CONTINUED

44 CONTINUED: (2)   44

                         BUFFY
            Don't. Just... kiss me.

And he does. They do. Tenderly - full of emotion. They lie
gently back on the bed and OUT OF FRAME.

                                        DISSOLVE TO:

45 INT. ANGEL'S APARTMENT - NIGHT   45

A CRASH OF LIGHTENING wakes ANGEL. Buffy is sleeping next to
him, the covers pulled up around her naked shoulders.

Angel sits on the side of the bed - holds his head in his
hands, clearly in terrible pain. He coughs, looks anxiously
to Buffy, afraid of waking her.

46 EXT. STREET NEAR ANGEL'S APARTMENT - NIGHT   46

It's still raining as Angel, dressed now, moves into the
street. He holds his coat close to him, staggers a few feet,
then falls to his knees.

CLOSE ON ANGEL

                         ANGEL
            Buffy...

He looks to the sky, racked with pain, desperate-

                                        BLACK OUT.

                    END PART ONE

BUFFY THE VAMPIRE SLAYER

"Innocence"

Written and Directed By

Josh Whedon

SHOOTING SCRIPT

December 2, 1997 (WHITE)
December 4, 1997 (BLUE-PAGES)
December 5, 1997 (PINK-PAGES)

BUFFY THE VAMPIRE SLAYER

"Innocence"

<u>CAST LIST</u>

BUFFY SUMMERS.......................... Sarah Michelle Gellar
XANDER HARRIS......................... Nicholas Brendon
RUPERT GILES.......................... Anthony S. Head
WILLOW ROSENBERG...................... Alyson Hannigan
CORDELIA CHASE........................ Charisma Carpenter
ANGEL................................. David Boreanaz

JOYCE SUMMERS......................... Kristine Sutherland
JENNY CALENDAR........................ Robia La Morte
SPIKE................................. James Marsters
DRUSILLA.............................. Juliet Landau
OZ.................................... Seth Green
GYPSY MAN............................. Vincent Schiavelli
THE JUDGE............................. Brian Thompson
WOMAN................................*Carla Madden
TEACHER..............................*James Lurie
STUDENT..............................*Parry Shen
SOLDIER..............................*Ryan Francis

BUFFY THE VAMPIRE SLAYER

"Innocence"

SET LIST

INTERIORS

SUNNYDALE HIGH SCHOOL
        HALL
        LIBRARY
                GILES' OFFICE
        LOUNGE
        CLASSROOM
BUFFY'S HOUSE
        BUFFY'S BEDROOM
        KITCHEN/DINING ROOM/STAIRS
        LIVING ROOM
ANGEL'S APARTMENT
        HALL OUTSIDE ANGEL'S APARTMENT
FACTORY
GYPSY'S ROOM
ARMORY
OZ'S VAN
MULTIPLEX/MALL
GILES' CAR

EXTERIORS

BUFFY'S HOUSE
ALLEY
GRAVEYARD
OUTSIDE ARMY BASE
BY THE ARMORY

BUFFY THE VAMPIRE SLAYER

"Innocence"

TEASER

1 INT. FACTORY - NIGHT   1

SPIKE wheels into frame impatiently. Behind him, THE JUDGE
sits calmly on the floor, his back to us. Spike turns to
DRU, speaks low.

>   SPIKE
>   I'm not happy, pet. Angel and the
>   Slayer are still alive, they know
>   where we are, they know about the
>   Judge... We should be vacating.

>   DRUSILLA
>   Nonsense. They'll not disturb us
>   here. My Angel is too smart to face
>   the Judge again.

>   SPIKE
>   (glancing over)
>   What's the Big Blue up to, anyway? He
>   just sits there.

Even across the room, The Judge can hear Spike perfectly.
Without looking back he replies:

>   THE JUDGE
>   I am preparing.

>   SPIKE
>   (wheels around to him)
>   Yeah, it's interesting to me that
>   preparing looks a great bit like
>   sitting on your arse. When do we
>   destroy the world already?

>   THE JUDGE
>   My strength grows. And every life I
>   take will increase it further.

>   SPIKE
>   So let's take some! I'm bored!

>   THE JUDGE
>   I fought an army. They hacked me to
>   pieces.
>   (more)

CONTINUED

1 CONTINUED: 1

                         THE JUDGE (cont'd)
                For six hundred years my living head
                lay in a box buried in the ground.
                         (turns to Spike)
                I've learned to be patient.

                         SPIKE
                Yeah, well, we're gonna need more
                than patience if Angel and the Slayer
                are --

Dru cries out -- a sharp pain hitting her. She trembles,
stumbles back.

                         SPIKE (cont'd)

                Dru?

                         DRUSILLA
                Angel...

She cries out in orgasmic pain, dropping to the ground.

                         SPIKE
                Dru! What is it? Dru!

She is breathing hard and fast, like an injured bird. Spike
wheels up to her.

                         SPIKE (cont'd)
                Darling, do you see something?

CLOSE UP: DRUSILLA

As the pain on her face washes away, replaced first by
wonder, and then finally a smile.

2 INT. ANGEL'S APARTMENT - NIGHT   2

CLOSE ON: BUFFY

as she slowly wakes up. A moment to remember where she is
and what has happened, then she turns to look at Angel.

He's gone.

She peers into the darkness of the room, pulling the blanket
up as she sits. Finally calling out shyly:

                         BUFFY
                Angel?

                                                        CONTINUED

2 CONTINUED: 2

   There is no answer. She sits, a bit thrown. There is a
flash of lightning and the following thunder takes us to:

3 EXT. ALLEY - NIGHT   3

   Where the rain is still coming down. The camera finds ANGEL
on his knees, in terrible pain. Lightning flashes again.

                 ANGEL
       Buffy... Oh, no...

   A terrible certainty crosses his face.

   ANGLE: A WOMAN

   of ill, if not actively professional, repute. She comes down
the alley tentatively, a cigarette in her hand.

                 WOMAN
       Hey. Are you okay?

   He is bent down, facing away from her. He slowly rises.

                 WOMAN (cont'd)
       You want me to call 911?

                 ANGEL
       No... the pain... is gone.

                 WOMAN
       You're sure?

   She takes a big drag on her cigarette, looking curiously at
his back.

   He spins, vampire face on, and buries his fangs deep in her
throat. Sucks hungrily for a few moments, the woman
paralyzed and dying.

   ANGLE: HER CIGARETTE

   Falls in slow motion to the ground.

   Angel lets her fall. Smiles, and blows out the smoke she had
inhaled.

                                   CONTINUED

3 CONTINUED: 3

                          ANGEL
              I feel just fine.

                                              BLACK OUT.

                  END OF TEASER

ACT ONE

4 INT. BUFFY'S HOUSE - MORNING   4

Buffy enters through the kitchen, tentatively. Her clothes
are no longer wet but she is decidedly rumpled.

She listens a moment for encroaching Mother. Coast is clear.

She moves through the dining room and starts up the stairs.
She's halfway up when JOYCE enters from the living room.
Before seeing Buffy she calls out --

                    JOYCE
          Good morning.

Buffy instantly turns around and starts coming back down.

                    BUFFY
          Good morning...

She stops at the base of the stairs, waiting to see if Joyce
knows she was out.

                    JOYCE
          Did you have fun last night?

                    BUFFY
          Fun?

                    JOYCE
          At Willow's.

                    BUFFY
          Oh. Right. Always fun at Willow's.
          She's a fun machine.

                    JOYCE
          You hungry?

                    BUFFY
          Not really. I ate at a little. I'm
          just gonna take a shower.

                    JOYCE
          Well, hurry up and I'll run you to
          school.

                    BUFFY
          Thanks.

Buffy absently picks a bit of fluff off Joyce's shoulder.
Joyce looks at her a moment.

                                              CONTINUED

4 CONTINUED: 4

                         JOYCE
          Is something wrong?

                         BUFFY
          No. What would be wrong?

                         JOYCE
          I don't know. You just look...

She shrugs it off, heads into the kitchen. Buffy watches her
go, then slowly heads upstairs.

5 INT. LIBRARY - MORNING   5

XANDER enters the library in a bit of a huff. Everyone else
(WILLOW, CORDELIA, GILES and JENNY) are there. They turn to
him, uniformly worried.

                         XANDER
          Well, the bus station was a total
          washout and may I say what a fine
          place to spend the night? What a
          vibrant cross section of Americana.

                         GILES
          You saw no vampires transporting
          boxes?

                         XANDER
          No, but a 400 pound wino offered to
          wash my hair...
                    (seeing their
                     expression)
          What's up? Where's Buffy?

                         WILLOW
          She never checked in.

                         JENNY
          Neither did Angel.

                         GILES
          And if the bus station was as empty
          as the docks and the airport...

                         XANDER
          You think this Judge guy might
          already be assembled?

Giles nods.

                                                          CONTINUED

5 CONTINUED: 5

                        XANDER (cont'd)
            Then Buffy could... We gotta find
            them! We gotta go to that place,
            that factory. That's where they're
            holed up, right? Let's go!

                        CORDELIA
            And do what? Besides be afraid and
            die.

                        XANDER
            Nobody's asking you to go, Cordy. If
            the vampires need grooming tips,
            we'll give you a call.

Cordelia glares at him, stung.

                        GILES
            Cordelia has a point. If Buffy and
            Angel were... harmed, we don't stand
            to fare much better.

                        XANDER
            Yeah, well those of us who were born
            with feelings are gonna do something
            about this.

                        JENNY
            Xander...

Willow jumps up and joins Xander.

                        WILLOW
            No, Xander's right. My God! You
            people are all... Well... I'm upset
            and I can't think of a mean word
            right now but that's what you are and
            we're going to the factory!

They start out - and run into Buffy herself.

                        WILLOW (cont'd)
            Buffy!

                        XANDER
            We were just going to rescue you.

                        WILLOW
            Well, some of us were...

                        GILES
                  (defensively)
            I would have...

5 CONTINUED: (2)   5

                    JENNY
Where's Angel?

                    BUFFY
He didn't check in with you guys?

                    GILES
No...

                    CORDELIA
What happened?

                    GILES
Is the Judge...?

                    BUFFY
                 (nodding)
No assembly required. He's active.

                    GILES
Dammit.

                    BUFFY
He nearly killed us. Angel got us
out.

                    GILES
Why didn't you call? We thought...

                    BUFFY
Well, uh, we had to hid... stuck in
the sewer tunnels... and with the
hiding... we split up and nobody's
heard from him?

                    WILLOW
No...

                    JENNY
He didn't say where he was going?

                    BUFFY
No, we just... we just split up.

                    WILLOW
I'm sure he'll come by.

                    BUFFY
                 (not convinced)
You're right. I'm sure.

                                                    CONTINUED

                          GILES
              Buffy, the Judge. We have to stop
              him.

                          BUFFY
              I know.

                          GILES
              What can you tell us?

                          BUFFY
              Not much. I just touched him --
              kicked him -- and it was like a
              sudden fever. If he'd gotten his
              hands on me --

                          GILES
              In time he won't have to. The
              stronger he gets... he'll be able to
              burn us all with a look.

                          BUFFY
              Also not the prettiest man in town.

                          GILES
              I'll just have to keep researching,
              look for a weakness. You all should
              get to your classes.

The kids start out.

                          JENNY
              I better go too. I'll go on the net
              and search for anything on the Judge.

                          GILES
              Thank you.

                          XANDER
              We'll stop in after classes, help you
              research.

                          CORDELIA
                   (to Xander)
              Yeah, you might find something
              useful -- if it's in an I-Can-Read
              book.

She strides out. He follows, all a-huff. Willow and Buffy
bring up the rear, coming out into:

6 INT. SCHOOL HALL - CONTINUOUS - DAY   6

Buffy's pensive. Willow looks at her, asks:

                    WILLOW
          You don't think Angel would have gone
          after the Judge himself, do you?

                    BUFFY
          No... He'd know better than that.
          Maybe he needed to... I don't know.
          I just wish he'd contact me. I need
          to talk to him.

ANGLE: JENNY

Watches the girls walk off, concerned herself.

7 INT. CLASSROOM - AFTERNOON   7

ANGLE: A CLOCK

Reads 1:43 pm.

Buffy sits as a TEACHER drones on about history. Buffy looks
out the window, looks at her hands, at the clock. Her mind
clearly not on her studies.

                    TEACHER
          So, can somebody tell me some of the
          differences between the Bolsheviks
          and the Mensheviks? What really
          separated them? Anyone?

The teacher looks to Buffy, who stares back for a moment.

Buffy rises and walks out of the class.

                    TEACHER (cont'd)
          Miss Summers, I'm sorry, did you have
          somewhere important to be?

Buffy doesn't hear. She's gone.

ANGLE: WILLOW AND XANDER

Watch her go, puzzled.

8 INT. HALL OUTSIDE ANGEL'S APARTMENT - AFTERNOON   8

Buffy comes down the steps and knocks on Angel's door.
Nothing. She opens it and enters.

9   INT. ANGEL'S APARTMENT - CONTINUOUS - DAY   9

She walks tentatively in, looking about her.

                    BUFFY
          Angel?

She's alone.

10 INT. FACTORY - AFTERNOON   10

Spike is addressing a couple of his henchmen.

                    SPIKE
          Soon as it gets dark, I want you
          patrolling the street. Plus two men
          on the door and down in the tunnels
          at all times, is that clear? I don't
          want any more surprises.

They nod, because they are extras. Then they leave and Spike
wheels to Dru, who lies face up on the table.

                    SPIKE (cont'd)
          Are we feeling better, then?

                    DRUSILLA
          I'm naming all the stars.

                    SPIKE
          Can't see the stars, love. That's
          the ceiling. Also, it's day.

She giggles, never taking her eyes off the ceiling.

                    DRUSILLA
          I can see them. But I've named them
          all the same name, and there's
          terrible confusion. I fear there may
          be a duel.

                    SPIKE
          Recovered, then, have we? Did you
          see any further? Do you know what
          happens to Angel?

                    ANGEL
          Well, he moves to New York and tries
          to fulfill that Broadway dream. It's
          tough sledding, but one day he's
          working in the chorus when the big
          star twists her ankle!

                                              CONTINUED

10 CONTINUED: 10

He steps forward from the shadows as he speaks, smiling coldly.

                    SPIKE
          Angel.

                    ANGEL
          Still having trouble guarding your
          perimeter, brother. Your boys
          downstairs are going to wake up sore.

                    SPIKE
          You don't give up, do you?

                    ANGEL
               (noble tough guy)
          As long as there is injustice in this
          world... As long as scum like you is
          walking -- or, well, rolling -- the
          streets, I'll be around. Look over
          your shoulder. I'll be there.

                    SPIKE
          Yeah, uh, Angel... Look over your
          shoulder.

Angel does, to see the Judge standing right behind him.
Angel's eyes widen with fear. The Judge reaches out and puts
his hand to Angel's chest. Angel begins to shake.

Drusilla watches wide-eyed, as Spike just grins contentedly.

                    SPIKE (cont'd)
          Hurts, doesn't it?

                    ANGEL
          Well, you know, it kind of itches a
          little.

The Judge looks at him in consternation.

                    SPIKE
          Don't just stand there, burn him!

The Judge looks at his hand.

                    ANGEL
          Gee, maybe he's broken.

                    SPIKE
          What the hell is going on?

CONTINUED

                    DRUSILLA
               (gets it)
          Oh my...

                    THE JUDGE
          I cannot burn this one. He is clean.

                    SPIKE
          Clean? You mean he's --

                    THE JUDGE
          There is no humanity in him.

                    ANGEL
          Couldn't have said it better myself.

                    DRUSILLA
          Angel...?

                    ANGEL
          Yeah, baby. I'm back.

                              BLACK OUT.

               END OF ACT ONE

ACT TWO

11   INT. FACTORY - MOMENTS LATER - DAY   11

This news is still sinking in. Spike and Dru stare at Angel,
circling him.

                    SPIKE
          It's really true?

                    ANGEL
          It's really true.

                    DRUSILLA
          You've come home.

                    SPIKE
          No more of this "I've got a soul"
          crap?

                    ANGEL
          What can I say? I was going through
          a phase.

                    SPIKE
          This is great! This is so great.

                    DRUSILLA
          Everything in my head is singing.
          We're family again. We'll feed, and
          we'll play...

                    SPIKE
          I gotta tell you, it made me sick to
          my stomach seeing you being the
          Slayer's lapdog --

Angel grabs his throat suddenly, brings his face close to
Spike's. And then kisses his forehead. Lets him go.

                    DRUSILLA
          How did this happen?

                    ANGEL
          You wouldn't believe me if I told you.

                    SPIKE
          Who cares! What matters is he's
          back. Now it's four against one,
          which are the kind of odds I like to
          play.

                                        CONTINUED

                         DRUSILLA
          We're going to destroy the world. Do
          you want to come?

                         ANGEL
          Yeah, destroying the world...
          great... I'm really more interested
          in the Slayer.

                         SPIKE
          Well, she's **in** the world, so it
          should work out.

                         ANGEL
          Give me tonight.

                         SPIKE
          What do you mean?

                         ANGEL
          Lay low for a night. Let me work on
          her. I guarantee by the time you go
          public, she won't be anything
          resembling a threat.

                         SPIKE
          You've really got a yen to hurt this
          girl, haven't you?

                         ANGEL
          She made me feel like a human being.
          That's not the kind of thing you just
          forgive.

                         SPIKE
          What do you say, Dru? Do we let him
          play?

                         DRUSILLA
          Yes... there's going to be a river of
          blood...

                         ANGEL
          Be just like old times.

He runs his hand along Dru's arm.

Spike's smile slightly drains.

12 INT. LIBRARY - EVENING   12

Cordelia walks through the library, a book in hand. As she
exits frame we see that Giles is in his office, reading.
Willow is at the counter, on the phone. Xander, next to her,
is both reading and listening.

                    WILLOW
          Okay... No, no he didn't... but I'm
          sure he'll... Buffy, he probably has
          some plan and he's trying to protect
          you... well, I don't know what, I'm
          not in on the plan, it's his plan...
          No. NO. Don't even say that. Angel
          is not dead.

                    XANDER
          Say hi for me.

Willow shoots him a look.

                    WILLOW
                (into phone)
          Okay... Yeah, we'll be here. Of
          course. Bye.

She hangs up. Looks at Xander.

                    WILLOW (cont'd)
          Say hi for me?

                    XANDER
          What's the word?

                    WILLOW
          She checked every place she could
          think of. She even beat up Willy the
          snitch a couple times. Angel's
          vanished.

                    GILES
          He does do that on occasion, no?

                    WILLOW
          Yeah, but she's extra wigged this
          time -- I guess 'cause of her dreams.
          God, what if something did happen to
          him?

                    GILES
          Is she going to join us here?

                    WILLOW
          Yeah, she's just stopping at home
          first.

                                              CONTINUED

12 CONTINUED: 12

Willow goes back to her own book. Xander closes his --

> XANDER
> Nada.

-- and heads for the stacks.

ANGLE: BEHIND THE SHELVES

is Cordelia, who is also going through the old text. Xander
rifles through some shelves, then making sure the others
below can't see or hear him, he approaches Cordy.

> XANDER (cont'd)
> Anything?

> CORDELIA
> This book mentions the Judge, but...
> nothing useful... big scary, no
> weapon forged can stop him... took an
> army to take him down blah blah blah.

> XANDER
> We need some insight. A weak spot.

> CORDELIA
> Well, we're not gonna find it here.

She tosses the book on an already prodigious pile. As she
starts looking for a new one, Xander manages:

> XANDER
> I'm sorry I snapped at you before.

> CORDELIA
> Oh yeah, I'm reeling from that new
> experience.

> XANDER
> I was crazed. I wasn't thinking.

> CORDELIA
> You were too busy rushing off to die
> for your beloved Buffy.
> (pouting)
> You'd never die for me.

> XANDER
> (with playful
> intimacy)
> I might die from you, does that get
> me any points?

                                                     CONTINUED

12   CONTINUED: (2)   12

                              CORDELIA
                    No.

                              XANDER
                    Come on, let's kiss and make up.

                              CORDELIA
                    I don't wanna make up.

He starts to move away - she puts a hand on his shirt.

                         CORDELIA (cont'd)
                    But I'm okay with the other part.

They haben der big smootchen. Xander moves his mouth near
her ear and whispers:

                              XANDER
                    Isn't it better when we're friends?

He moves back to look at her - and Willow is revealed between
them, standing some 10 feet away. Eyes and mouth wide open,
pain on her face like a blush.

They see her, Xander stepping back in guilty shock.

                         XANDER (cont'd)
                    Willow! We were just--

But she's out of there.

ANGLE: GILES

As Willow blows past, he says:

                              GILES
                    Oh, Willow, did you find the index
                    to--

And she's out the door. Xander passes:

                         GILES (cont'd)
                    Any luck with--

And he's out the door as well.

                         GILES (cont'd)
                    Well. Yes. Interesting children.

He turns back to his volumes, not even trying to guess.

13 INT. SCHOOL HALL - CONTINUOUS - NIGHT 13 *

Willow is almost out of it as Xander stops her with:

> XANDER
> Willow, come on!

> WILLOW
> I knew it! I knew it! Well, not
> "knew it" in the sense of having the
> slightest idea, but I knew there was
> something I didn't know. You two
> were fighting way too much. It's not
> natural.

> XANDER
> I know, it's weird...

> WILLOW
> Weird? It's against all the laws of
> God and man! That's Cordelia!
> Remember? The "we hate Cordelia
> club," of which you are the treasurer?

> XANDER
> I was gonna tell you...

> WILLOW
> Gee, what stopped you? Could it be
> shame?

> XANDER
> All right! Let's overreact, shall
> we? We were kissing. It doesn't
> mean that much.

> WILLOW
> (softly)
> No. It just means you'd rather be
> with someone you hate... than be with
> me.

She goes. Xander moves to stop her, thinks better of it.

14 EXT. IN FRONT OF BUFFY'S HOUSE - NIGHT 14

Buffy walks along the street. It's dark and not altogether
uncreepy.

As she reaches her house, Angel steps out of the shadows.

> BUFFY
> Angel!

CONTINUED

14 CONTINUED   14

                         ANGEL
          Hey.

She goes up to him, embraces him. He doesn't exactly
reciprocate, but neither does he stop her.

                         BUFFY
          Oh, God, I was so worried...

                         ANGEL
          Didn't mean to frighten you...

                         BUFFY
          Where did you go?

                         ANGEL
          Been around.

                         BUFFY
          I was freaking out. You just
          disappeared...

                         ANGEL
          What, I took off.

                         BUFFY
          Well, you didn't even say anything.
          You just left.

                         ANGEL
          Yeah, like I really wanted to stick
          around after that.

                         BUFFY
               (totally thrown)
          After... What do you...

                         ANGEL
          You got a lot to learn about men,
          kiddo. Although I guess you proved
          that last night.

                         BUFFY
          What do you mean?

                         ANGEL
          Let's not make an issue out of it.
          In fact let's not talk about it at
          all. Does that work for you?

                         BUFFY
          Are you... not glad that we...

                                                    CONTINUED

                         ANGEL
                    Hey, it happened.

                         BUFFY
                    I don't understand. Was I... was
                    it... not good?

She can barely get this question out -- so it's like a kidney-
punch that he starts to laugh.

                         ANGEL
                    No, you were great! Really. I
                    thought you were a pro.

                         BUFFY
                    God, Angel, how can you talk to me
                    like that?

                         ANGEL
                    Lighten up. It was a good time.
                    Doesn't mean we have to make a big
                    deal.

                         BUFFY
                    It is a big deal! It's -- it's --

                         ANGEL
                    Fireworks. Bells ringing. A dulcet
                    choir of pretty little birdies. Come
                    on, Buffy, it's not like I've never
                    been there before.

He puts a friendly hand on her shoulder. She jerks away.

                         BUFFY
                    Get away from me.

                         ANGEL
                    I should have known you wouldn't be
                    able to handle it.

He starts to leave. She turns, a world of hurt in her eyes.

                         BUFFY
                         (a last plea)
                    Angel.... I **love** you.

The son of a bitch actually winks at her.

                         ANGEL
                    Love ya too.
                         (turns to go)
                    I'll call ya.

                                                    CONTINUED

14 CONTINUED: (3)   14

He walks away, laughing to himself. Buffy unable to move.

15 INT. GYPSY'S ROOM - NIGHT   15

It's shabby, but comfortingly homey little room. An armchair
and small coffee table sit by the bed. The GYPSY MAN is in
the armchair. Jenny sits facing him.

                    GYPSY MAN
          Do you know what it is, this thing
          vengeance?

                    JENNY
          Uncle, I have served you. I've been
          faithful and I need to know --

                    GYPSY MAN
          To the modern man, vengeance is an
          idea, a word. Payback, one thing for
          another, like commerce. Not for us.
          Vengeance is a living thing. It
          moves through generations. It
          commands. It kills.

                    JENNY
          Something has happened. Something
          has changed.

                    GYPSY MAN
          Everything has changed.

                    JENNY
          You told me to watch Angel. You told
          me to keep him from the Slayer. I
          tried. But there are other factors,
          there are terrible things happening
          here that we cannot control.

                    GYPSY MAN
          We control nothing. We are not
          wizards, Janna. We merely play our
          part.

                    JENNY
          Angel could be of help to us -- he
          may be the only chance we've got to
          stop the Judge.

                    GYPSY MAN
          It is too late for that.

                                                          CONTINUED

15 CONTINUED: 15

                          JENNY
              Why?

                          GYPSY MAN
              The curse... Angel was meant to
              suffer. Not to live as a human. One
              moment of true happiness, of
              contentment... one moment where his
              soul that we restored does not plague
              his thoughts -- and that soul is
              taken from him.

                          JENNY
              Then, if he somehow has... if it's
              happened, then Angelus is back.

                          GYPSY MAN
              I hoped to stop it. But I see now
              that it was arranged to be so.

                          JENNY
              Buffy loves him.

                          GYPSY MAN
              And now she will have to kill him.

She rises, in a fury.

                          JENNY
              Unless he kills her first! Uncle,
              this is insanity. People are going
              to **die.**

                          GYPSY MAN
              Yes. This is not justice that we
              serve. It is vengeance.

                          JENNY
              You're a fool. We're all fools.

She exits.

16 INT. SCHOOL LOUNGE - NIGHT   16

Xander is coming out of the bathroom (which is right off the
lounge, in case you didn't know) and sees Willow heading
toward the library.

                          XANDER
              Will!

                                                       CONTINUED

16 CONTINUED: 16

                    WILLOW
                (sullenly)
          Hey.

                    XANDER
          Where did you go?

                    WILLOW
          Home. Or, partway home. Then I came
          back. Now I'm here.

                    XANDER
          I'm glad you came back. We can't do
          this without you.

                    WILLOW
          Let's get this straight. I don't
          understand it. I don't want to
          understand it. You have gross
          emotional problems and things are not
          okay between us. But what's
          happening right now is more important
          than that.

                    XANDER
          Willow, I just --

                    WILLOW
          No.

                    XANDER
          Okay.

                    WILLOW
          What about the Judge? Where do we
          stand?

                    XANDER
          On a pile of really boring books that
          all say exactly the same thing.

                    WILLOW
          Let me guess. "No weapon forged..."

                    XANDER
          "It took an army..."

                    WILLOW
          Yeah, where's an army when you need
          one?

     Xander stops. Thinks.

                                                          CONTINUED

16   CONTINUED: (2)   16

                         WILLOW (cont'd)
              What?

                         XANDER
              Wow. Wow. I think I'm having a
              thought. I am. I'm having a
              thought. And now I'm having a plan.

The lights all go out.

                         XANDER (cont'd)
              And now I'm having a wiggins.

                         WILLOW
              What's going on?

                         XANDER
              Let's get back to the library.

ANGLE: FROM THE END OF THE HALL

As they turn to go, someone steps into frame behind them.
Angel.

                         ANGEL
              Willow? Xander?

They turn -- but in the dark, they can't see his face.

                         XANDER
              Angel!

                         WILLOW
              Thank god you're okay! Have you seen
              Buffy?

                         ANGEL
              Yeah. What's up with the lights?

                         XANDER
              I don't know. Listen, I think I
              might have an idea --

                         ANGEL
              That doesn't matter now. I've got
              something to show you.

                         WILLOW
              Show us?

                         ANGEL
              Come here. And Xander, get the
              others.

                                                     CONTINUED

16 CONTINUED: (3)   16

                              XANDER
                    Okay...

          He takes off down the hall a little perplexed. Willow starts
          toward Angel. She's a bit hesitant -- probably doesn't even
          know why.

                              WILLOW
                    What is it, Angel?

                              ANGEL
                    It's amazing.

A17 INT. HALL - CONTINUOUS - NIGHT   A17   *

          Xander is heading down, stops, turns, uncertain.   *

B17 INT. SCHOOL LOUNGE - CONTINUOUS - NIGHT   B17   *

          Willow comes closer to Angel -- and now someone ELSE steps   *
          into frame behind her.

                              JENNY
                    Willow, get away from him.

          Willow turns, confused.

                              WILLOW
                    What?

                              JENNY
                    Walk to me.

          She holds up a cross.

                              WILLOW
                    Ms. Calendar, what are you doing?
                    It's Angel.

          As she says this, Angel comes out of the shadows toward her.
          VAMP FACE on. Grin on as well.

          Xander bursts through the double doors, stops when he sees
          Angel GRAB Willow.

                              XANDER
                    Don't you do that...

                              ANGEL
                    Oh, I think I do that.

                                                              CONTINUED

B17 CONTINUED: B17

                  WILLOW
              (terrified)
    Angel...

                  JENNY
    He's not Angel anymore. Are you?

                                      CONTINUED

> ANGEL
> Wrong. I am Angel. Angelus. At
> last.

> XANDER
> (gets it)
> Oh my God...

> ANGEL
> I've got a message for Buffy.

> BUFFY
> Then give it to me yourself.

She comes out of the darkness, down the hall he came down.
He spins to see her. She is trying to be strong, but she is
shaking.

> ANGEL
> Well, it's not really the kind of
> message you tell. It sort of
> involves finding the bodies of all
> your friends.

> BUFFY
> This can't be you...

> ANGEL
> We already covered this subject.

As they talk, Xander, who is now behind Angel, takes the
cross from Jenny and starts moving slowly toward Angel.

> BUFFY
> Angel... there must be some part of
> you inside that remembers who you
> are...

> ANGEL
> Dream on, schoolgirl. Your boyfriend
> is dead. You're all gonna join him.

> BUFFY
> Just leave Willow alone. Deal with
> me.

> ANGEL
> But she's so cute and helpless. It's
> really a turn on --

Xander reaches around and shoves the cross in Angel's face.
Angel roars, let's go of Willow. He knocks Xander to the
ground -- Buffy comes forward --

CONTINUED

B17 CONTINUED: (3)   B17*

Angel leaps at Buffy, grabs her. She is too wigged to do
much more than stare at him.

              ANGEL (cont'd)
Things are about to get very
interesting.

He kisses her, hard - she tries to move her hand away -- then
he tosses her to the ground like a rag doll and takes off,
the double door swinging shut behind him.

Buffy is still semi-prone on the ground as the others come up
to her.

              XANDER
Buffy, are you okay?

              WILLOW
Buffy?

She just stares at the doors he exited by. She can't even
speak.

                      BLACK OUT.

          END OF ACT TWO

ACT THREE

17 INT. LIBRARY - EVENING   17

It's maybe ten minutes later. Everyone is gathered in the
library, in various stages of freakingdom. We do not see
Buffy yet.

                    GILES
          And we're absolutely certain that
          Angel has reverted to his former self?

                    XANDER
          We're certain. Anybody not feeling
          certain here?

                    WILLOW
          Giles, it was just -- you wouldn't
          have believed him. He was so... He
          came here to kill us!

                    CORDELIA
          What are we gonna do?

                    GILES
          I'm leaning toward blind panic,
          myself.

                    JENNY
          Rupert, don't talk like that. The
          kids.

                    GILES
          I'm sorry. It's just, things are bad
          enough with the Judge here. Angel
          crossing to the other side... I just
          wasn't prepared to deal with that.

                    JENNY
          None of us was.

And the camera finds Buffy, sitting off to the side by
herself. Willow approaches her.

                    WILLOW
          Are you okay?

Buffy shakes her head.

                    WILLOW (cont'd)
          Is there anything I can do?

                                              CONTINUED

17 CONTINUED: 17

                              BUFFY
                    I should have known. I saw him... at
                    home and he was... different. the
                    things he said...

                              GILES
                         (coming near)
                    What things?

                              BUFFY
                    It's private.

                              JENNY
                    But you didn't know he had turned bad.

                              WILLOW
                         (to Jenny)
                    How did you?

                              JENNY
                    What?

                              WILLOW
                    You knew. You told me to get away
                    from him.

                              JENNY
                    Well, I saw his face.

          Before Willow has time to consider that answer, Giles
          interrupts:

                              GILES
                    If we only knew how it happened...

                              BUFFY
                    What do you mean?

                              GILES
                    Well, something set it off. Some
                    event must have triggered his
                    transformation.

          This hits Buffy hard.

                              GILES (cont'd)
                    If anyone would know, Buffy, it
                    should be you.

                              BUFFY
                    I don't... I...

CONTINUED

17 CONTINUED: (2)   17

                         GILES
               Did anything happen last night that
               might --

                         BUFFY
               Giles, please. I can't... now now.

She starts out, distraught. Willow has her eyes locked on
Buffy, realization sinking in.

                         GILES
               Buffy, I'm sorry but we can't afford
               to... Buffy!

                         WILLOW
               Giles, shut up.

She says it levelly, eyes still on the departing figure of
Buffy.

18 INT. SCHOOL HALL - CONTINUOUS - NIGHT   18

Buffy comes out and takes off at a good clip. Completely
unable to deal.

19 INT. LIBRARY - CONTINUOUS - NIGHT   19

The others all react to Buffy's departure.

                         CORDELIA
               This is great. There's an unkillable
               demon in town, Angel's joined his
               team and the Slayer is a basket case.
               I'd say we've hit bottom.

                         XANDER
               I have a plan.

                         CORDELIA
               Oh, no, here's a lower place.

                         XANDER
               I don't know what's up with Angel,
               but I may have a way to deal with
               this Judge guy.

                         WILLOW
               What do we do?

                         XANDER
               I'm gonna need... I think I'm gonna
               need Cordelia on this one.

                                              CONTINUED

19 CONTINUED: 19

Boy, is that not lost on Willow.

                    XANDER (cont'd)
          And we'll need wheels.

                    CORDELIA
          Well, my car --

                    XANDER
          It might need to be bigger.

                    WILLOW
                (steely-eyes, to
                Xander)
          No problem. I'll get Oz. He has a
          van.

Nor is that lost on Xander. But he's grown-up enough to
ignore it.

                    XANDER
          Good. Okay.

                    CORDELIA
          Care to let me in on the plan that
          I'm a part of?

                    XANDER
          No.

                    CORDELIA
          Why not?

                    XANDER
          'Cause if I tell you what it is, you
          won't do it. Just meet me at
          Willow's in half an hour. And wear
          something trashy -- er.

                    GILES
          I'm not sure what we should do about
          Buffy.

                    JENNY
          Assuming they don't attack tonight,
          I think we should let her be.

                    WILLOW
          I agree.

                    GILES
          I can't imagine what she's going
          through right now.

                                          CONTINUED

19 CONTINUED: (2)   19

                         WILLOW
          I don't think any of us can.

20 INT. FACTORY - NIGHT   20

Angel is having a very different conversation with Spike and
Dru.

                         ANGEL
          You should have seen her face. It
          was priceless. I'll never forget it.

                         SPIKE
          So, you didn't kill her then?

                         ANGEL
          Of course not.

                         SPIKE
          I know you haven't been in the game
          for a while, mate, but we do still
          kill people. It's sort of our raison
          d'etre, you know.

                         DRUSILLA
          You don't want to kill her, do you?
          You want to hurt her. Just like you
          hurt me.

She smiles with such affection when she says it...

                         ANGEL
          Nobody knows me like you do, Dru.

                         SPIKE
          She'd better not get in our way.

                         ANGEL
          Don't worry about it.

                         SPIKE
          I do.

                         ANGEL
          Spike, my boy, you really don't get
          it. You tried to kill her and you
          couldn't. Look at you. You're a
          wreck. She's stronger than any
          Slayer you've faced. Force won't get
          it done. You gotta work from the
          inside. To kill this girl... you
          have to love her.

21 INT. BUFFY'S BEDROOM - NIGHT   21

She enters quietly, shuts the door behind her. She stares
ahead blankly, trying to hold herself together. Goes to the
dresser.

ANGLE: MIRROR

Hanging over it is the cross Angel gave her last year. She
looks at it, then at herself in the mirror. Beginning to
tremble, she looks at her hand.

ANGLE: THE CLADDAGH RING

Still on her finger. She pulls it off abruptly, letting it
drop to the floor as the vast vestige of her resolve crumbles.

She cries.

Moves blindly to the bed, sitting. Lying, curling up, unable
to stop the tears.

                              FADE TO BLACK.

LIGHTNING FLASHES

22 INT. ANGEL'S APARTMENT - NIGHT (DREAM SEQUENCE)   22

As we see EXTREME CLOSE UPS of Buffy and Angel together --
her hand on his back, his face in her neck, her eyes opening.

                    ANGEL
          I love you...

ANGLE: VAMPIRE ANGEL

ROARS at us in close up, then disappears.

23 EXT. GRAVEYARD - DAY   23

Buffy stands at Angel's grave. Behind her and to the right
stands a woman in black with a veil. Buffy looks behind her
as the woman lifts the veil -- to reveal Jenny, who looks
straight ahead, ignoring her.

Buffy turns back and Angel is standing, in broad daylight, by
his grave. He says serenely:

                    ANGEL
          You have to know what to see.

Buffy looks behind her again, but Jenny is gone.

24 INT. BUFFY'S BEDROOM - MORNING   24

She awakens, still in her clothes. Steely purpose in her
eyes.

25 INT. SCHOOL HALL - DAY   25

Buffy strides through the mass of students, paying no
attention to anything around her.

26 INT. COMPUTER CLASS - CONTINUOUS - DAY   26

Jenny is standing before her desk talking in low tones to
Giles. A few students sit at computers, working silently.

Buffy strides in, the grown-ups looking up as Buffy crosses
the room to them.

She never breaks stride. It's one swift motion from walking
to taking Jenny by the neck and slamming her down onto her
desk.

Pencils and disks fly everywhere. Kids look up, stand,
shocked as Giles --

                    GILES
          Buffy!

-- tries to grab her, Buffy shoving him away without even
looking at him.

                    BUFFY
                (to Jenny)
          What do you know?

Jenny is wide eyed -- Buffy is choking her, a murderer's calm
in her eyes.

Giles stands again, coming forward --

                    GILES
          Buffy, stop it!

Buffy lets Jenny up, who gasps for breath.

                    STUDENT
          Should I get the principal --

                    GILES
          I'll handle this. You're all
          dismissed.

The kids file out. Buffy never takes her eyes off Jenny.

                                                    CONTINUED

26 CONTINUED: 26

                          BUFFY
          Did you do it? Did you change him?

                          GILES
          For God's sake, calm down!

                          BUFFY
                  (ignores him)
          Did you know what was gonna happen?

                          GILES
          Buffy, you can't just go accusing
          everyone around you of --

                          JENNY
          I didn't know exactly.

Giles stops, stares at Jenny. She cannot even look at the
two of them as she continues.

                          JENNY (cont'd)
          I was told... I was sent here to
          watch you. When they told me to keep
          you and Angel apart, they never told
          me what would happen.

                          GILES
          Jenny...

                          JENNY
          I'm sorry, Rupert. Angel was
          supposed to pay for what he did to my
          people.

                          BUFFY
          And me? What was I supposed to be
          paying for?

                          JENNY
          I didn't know what would happen until
          after. I swear I would have told
          you...

                          BUFFY
          So it was me. I did it.

                          JENNY
          I think so. I mean, if you...

                          GILES
          I don't understand.

                                                        CONTINUED

26 CONTINUED: (2)   26

                         JENNY
            The curse. If Angel achieved true
            happiness, just a moment of... he
            would lose his soul.

                         GILES
            But how do you know that you were
            responsible... Oh.

    Buffy nods. There is a moment of uncomfortable silence.

                         JENNY
            If I could do anything --

                         BUFFY
            Curse him again. Can't you do that?

                         JENNY
            Those majicks are long lost, even to
            my people.

                         BUFFY
            But you did it once, I mean it may
            not be too late to save him...

                         JENNY
            It can't be done. I can't help you.

                         BUFFY
            Then take me to someone who can.

27 INT. GYPSY'S ROOM - NIGHT   27

    He sits in the armchair, his back to us, when he hears the
    footsteps. He turns his head only slightly.

                         GYSPY MAN
            I knew you would come. I suppose you
            want answers.

                         ANGEL
            Not really.

    The Gypsy Man stands, spins, terror in his eyes.

                         ANGEL (cont'd)
            But thanks for the offer.

                         GYPSY MAN
            You! Evil one...

                                                         CONTINUED

27 CONTINUED: 27

                        ANGEL
          Evil one? Oh, man, now I've got
          hurty feelings.

                        GYPSY MAN
                    (backing away)
          What do you want?

                        ANGEL
          A whole lot. Got a lot of lost time
          to make up for. Say, I guess that's
          kind of your fault, isn't it?

The Gypsy holds up a cross, which Angel knocks out of his
hand, grabbing his neck.

                        ANGEL (cont'd)
          You gypsy types, you go and curse
          people, you really don't care who
          gets hurt. Of course, you did give
          me an escape clause, so I gotta thank
          you for that.

He pushes the old man back so he's sitting on the bed.

                        GYPSY MAN
          You are an abomination. The day you
          stop suffering for your crimes, you
          are no longer worthy of a human soul.

                        ANGEL
          Well, that pesky critter's all gone.
          So we can get down to business.

He kneels in front of the old man.

                        ANGEL (cont'd)
          Don't worry, it won't hurt a bit...
          after the first hour.

Off the Gypsy's look...

28 EXT. OUTSIDE AN ARMY BASE - NIGHT   28

Oz's Van pulls up by a wall (the back of the armory) with a
high window in it. Oz is driving, Willow beside him.

The back door slides open and Xander and Cordy pile out. She
is dressed less sophisticatedly than usual. He has a tight
hawaiian shirt and dockers. Hair very neat, ala Reptile Boy.
He moves to Oz's window.

                                                        CONTINUED

28 CONTINUED: 28

                    XANDER
          Wait here. When you hear that window
          open, get the ladder out, go up and
          we'll pass you the package. Okay?

                    OZ
          Okay.

                    WILLOW
          Be careful.

Xander and Cordy head around a corner.

29 EXT. BY THE ARMORY - MOMENTS LATER - NIGHT   29

They squeeze through the edge of a cyclone fence that runs to
the armory, head down the length of the building.

                    XANDER
          Security here is a joke. I really
          should report it.

                    CORDELIA
          Who are we supposed to be again?

                    XANDER
          You're supposed to be a girl. Think
          you can handle it?

A couple of soldiers pass. Xander suavely nods to them.
They nod back and pass without comment, because they are
extras.

ANGLE: THE ARMORY DOOR

As Xander and Cordelia round the corner and head for it.
They are almost there when:

                    SOLDIER
          Halt!

He's the guard on duty. Not huge, but tough. Eyeballs
Xander. Xander looks slightly busted. Tries not to stammer.

                    SOLDIER (cont'd)
          Identify yourself right the Hell now.

                    XANDER
          Private Harris, with the... 33rd.

                    SOLDIER
          33rd are on maneuvers.

                                              CONTINUED

                         XANDER
          Right. And I'm on leave. From them.

                         SOLDIER
          You always spend your leave sneaking
          into the armory, buddy? And who is
          she?

                         CORDELIA
          Hi. I'm not a soldier.
                 (to Xander)
          Right?

Xander pulls the soldier aside.

                         XANDER
          Look, I just want to give her the
          tour, you know what I'm saying?

                         SOLDIER
          The tour?

                         XANDER
          Well, you know the ladies... they
          love to see the big guns. Gets 'em
          all hot and bothered. Can you cut me
          some slack, give me a blind eye?

                         SOLDIER
                 (still suspicious)
          Why should I?

Cordy watches them. It looks like Xander's going down in
flames.

                         XANDER
          Well if you do, I won't tell Colonel
          Newsome that your shoes ain't
          regulation, your oakleafs are on
          backwards and you hold your gun like
          a sissy girl.

He takes the gun and positions it correctly in the soldier's
hands. Smiles winningly. Begrudgingly, the soldier smiles
back.

                         SOLDIER
          You got twenty minutes, nimrod.

                         XANDER
          I only need five.

He herds Cordy in, pokes his head back out to say --

                                                        CONTINUED

29 CONTINUED: (2)   29

                    XANDER (cont'd)
            Uh, forget I said that last part.

He shuts the door as the soldier moves on.

30 INT. ARMORY - CONTINUOUS - NIGHT   30

All we see (or ever shall) is a very dark room full of crates
that cut off our view of the rest of the room.

                    CORDELIA
            Okay, what was that? And also, who
            are you?

                    XANDER
            Remember Halloween? I got turned
            into a soldier?

                    CORDELIA
            Yeah...

                    XANDER
            I still remember all of it! I know
            procedure, ordinance, access codes,
            everything. I know the whole layout
            of this place and I'm pretty sure I
            can put together an M16 in fifty
            seven seconds.

                    CORDELIA
            Well, I'm sort of impressed. But
            let's just find the thing and leave.

                    XANDER
            Okay.

They start looking.

                    CORDELIA
            So looking at guns makes girls want
            to have sex? That's scary.

                    XANDER
            Yeah, I guess...

                    CORDELIA
            Well, does looking at guns make **you**
            wanna have sex?

                    XANDER
            I'm seventeen. Looking at **linoleum**
            makes me wanna have sex.

31 INT. OZ'S VAN - NIGHT   31

As Oz and Willow wait for the others in not entirely
comfortable silence...

                    WILLOW
          I wish they'd hurry...

                    OZ
          So, do you guys steal weapons from
          the army a lot?

                    WILLOW
          Well, we don't have cable, so we have
          to make our own fun.

                    OZ
          I get you.

                    WILLOW
          Do you want to make out with me?

                    OZ
          What?

                    WILLOW
          With me. Make out. Do you want to?

                    OZ
          That time you said it backwards.

                    WILLOW
          Forget it. I'm sorry.
                    (beat)
          Well do you?

                    OZ
          Sometime when I'm sitting in class,
          I'm not thinking about class, 'cause,
          that could never happen, and I'll
          think about kissing you and then
          everything stops. It's like, freeze
          frame. Willow kissage.

She is drawn in by this -- so a bit taken aback when instead
of kissing her, he just looks out the window again. There is
a moment of confused silence before he remembers himself and
speaks again.

                    OZ (cont'd)
          I'm not gonna kiss you.

                    WILLOW
          What? But... freeze frame...

                                                    CONTINUED

31 CONTINUED: 31

>   OZ
>   Well, to the casual observer, it
>   looks like you want to make your
>   friend Xander jealous. Or even the
>   score, or something. That's on the
>   empty side. You see, in my fantasy,
>   when I'm kissing you... you're
>   kissing me.

She can't reply -- she's touched, but she knows he's right about Xander. Oz smiles at her, serene.

>   OZ (cont'd)
>   It's okay. I can wait.

We hear the window opening, as do they.

>   OZ (cont'd)
>   We're up.

He gets out of the van. Willow watches him, real affection suffusing her gaze.

32 INT. GYPSY'S ROOM - NIGHT   32

Buffy, Giles and Jenny enter. They stop, Jenny putting her hand over her mouth.

We don't see much -- maybe a hand -- but we can hear flies buzzing around the remains.

Buffy looks down at the body -- then her eyes drift over to the wall.

ANGLE: THE WALL

on it is written: WAS IT GOOD FOR YOU TOO?

It isn't written in ink.

>   JENNY
>   God...

>   GILES
>   Buffy, he's doing this deliberately.
>   He's trying to make it harder for you.

>   BUFFY
>   He's just making it easier. I know
>   what I have to do.

                                                       CONTINUED

32 CONTINUED: 32

                         GILES
          What?

She looks at him, summoning her resolve.

                         BUFFY
          Kill him.

                                        BLACK OUT.

          END OF ACT THREE

ACT FOUR

33   INT. FACTORY - NIGHT   33

The Judge steps forward as two vampires put a coarse, monkish robe around his shoulders.

                    THE JUDGE
          I am ready.

                    SPIKE
          'Bout time.

Drusilla breezes in, all excited. She places herself on Spike's lap.

                    SPIKE (cont'd)
          Have a good time.

                    DRUSILLA
          You'll be able to hear screams.
          I promise.

Angel also joins them.

                    ANGEL
                (to Spike)
          Too bad you can't come with. We'll
          be thinking of you.

                    SPIKE
                (glares at him)
          I won't be in this chair forever.
          What if your girlfriend shows up?

                    ANGEL
          I'm gonna give her a kiss.

Drusilla plants a huge kiss on Spike, then takes Angel's hand and leads him out. As Angel passes the Judge he remarks:

                    ANGEL (cont'd)
          Don't you look spiffy.

34   INT. GILES' OFFICE - NIGHT   34

Xander and Oz set an oblong wooden crate down on the desk.
Buffy comes up to it as Giles starts to open it with a
crowbar. (Willow and Cordy may be visible in the background,
loading weapons into a gymbag).

                                                    CONTINUED

34 CONTINUED: 34

                        XANDER
            Happy Birthday, Buffy. Hope you like
            the color.

                        BUFFY
            Giles, we'll hit the factory first
            but we may not find them. If they're
            on the offensive we need to figure
            out where they'll go.

                        GILES
            Agreed.

He pries it open. Jenny comes into the office tentatively.
Buffy still looks at the box.

                        BUFFY
            This is good.

                        JENNY
            Do you... is there something I can do
            to --

                        BUFFY
            Get out.

Buffy never looks at her. Everyone is made plenty
uncomfortable by the silence.

                        JENNY
            I just want to help...

She looks pleadingly at Giles. There's no joy, nor anger in
his reply. Just a decision.

                        GILES
            She said get out.

Slowly, Jenny does. A moment before Xander turns to Buffy

                        XANDER
            Do you want me to show you how to use
            it?

                        BUFFY
                 (all business)
            Yes I do.

35 INT. FACTORY - NIGHT   35

Buffy and Giles enter the empty space, the others waiting at
the door.

CONTINUED

35 CONTINUED: 35

                         BUFFY
              I knew it.

                         GILES
              And we haven't a bead on where they
              would go?

                         BUFFY
              I don't know.

ANGLE: SPIKE

hides in the shadows, chair behind the boiler.

                         BUFFY (cont'd)
              Somewhere crowded. The Judge is
              gonna need bodies.

                         WILLOW
              The Bronze?

                         XANDER
              It's closed tonight.

                         CORDELIA
              There's not a lot of choices in
              Sunnydale. It's not like people are
              gonna line up to get massacred.

That strikes a chord with Oz.

                         OZ
              Uh, guys? If I was gonna line up, I
              know where I'd be.

36 INT. MULTIPLEX\MALL - NIGHT   36

We see people, not surprisingly, lined up, waiting inside for
movies to open. They are in a huge, arched hallway. At one
end is a domed room with a giant concession stand in the
middle. At the other end is the mall, a large balcony
overlooking the area and facing the concession stand.

We see various angles of the busy space -- people shopping,
waiting, buying tickets or popcorn. Then we see:

ANGLE: THE DOORS ON THE BALCONY LEVEL

open, the Judge striding in. Dru and Angel flanking him, the
other vamps (say, three) behind.

                                                    CONTINUED

36   CONTINUED: 36

A businessman is on his way out, head down, oblivious. The
Judge gestures at him -- no touching -- and the man shakes,
burns (CGI), drops.

                    ANGEL
               (to the vamps)
          Lock the exits, boys.

The vamps spread out.

                    ANGEL (cont'd)
               (to the Judge)
          It's all yours.

37   INT. MALL HALLWAY - CONTINUOUS - NIGHT   37

As Buffy and the gang arrive from another entrance, full of
purpose. Xander and Giles still carry the box by its rope
handles.

                    BUFFY
          Everybody keeps back. Damage control
          only. Take out any lesser vamps if
          you can. I'll handle the smurf.

38   INT. BALCONY SECTION OF THE MALL - CONTINUOUS - NIGHT   38

The Judge comes to the center of the balcony, looks down on
the people who are too busy shopping to notice him.

There are two staircases leading down from the balcony,
people on both.

The Judge spreads his arms and connects with the nearest two
on either stair. They start to burn, slowly, eyes wide, then
we CUT WIDE as the energy from the Judge shoots from them to
more people, and more, till he has created a huge web of
energy, scores of people caught in it, starting to shake.

                    DRUSILLA
          Oh, goodie!

An arrow suddenly whips into the Judge's chest. He stumbles
back, the power cut off.

ANGLE: HIS VICTIMS

We see some of them fall to the ground, hurt but alive.

The Judge pulls the arrow out of his chest, quietly seething.

                                                    CONTINUED

                          THE JUDGE
                    Who dares...?

ANGLE: THE CONCESSION STAND

As we ARM up it, up the center, to find Buffy standing on top
of the popcorn machine (or highest point of the stand),
holding her crossbow.

                          BUFFY
                    I think I got his attention...

The Judge sees her, takes a step forward, throwing down the
arrow.

                          THE JUDGE
                    You are a fool. No weapon forged can
                    stop me.

Buffy drops the crossbow --

                          BUFFY
                    That was then.

-- and hoists the rocket launcher Xander has procured for her.

                          BUFFY (cont'd)
                    This is now.

And then everything happens very slowly.

DRUSILLA

Sees the rocket launcher, starts to dive out of the way --

ANGEL

Does the same --

BUFFY

flicks a switch and sights up --

THE JUDGE

looks at the thing in confusion and just a touch of worry.

                          THE JUDGE
                    What's that do?

And Buffy fires.

                                                       CONTINUED

38 CONTINUED: (2)   38

The rocket streaks across the hall, high above the heads of
the bystanders -- straight toward the Judge --

-- and IMPACTS with a shuddering blast.

Drusilla gets pelted with debris. She looks back at the
Judge.

Or rather, the place he was. It's smoke, rubble, and small
fires.

Drusilla, whimpering, bails, her henchvamps following.

ANGLE: THE GANG

Come out from behind the concession stand as Buffy climbs
down, tossing the launcher to Xander.

                    BUFFY
          My best present ever.

                    XANDER
          Knew you'd like it.

                    WILLOW
          Do you think he's dead?

Buffy is looking around her, her guard still up.

                    BUFFY
          You guys pick up the pieces. Keep
          'em separate.

As they move to comply --

                    CORDELIA
          Pieces? We're getting pieces? Our
          job sucks!

Buffy is still looking about -- and then she spots him, off
to the right.

ANGLE: ANGEL

Slips around a corner, past panicking civilians.

Buffy pursues.

ANGLE: SPRINKLERS

Rising smoke sets them off.

39 INT. MALL HALLWAY\CUL DE SAC - NIGHT   39

Buffy makes her way quickly but cautiously along, water
cascading down everywhere.

She turns a corner, looking around her. This cul de sac has
a pastry and coffee counter, not much else. Everything being
soaked by the sprinklers. Buffy stops, listening.

She spins -- and a fist knocks her hard to the ground.

Angel steps up, grinning. (Human face still on).

                    ANGEL
          You know what the worst part was?
          Pretending I loved you. If I'd known
          how easily you'd give it up, I
          wouldn't have bothered.

She rises, her fury bottled in calm.

                    BUFFY
          That doesn't work any more. You're
          not Angel.

                    ANGEL
          You'd like to think that, wouldn't
          you? Doesn't matter. The important
          thing is, you made me the man I am
          today.

She comes at him -- and they trade vicious blows, Angel
getting the upper hand.   *

A40 INT. MALL - CONTINUOUS - NIGHT   A40   *

In the wet, Xander and Willow look for Judge parts. Behind   *
them, Oz finds: *

                    OZ   *
          Arm.   *

They go to look.   *

B40 INT. MALL HALLWAY/CUL DE SAC - CONTINUOUS - NIGHT B40   *

Angel drives Buffy back, toward the glass counter.   *

She hesitates, out of breath and frightened. He beckons to
her.

                                              CONTINUED

B40 CONTINUED: B40

                           ANGEL
                Not quitting on me already, are you?
                Come on, Buffy. You know you want it.

Okay, well, that's just it. She hits him in the stomach like
a pile driver -- He doubles over in pain -- and she grabs
him, **thrusts** his head right through the glass of the pastry
case -- then pulls him roughly up so the back of his head
smashes through the glass **top** of the case.

And then she wails on him. Punching his face, round-housing
him, just pummelling the guy, everything she's gone through
pouring out in a hail of blows.

She sends him slamming back into the wall. He staggers back
toward her, face cut and bloody, as she pulls a stake out and
pulls back, ready to plunge --

                                                      CONTINUED

B40   CONTINUED: (2)   B40

She hesitates. Pain running through her face. Hand
trembling. And finally lets the stake drop to the floor.
Angel smile is aggravatingly charming.

                    ANGEL (cont'd)
          You can't do it. You can't kill me.

She kicks him between the legs, just about as hard as a
person can.

He drops to his knees, mouth open in in an extreme of agony
that cannot even scream. She turns.

                    BUFFY
          Give me time.

She walks away, leaving him gasping in the artificial rain.

40   EXT. IN FRONT OF BUFFY'S HOUSE - NIGHT   40

Giles' car pulls up, Giles at the wheel, an extremely subdued
Buffy beside him. For a moment, they both sit in silence.

                    GILES
          It's not over. I suppose you know
          that.

Buffy nods, not looking at him.

                    GILES (cont'd)
          He'll come after **you** particularly.
          His profile -- well, he'll strike out
          at the things that made him the most
          human.

                    BUFFY
          You must be so disappointed in me.

                    GILES
          No, I'm not.

                    BUFFY
          But... this is all my fault.

                    GILES
          I don't believe it is.

Buffy looks at him. She is close to crying.

                                                          CONTINUED

40 CONTINUED: 40

                         GILES (cont'd)
          Do you want me to wag my finger at
          you and tell you you acted rashly?
          You did, and I can. But I know you
          loved him, and he has proven more
          than once that he loved you. You
          couldn't have known what would
          happen. The coming months are going
          to be very hard -- I suspect on all
          of us. Buf if you're looking for
          guilt, Buffy, I'm not your man. All
          you will have from me is my
          support... and my respect.

She says nothing, spilling eloquent tears.

41 INT.   BUFFY'S LIVING ROOM - NIGHT   41

ANGLE: A T.V. (old movie) (comforting musical)

We pan off it to find Joyce entering the living room, holding
a plate with a couple of cupcakes on it, and a mug of cocoa.

Buffy is on the couch. Joyce joins her, setting the food
down on the coffee table.

                         JOYCE
          Did I miss anything?

                         BUFFY
          Some singing. And some running
          around.

Joyce sets a candle in one of the cupcakes.

                         JOYCE
          Here we go... I'm sorry I didn't have
          time to make you a real cake.

                         BUFFY
          This is perfect.

                         JOYCE
          But we're still going shopping
          tomorrow.

Buffy nods as Joyce gets matches.

                         JOYCE (cont'd)
          So, did you have a fun birthday?
          What'd you do?

                                                        CONTINUED

41 CONTINUED: 41

                          BUFFY
               I got older.

                          JOYCE
               You still look the same to me.

          She lights the candle, pushes the cupcake over to Buffy.

                          JOYCE (cont'd)
               Happy birthday. I don't have to
               sing, do I?

          Buffy shakes her head, looks at the candle.

                          JOYCE (cont'd)
               Well, go on. Make a wish.

          A moment before she replies.

                          BUFFY
               I'll just let it burn.

          Joyce puts her hand to Buffy's hair, touching it softly.
          Affection and vague concern on her face. Buffy puts her head
          in her mother's lap, brings her feet up onto the couch.

          They sit, Joyce playing gently with her daughter's hair.
          Buffy letting her eyes drift shut. The candle flickering
          bravely in the dark.

                                        FADE TO BLACK.

                         END OF SHOW

BUFFY THE VAMPIRE SLAYER

"Phases"

Written By

Rob DesHotel
&
Dean Batali

Directed By

Bruce Seth Green

SHOOTING SCRIPT

December 15, 1997 (WHITE)

BUFFY THE VAMPIRE SLAYER

"Phases"

CAST LIST

BUFFY SUMMERS........................ Sarah Michelle Gellar
XANDER HARRIS........................ Nicholas Brendon
RUPERT GILES........................ Anthony S. Head
WILLOW ROSENBERG...................... Alyson Hannigan
CORDELIA CHASE....................... Charisma Carpenter
ANGEL............................... David Boreanaz

OZ.....................................*Seth Green
LARRY.................................
GIB CAIN.............................
MISS LITTO...........................
THERESA.............................
NEWS ANNOUNCER.......................

THE BAND..............................*Lotion

BUFFY THE VAMPIRE SLAYER

"Phases"

SET LIST

INTERIORS

SUNNYDALE HIGH SCHOOL
     HALL
     LOUNGE
     LIBRARY
     GYMNASIUM
     LOCKER ROOM

CORDELIA'S CAR

THE BRONZE
     UPPER LEVEL
     *BACKSTAGE

OZ'S HOUSE
     ANOTHER PART OF HOUSE

FUNERAL PARLOR VIEWING ROOM

CAIN'S VAN

EXTERIORS

SUNNYDALE HIGH SCHOOL
     SCHOOL PARKING LOT
     COURTYARD

*SUNNYDALE (STOCK)

THE BRONZE

MAKEOUT PARK

SUNNYDALE STREET

SUNNYDALE WOODS

BUFFY THE VAMPIRE SLAYER

"Phases"

TEASER

1 EXT. SUNNYDALE HIGH - MORNING (STOCK)   1

The start of another school day. STUDENTS head inside with
ambitious hopes about what the day will bring them.

                                        CUT TO:

2 INT. HALLWAY/INT. LOUNGE - MORNING   2

WILLOW comes inside and sees OZ studying something in the
trophy case. She goes over to him. He looks up; smiles.

                    WILLOW
          Hi.

                    OZ
          That's what I was going to say.

                    WILLOW
          Whatcha looking at?

                    OZ
          This cheerleader trophy. It's like
          its eyes follow you wherever you go.

He LEANS to one side, then the other.

                    OZ (cont'd)
          I like it.

He and Willow walk together.

                    WILLOW
          So, did you like the movie last night?

                    OZ
          I don't know. Today's movies are
          kind of like popcorn. You forget
          about them as soon as they're done.
          I do remember I like the popcorn,
          though.

                    WILLOW
          Yeah, it was good. And I had a
          really fun time at the rest. I mean,
          the part with you.

                                        CONTINUED

                         OZ
               That's great, because my time was
               also of the good.

                         WILLOW
               Mine, too.

Willow waits expectantly, hoping for a kiss.

                         WILLOW (cont'd)
               Well, then...

Oz stands there. Then stands there some more. It's
beginning to get awkward. Willow sees an escape.

                         WILLOW (cont'd)
               Oh, there. I have... my friend. So
               I will go to her.

                         OZ
               I'll see you, then. Later.

Willow joins BUFFY in the lounge as LARRY and some LARRYETTES
come over to Oz. Larry stares leeringly off at the girls.

                         LARRY
               Man, Oz, I would love to get me some
               of that Buffy and Willow action, if
               you know what I mean.

                         OZ
               Good job, Larry. You've really
               mastered the single entendre.

A GIRL (could be Theresa) walks by. Larry 'accidentally'
KNOCKS the books out of her hands.

                         LARRY
               Oops.

The girl BENDS OVER to pick up her books. Larry and the
Larryettes enjoy the view.

                         LARRY (cont'd)
               Thank you, Thighmaster!

The Larryettes LAUGH BRAINLESSLY.

                         LARRY (cont'd)
               So, Oz, an, what's up with that?
               Dating a Junior? Let me guess - that
               innocent school-girl thing is just an
               act, right?

                                                        CONTINUED

                    OZ
          Yeah, she's actually an evil
          Mastermind. It's fun.

                    LARRY
          She's gotta be putting out, or what's
          the point? What are you gonna do,
          talk? Come on, fess up - how far
          have you got?

A3 EXT. SCHOOL - DAY   A3   *

    ANGLE: BUFFY AND WILLOW

    sitting at a table.

                    WILLOW
          Nowhere! I mean, he said he was
          gonna wait till I was ready, but...
          I'm ready! Honest. I'm good to go
          here.

                    BUFFY
          I think it's nice he's not just being
          an animal.

                    WILLOW
          It is nice. He's great. We have a
          lot of fun. But I want some
          smootchies.

                    BUFFY
          Have you dropped any hints?

                    WILLOW
          I've dropped anvils.

                    BUFFY
          He'll come around. What guy could
          resist your wily, Willow charms?

                    WILLOW
          At last count? All of them. Maybe
          more.

                    BUFFY
          Well, none of them know a thing.
          They all get an 'F' in Willow.

                    WILLOW
          But I want Oz to get an 'A.' And,
          ooh, one of those gold stars.

                                                        CONTINUED

                              BUFFY
            He will.

                                              CONTINUED

                    WILLOW
          Well he better hurry. I don't want
          to be the only girl in school without
          a real boyfriend.

Buffy looks down, thinking of Angel.

                    WILLOW (cont'd)
          Oh, I'm such an idiot, I'm sorry. I
          shouldn't even be talking about... do
          you want me to go away?

                    BUFFY
          I wish you wouldn't.

Willow cautiously tests the waters.

                    WILLOW
          How are you holding up, anyway?

                    BUFFY
          I'm holding.
                    (looks at watch)
          I was going on close to two minutes
          there without thinking of Angel.

                    WILLOW
                    (encouraging)
          Well, there you go!

                    BUFFY
          But I'd be holding better if you and
          Xander and I could do that 'sharing
          our misery' thing tonight.

                    WILLOW
          Great! I'll call Xander, ask him to
          join us. What's his number? Oh,
          yeah: '1-800-I'm-Dating-A-Skanky-Ho.'

                    BUFFY
          Me-ow!

                    WILLOW
          Really? Thanks! I've never gotten
          a 'me-ow' before.

                    BUFFY
          Well deserved.

                                              CONTINUED

                    WILLOW
      Darn tootin'! I'm just saying,
      Xander and Cordelia? What does he
      see in her, anyway?

                                CUT TO:

3 INT. CORDELIA'S CAR/EXT. MAKEOUT PARK - NIGHT   3

  XANDER and CORDELIA are in Cordelia's car, in the middle of
  a very serious make-out session. Suddenly, Xander pulls away.

                    XANDER
      But what could she possibly see in
      him?

                    WILLOW
         (exasperated)
      Excuse me, we did not come here to
      talk about Willow. We came here to
      do things I can never tell my father
      about because he still thinks I'm a
      good girl.

                    XANDER
      I just don't trust Oz with her. He's
      a senior, he's attractive. Okay, not
      to me, but... Oh, and he's in a
      band. We all know what element that
      kind attracts.

                  CORDELIA
         (offended)
      I've dated lots of guys in bands.

                    XANDER
         (point proven)
      Thank you!

                  CORDELIA
      Do you even want to be here?

                  XANDER
      I'm not running away.

                  CORDELIA
      Because when you're not babbling
      about poor, defenseless Willow,
      you're raving about the all-powerful
      Buffy.

                            CONTINUED

3 CONTINUED: 3

> XANDER
> I do not babble. I occasionally run-
> on. And every now and then I yammer--

> CORDELIA
> (gently)
> Xander, look around. We're in my
> car. Just the two of us. There's a
> big, full moon. It doesn't get any
> more romantic than this.
> (then)
> So shut up!

She angrily GRABS him and they go back to kissing.

A4   EXT. SUNNYDALE - NIGHT (STOCK)   A4   *

ANGLE: THE MOON

ROUND and BRIGHT in the sky.

TILT DOWN, into the darkness.

B4   EXT. MAKEOUT PARK - NIGHT   B4   *

A BEASTLY FACE, half-human, half-animal, stares out from the
bushes. It GROWLS softly.

BLACK OUT.

END OF TEASER

ACT ONE

4 INT. CORDELIA'S CAR/EXT. MAKEOUT PARK - NIGHT   4

   Xander and Cordelia are still doing their thing. Xander
   hears a noise; breaks the kiss.

                    XANDER
          Did you hear that?

                    CORDELIA
                (evenly)
          What is it now?

                    XANDER
          I thought I heard something.

                    CORDELIA
          Oh, is Willow sending some sort of
          distress signal that only you can
          hear?

   He looks out the window into the darkness. Nothing.

                    XANDER
          Hunh...

   They lean in towards each other again. He JOLTS back.

                    XANDER (cont'd)
          Okay, now I know I heard something.

                    CORDELIA
                (moving away)
          That's it! Your mind has been not
          here all night. How about I just
          drop you off at--

   A LARGE PAW RIPS THROUGH the convertible top of the car and
   SWIPES between them.

   The two of them SCREAM and pin themselves against the doors.

   A HAIRY, SNOUTED FACE peers through the rip. It's a WEREWOLF.

                    XANDER
          Get us out of here!

   Cordelia reaches for the ignition.

                    CORDELIA
          Where're the keys!

                                                    CONTINUED

4 CONTINUED: 4

Cordelia frantically feels around on the floor as the
werewolf SLASHES at the roof. Xander fights it off, KICKING
at it with his feet.

                    XANDER
          We should be moving! Let's go!

Cordelia finds the keys--

                    CORDELIA
          Got 'em!

--STARTS the car, and THROWS it into gear.

The werewolf CLINGS to the top as the car BACKS UP. The car
stops and LURCHES forward, THROWING the werewolf off.

Cordelia and Xander SPEED AWAY into the night.

                    XANDER (O.C.)
          Told you I heard something.

                                              CUT TO:

5 EXT. SCHOOL PARKING LOT - DAY   5

Buffy, Willow, and Oz surround Cordelia's car, looking at the
shredded convertible top as Xander and Cordelia fill them in.

                    BUFFY
          And you're sure it was a werewolf?

                    XANDER
          Let's see: six feet tall, claws, big
          ol' snout right in the middle of a
          face like a wolf. Yeah, I'm sticking
          with my first guess.

                    OZ
          Seems wise.

                    XANDER
          Oh, and there was that little thing
          where it tried to bite us.

Cordelia buries her head in Xander's shoulder.

                    CORDELIA
          It was so awful.

                    XANDER
          I know...

                                              CONTINUED

                         CORDELIA
               I just had this car detailed.

          GILES comes over, carrying a newspaper.

                         BUFFY
               What's the word on the street?

                         GILES
                    (shows headline)
               Seems there were a number of other
               attacks by a 'wild dog' around town.
               Several animal carcasses were found
               mutilated.

                         WILLOW
               Ohh... you mean bunnies and stuff?
                    (then)
               No, don't tell me.

                         OZ
                    (to Willow)
               Don't worry. They may not look it,
               but bunnies can really take care of
               themselves.

                         WILLOW
               Yeah.

                         GILES
               Fortunately, no people were injured.

                         BUFFY
               That falls into the 'that's a switch'
               column.

                         GILES
               For now. But my guess is this
               werewolf will be back at next month's
               full moon.

                         WILLOW
               What about tonight's full moon?

                         GILES
               Pardon?

                         WILLOW
               Last night was the night before the
               full moon. Traditionally known as...
               the night before the full moon.

                                                  CONTINUED

5 CONTINUED: (2)   5

>   GILES
> Meaning the accepted legend that
> werewolves only prowl during the full
> moon might be erroneous.

>   CORDELIA
> Or it could be a crock.

>   XANDER
> Unless our werewolf is still using
> last year's almanac.

>   BUFFY
> Looks like Giles has some schoolin'
> to do.

>   GILES
> I must admit, I'm intrigued. A
> werewolf? It's one of the classics.
> I'm sure my books and I are in for a
> fascinating afternoon.

They watch as Giles goes off.

>   BUFFY
> He needs to get a pet.

>   PRELAP:

>   MISS LITTO (V.O.)
> Sunnydale is becoming more dangerous
> all the time. And a full moon like
> tonight tends to bring out the
> crazies.

>   CUT TO:

6 INT. GYMNASIUM - DAY   6

MISS LITTO (a formidable-looking woman) speaks to STUDENTS
who stand on MATS. A number of the students have BODY PADS,
GLOVES, etc.

>   MISS LITTO
> But with some simple basics of self-
> defense, each of you can learn how to
> protect yourself...

She CONTINUES TO TALK as we:

                                                    CONTINUED

ANGLE: BUFFY, WILLOW AND OZ

                    BUFFY
          Here's a suggestion: move away from
          the Hellmouth.

Oz REACHES for the collar on the back of Willow's shirt and
fixes something. Willow turns to him.

                    OZ
                (explaining)
          Tag.

Xander, who is with Cordelia, SEES this.

                    XANDER
          Would you look at that? He's all
          over her!
                (whispers over)
          Hey, buddy, you're in a public forum
          here!

                    CORDELIA
                (to Xander)
          I think you splashed a little too
          much 'Obsession for Dorks.'

                    MISS LITTO
          ...Okay, everyone get into your
          assigned groups.

The students separate into GROUPS. Larry removes his jacket
to reveal a large BANDAGE on his arm.

                    XANDER
          What happened to you?

                    LARRY
          Ah, last week some huge dog jumped
          out of the bushes and bit me. Thirty-
          nine stitches. They ought to shoot
          those strays.

                    OZ
          I been there, man.

He holds up a finger.

                                              CONTINUED

> OZ (cont'd)
> My cousin Jordy. Just got his grown-
> up teeth in. Does not like to be
> tickled.

> WILLOW
> (leaning in)
> Looks like it healed already.

> OZ
> The emotional scar is still there.

Larry approaches THERESA, a small, timid-looking girl (who we may or may not have already seen in the teaser).

> LARRY
> Theresa, be still my shorts. We're
> in the same group.
> (smiling cruelly)
> I may have to attack you.

> THERESA
> (anxious)
> No, I think, actually, in our group,
> they're a few of us--

Buffy STEPS BETWEEN Larry and Theresa.

> BUFFY
> (to Larry)
> Yeah. And I'm one of the few.

Theresa backs away to safety as Willow pulls Buffy aside.

> WILLOW
> Don't forget, you're supposed to be
> a meek little girlie-girl like the
> rest of us.

> BUFFY
> Spoil my fun.

Willow JOINS Xander and Cordelia in their group. Xander is pulling a large PADDED HELMET over his head.

> XANDER
> Be gentle with me.

> CORDELIA
> (to Willow)
> You first. I wouldn't want to be
> accused of taking your place in line.

                                                        CONTINUED

                     WILLOW
Oh, I think you pushed your way to
the front long before this.

                     CORDELIA
Hey, I can't help it if I get the
spotlight just because some people
blend into the background.

                     WILLOW
Well, maybe some people could see
better if you weren't standing on the
auction block, shaking your wares.

                     CORDELIA
Sorry, we haven't all perfected that
phony 'girl next door' bit.

                     WILLOW
You could be the girl next door, too.
If Xander lived next to a brothel!

They BORE INTO EACH OTHER, breathing heavily. Xander,
completely suited up, calls out to them.

                     XANDER
                    (innocently)
Okay, who wants a piece of me?

Cordelia and Willow look at one another.

                            SMASH CUT TO:

BAM!

Xander reels from a PUNCH thrown by Cordelia.

OOF!

He buckles over from a KICK, administered by Willow.

The girls WORK TOGETHER, eventually taking Xander to the
ground. He looks up at them, confused and pleading:

                     XANDER
Why...?

ANGLE: MISS LITTO.

                     MISS LITTO
Okay, everyone, listen up. I want to
show you what to do should you be
attacked from behind.

                                   CONTINUED

                                                                   *

Larry puts his arms around Buffy from behind. The students
watch as Miss Litto explains the procedure.

                    MISS LITTO (cont'd)
          In this situation, bend forward,
          using your back and shoulders to flip
          your assailant over and to the ground.

Buffy 'tries' to flip him.

                    BUFFY
          Unh! Mnh!

                    LARRY
          You're turning on me, Summers.

Larry reaches down and GRABS A HANDFUL of Buffy's butt. No
more girlie-girl. In the blink of an eye, Buffy GRABS hold
of Larry, LIFTS him, and SLAMS him into the mat. Oz looks
down at Larry:

                    OZ
          That works, too.

                                        CUT TO:

7 INT. LIBRARY - LATER THAT DAY   7

Giles uses a GLOBE OF THE EARTH, a MODEL OF THE MOON and a
LAMP as he explains things to Buffy, Willow, and Xander.

                    GILES
          ...and while there is no scientific
          explanation for lunar effect on the
          human psyche, the phases of the moon
          do exert a great deal of
          psychological influence. And a full
          moon tends to bring out our darkest
          qualities.

                    XANDER
          Yet, ironically, also led to the
          invention of the moon pie.

Buffy and Willow shoot Xander a look, then look back to Giles.

                                        CONTINUED

                    GILES
               (chuckling to himself)
          Moon pie...

Willow and Buffy stare at Giles. He composes himself.

                    GILES (cont'd)
          You see, a werewolf is such a potent,
          extreme representation of our inborn,
          animalistic traits that it emerges
          for three consecutive nights -- the
          full moon, and the two nights
          surrounding it.

                    WILLOW
          Quite the party animal.

                    GILES
          Quite. It acts on pure instinct,
          without conscience, predatory and
          aggressive--

                    BUFFY
          In other words, your typical male.

                    XANDER
          On behalf of my gender: hey!

                    GILES
          Let's not jump to conclusions--

                    BUFFY
          I didn't jump. I took a tiny step.
          And there conclusions were.

                    GILES
          The point is, our wolfman could also
          be a wolf-woman. Or anyone who's
          been bitten by a werewolf.

                    XANDER
               (looks at wach)
          And whoever it is will be changing at
          any moment.

                    WILLOW
          'Cause it'll be night soon.

She reaches over and SPINS THE GLOBE half a turn (as a visual
representation of the earth's rotation, which spins away from
the sun into darkness, hence the night).

                                                  CONTINUED

7 CONTINUED: (2)   7

>   XANDER
>   So, then. I'm guessing your standard-
>   issue silver bullets are in order
>   here.
>
>   GILES
>   No. No bullets. No matter who this
>   werewolf is, it's still a human
>   being. Who might be completely
>   unaware of his, or her, condition.
>
>   BUFFY
>   So tonight we bring 'em back alive.

>   DISSOLVE TO:

8 EXT. MAKEOUT PARK - NIGHT   8

Parked CARS. With KIDS in them. Doing the things kids do in
parked cars. The FULL MOON illuminates it all.

Buffy and Giles (who carries a bag of hunting supplies) MEET
UP between two cars.

>   GILES
>   Anything yet?
>
>   BUFFY
>   Yes. And you won't believe it! Lisa
>   Hamm is over there making out with
>   Tim Bushway! But he's dating Mandy
>   Donaldson. If she ever finds out--
>   (off Giles' look)
>   Nothing. Not a werewolf in sight.
>   You?
>
>   GILES
>   The same. I thought we might knock
>   on a few windows, ask if anyone has
>   seen anything.
>
>   BUFFY
>   (how old are you?)
>   Giles? No one's seen anything.
>
>   GILES
>   Yes. Of course not.

They split up again.

Buffy searches near the edge of the park. She hears a NOISE
in the bushes and TURNS. SOMETHING catches her eye.

>   CONTINUED

8 CONTINUED: 8

She LUNGES into the darkness.

And is promptly LIFTED into the air by a NET that has been
laid as a trap.

A ROUGH-LOOKING GUY emerges from the shadows. He wears dark
clothing and boots. A number of SHARP TEETH hang from a
string around his neck.

This is The Hunter: GIB CAIN.

He aims a RIFLE at the thing that FLAILS ABOUT overhead.

                    CAIN
          Gotcha!

                                        BLACK OUT.

                    END OF ACT ONE

ACT TWO

9 EXT. MAKEOUT PARK - NIGHT (AN INSTANT LATER)   9

Cain has his rifle trained on his catch. Buffy SCREAMS out:

                    BUFFY
          Giles...!

Cain lowers his rifle, confused. He POKES at what he's
caught with the tip of the rifle.

                    BUFFY (cont'd)
          Ow!

Giles comes running over.

                    GILES
          Hey!

Cain turns his gun towards Giles, who STOPS and throws his
hands in the air.

                    GILES (cont'd)
          Whoa, now...

                    CAIN
          The hands are good right about
          there...

                    GILES
          Who are you? What are you doing?

                    CAIN
          The name's Cain. I'm the one with
          the gun. Which means I'm the one who
          gets to do the interviewing.

                    BUFFY
          You know, before we get all chummy,
          could we do something about this 'me
          being in a net' thing?

Cain looks up at Buffy, takes a knife from his belt and
SLICES through a rope...

...which DROPS the net -- and Buffy -- to the ground. Giles
helps Buffy UNTANGLE herself.

                    GILES
          Are you all right?

                                                    CONTINUED

                         BUFFY
          I could have done without the poking.

Cain looks at Buffy, then at Giles.

                         CAIN
          I got to say, I'm impressed.

                         GILES
          Excuse me?

                         CAIN
               (off Buffy)
          It's good to get the fruit while it's
          fresh.

Giles stares at him.

                         GILES
          You'd be wise to take that back.

                         CAIN
          Hey, what a man and a girl are doing
          in Lovers' Lane at night is
          nobody's--

Giles makes a move towards Cain.

Buffy stops Giles, moving in front of him.

                         BUFFY
          It's not what you think, repulsive
          brain.
               (off Cain's look)
          We're hunting a werewolf.

A beat. Cain breaks into raucous LAUGHTER.

                         BUFFY (cont'd)
          Sure, it's funny if you don't believe
          in werewolves...

                         CAIN
          No, it's funny thinking about you two
          catching one!
               (re: Giles)
          This guy looks like he's auditioning
          to be a librarian. And you, well,
          you're a girl.

                         GILES
          I assure you, she's more than capable.

                                             CONTINUED

                         CAIN
               Uh-huh.
                    (to Buffy)
               Let me ask you something, sweetheart.
               Exactly how many of these animals
               have you taken out?

                         BUFFY
                    (hedging)
               As of today?

Cain shows the collection of TEETH on his necklace.

                         CAIN
               I tore a tooth from the mouth of
               every werewolf that I killed. This
               next one will bring the total to an
               even dozen.

Buffy looks at Giles, then back at Cain.

                         BUFFY
               You're just going to kill it?

                         CAIN
               Well, see, that's the thing. Their
               pelts fetch a pretty penny in Sri
               Lanka, and it's a little hard to skin
               'em when they're alive.

                         GILES
                    (incredulous)
               You're hunting werewolves for sport.

                         CAIN
               Oh, no. I'm in it purely for the
               money.

                         BUFFY
               And it doesn't bother you just a
               smidge that werewolves are people 28
               days out of the month?

                         CAIN
               You know, it does bother me. Quite
               a bit.
                    (grinning)
               That's why I only hunt them the other
               three.

Cain smiles and starts to pack up his gear.

                                                      CONTINUED

                         CAIN (cont'd)
               I'd really love to stay and chat, but
               I'm on a tight schedule. Any idea
               where else the boys and girls like to
               get together in this town?

                         BUFFY
               You looking for a party?

                         CAIN
               No, but the werewolf is. They're
               suckers for that whole 'sexual heat'
               thing. Sense it miles away. But
               since the little doggie ain't here,
               it must have found another place.

                         BUFFY
                    (covering)
               Wish we could help you, but--

                         CAIN
               You don't know squat? Gee, what a
               surprise.

He goes off. Buffy grabs the bag of hunting supplies out of
Giles' hand and starts away. Giles moves with her.

                         GILES
               Where are we going?

                         BUFFY
               I think I know where to look. We
               just have to make it there before
               Mein Furrier.

                                                  CUT TO:

10 EXT. SUNNYDALE - NIGHT (A LITTLE LATER)   10

Theresa walks along, her bookbag on her back. She clearly
doesn't like being alone. She nervously GLANCES AROUND,
bunches up her coat, and MOVES ALONG briskly.

A NOISE startles her. She stops, looks back.

POV: SOMETHING IS WATCHING HER

from a hidden place behind some bushes.

Theresa TURNS and starts walking QUICKLY away.

                                                  CONTINUED

10 CONTINUED: 10

POV: MOVES OUT FROM BEHIND THE BUSHES

and follows after her, GROWLING.

Theresa HEARS the growl and PICKS UP THE PACE. She glances
over her shoulder, then starts to RUN.

POV: RUNS AFTER HER.

Theresa is on the run. She LOOKS BEHIND her again,
frightened, then turns back:

                    THERESA
          Ah!!!

ANGEL stands there (in regular-guy mode). He SMILES.

                    ANGEL
          Everything okay?

                    THERESA
          I-- thought I heard something.
          Behind me.

Angel scopes out the area. Whatever was there is gone.

                    ANGEL
          No one there.

                    THERESA
          Oh... I guess not. I could have
          sworn--

                    ANGEL
          It's okay. It can get pretty scary
          out here, all alone at night.

                    THERESA
               (uneasy)
          Yeah.

Angel looks at her.

                    ANGEL
          Hey, do I know you from somewhere?
          Don't you go to school with Buffy?

                    THERESA
          You know Buffy?

                    ANGEL
          I do. Very well.

                                              CONTINUED

10 CONTINUED: (2)   10

    She smiles, feeling a bit safer.

                    ANGEL (cont'd)
        Come on, I'll get you home.

    They walk off.

                            CUT TO:

11 INT. BRONZE - SAME TIME - NIGHT   11

    Lots of touchy-feely going on. AN AMOROUS COUPLE kiss their
    way up the stairs, heading for some privacy.

    Cordelia is at a table, TALKING to someone we don't yet see.

                    CORDELIA
        I mean, with Xander it's always
        'Buffy did this' or 'Willow said
        that.' Buffy, Buffy. Willow,
        Willow. It's as if I don't even
        exist.

    REVEAL she is talking to Willow.

                    WILLOW
        I sometimes feel like that.

                    CORDELIA
        And then when I call him on it, he
        acts all confused, like I'm the one
        with the problem.

                    WILLOW
        His 'Do I smell something?' look.

                    CORDELIA
            (nodding)
        All part of his little guy-games.
        He's there, then he's not there. He
        wants it, but he doesn't want it.

                    WILLOW
        He's so busy looking around at
        everything he doesn't have that he
        doesn't even realize what he does
        have.

                    CORDELIA
        But he should at least realize that
        <u>you</u> have Oz.

                          CONTINUED

11 CONTINUED: 11

Willow frowns.

                    WILLOW
          I'm not sure I do. Right now, Oz and
          I are in some sort of holding
          pattern. Only without the holding.
          Or anything else.

                    CORDELIA
          Well, what's he waiting for? What's
          his problem?
                    (then)
          Oh, that's right. He's a guy.

                    WILLOW
          Yeah. Him and Xander. Guys.

                    CORDELIA
          Who do they think they are?

                    WILLOW
          A couple of guys.

They nod in agreement--

--and are interrupted when the werewolf CRASHES down on their
table. Willow and Cordelia's drinks go FLYING as they
SCRAMBLE out of their chairs.

                    WILLOW (cont'd)
          Come on! This way!

PANDEMONIUM ensues as EVERYONE heads for the doors.

                                        CUT TO:

12 EXT. BRONZE - NIGHT (SAME TIME)   12

Kids pour out, SCREAMING in a rush to escape. Buffy and
Giles run up.

                    GILES
                (to Buffy)
          Looks like your hunch was right.

                    BUFFY
          How could a werewolf resist
          Sunnydale's own House o' Hormones?

She and Giles fight through the crowd. They BUMP INTO a
frantic Willow and Cordelia at the door.

                                        CONTINUED

12 CONTINUED: 12

>   WILLOW
>   The werewolf! It's in there!

Cordelia turns to the DOORMAN.

>   CORDELIA
>   (half-crazed)
>   You could be a little more
>   discriminating with that velvet rope!

>   WILLOW
>   (to Buffy)
>   It went upstairs!

Buffy pulls a LONG CHAIN from the bag, tosses the bag at
Giles, and heads inside.

>   CUT TO:

13 INT. BRONZE/BACKSTAGE - A MOMENT LATER - NIGHT   13   *

Dark and creepy. Buffy quietly MAKES HER WAY UP the stairs,
the chain dangling at her side.

The now not-so-amorous couple comes SCRAMBLING down the
stairs, PLOWING into Buffy. They point upstairs. Buffy
nods, CONTINUES UP, and takes a few steps into the darkness.

She looks around. A MOVEMENT catches her eye. She turns her
head. She's looking straight at a MIRROR -- the movement was
in the reflection -- and the werewolf is right behind her.

It JUMPS.

Buffy fights it off. It comes back at her. She PUNCHES it
in the face, and it reacts, STARTLED.

Buffy SWINGS the chain so that it WRAPS around the werewolf's
neck. She's got it! She holds on tight to the chain.

The werewolf YANKS away, sending Buffy FLYING across the room.

The werewolf BREAKS the chain apart, LEAPS for a window...

>   CUT TO:

14 EXT. WINDOW - CONTINUOUS - NIGHT   14

...and CRASHES through.

>   CONTINUED

14   CONTINUED: 14

The werewolf HITS THE GROUND, HOWLS, and TAKES OFF into the
night.

                                                    DISSOLVE TO:

15   INT. BRONZE - A LITTLE LATER - NIGHT   15

Cain is there with Buffy and Giles. He seems not at all
surprised that:

                    CAIN
          You let it get away.

                    BUFFY
          I didn't let it do anything. I had
          the chain around its neck--

                    CAIN
          Chain? What were you going to do,
          take it for a walk?

                    BUFFY
          I was trying to lock it up.

                    CAIN
          That's beautiful.
               (shakes his head)
          This is what happens when a woman
          tries to do a man's job.

                    GILES
          Mr. Cain, this girl put her life at
          risk to capture a beast which you
          haven't even been able to find!

                    CAIN
          Uh-huh. And daddy's doing a great
          job carrying her bag of Milk Bones.
               (in Buffy's face)
          You know, sis, if that thing out
          there harms anyone? It's going to be
          on your pretty little head.

Buffy doesn't respond.

                    CAIN (cont'd)
          I hope you can live with that.

He moves away and starts for the door.

                                                    CONTINUED

15   CONTINUED: 15

                              BUFFY
                          (to herself)
                    I live with that every day.

Cain heads out, mumbling to himself.

                              CAIN
                    First they tell me I can't shoot an
                    elephant for its ivory. Now I've got
                    to deal with People for the Ethical
                    Treatment of Werewolves.

He goes off. Buffy stands there for a beat. Giles ZIPS up
the bag, looks at Buffy.

                              GILES
                    Let's move out.

They go.

                                             CUT TO:

16   EXT. SUNNYDALE RESIDENTIAL STREET-NIGHT (A LITTLE LATER) 16   *

The werewolf wanders through the night. It PICKS UP A SCENT
and finds a trail of BLOOD DROPLETS. It follows the trail,
PICKING UP SPEED, when:

A BODY thumps to the ground in front of the werewolf. It's
Theresa. And she's DEAD. Angel stands over her (in VAMP-
MODE), post feeding.

Angel locks eyes with the werewolf and HISSES loudly. The
werewolf SWIPES defensively and HISSES back. They face-off
for a beat. Angel backs away, then disappears into the dark.

The werewolf goes to the dead body. SNIFFS.

It HOWLS up at the moon and the sound carries over as we:

                                             DISSOLVE TO:

17   EXT. MAKEOUT PARK - NIGHT   17   *

                                                                 *

A lone car -- Giles' car -- sits there, its LIGHTS still on.
We hear the TINNY SOUND of a news station from the radio.

                                             CONTINUED

                         NEWS ANNOUNCER (V.O.)
               ...the negotiations were tabled when
               West-leader Petrie could not come to
               terms with the leader from the East.
               Petrie said a strike is inevitable.

The NEWSCAST CONTINUES in the background as Buffy comes into
view. She sees the empty car.

                         BUFFY
               Giles?

She RUNS to the car, panicked, and opens the door. A
startled Giles BOLTS upright, scared half to death.

                         GILES
               Blaerg!

                         BUFFY
                    (relieved)
               Oh. I didn't see you there.
                    (gets in car)
               I thought something happened.

                         GILES
                    (groggy)
               No, no. I'm okay. I was just... I'm
               okay.
                    (then)
               Any sign of the werewolf?

                         BUFFY
               No. I'm guessing you didn't see
               much, either, from that vantage point
               of having your eyes closed.

Giles looks at his watch, then out the window.

                         GILES
               It's starting to get light. I
               suppose we should be heading--

                         BUFFY
               Shh.

Buffy silences Giles and TURNS UP the radio.

                         NEWS ANNOUNCER (V.O.)
               ...apparently connected to the animal
               mutilations which occurred two nights
               ago.
                    (more)

                                                       CONTINUED

                        NEWS ANNOUNCER (cont'd; V.O.)
              The coroner's office has identified
              the body as that of Theresa
              Klusmeyer, 17. The family asks that
              in lieu of flowers--

Giles turns off the radio. Buffy SLUMPS DOWN into the seat,
devastated. Giles assures her:

                        GILES
              Buffy, we're going to get this thing.
              We've got another whole night.

Buffy just stares off.

                        GILES (cont'd)
              Right now there's nothing we can do.
              The sun is rising. That werewolf
              isn't a werewolf anymore.

                                            CUT TO: *

A18 EXT. SUNRISE (STOCK)   A18   *

                                            CUT TO:

18 EXT. SUNNYDALE WOODS - SAME TIME - DAY   18

We BEGIN TO PAN UP the body of the werewolf as it lies,
curled up, beneath a tree. It GROWLS softly.

The growling turns into a human kind of MOANING.

By the time WE REACH THE HEAD of the werewolf, it has fully
transformed into a human state.

The state of Oz.

Oz takes note of his outdoor surroundings. And the fact that
he's wearing no clothes.

                        OZ
              Whoa.

                                            BLACK OUT.

                        END OF ACT TWO

ACT THREE

19   INT. OZ'S HOUSE - MORNING   19

Oz picks up a PHONE and dials a number. He sits down and
waits for someone to answer.

                    OZ
                (into phone)
          Hey, Aunt Maureen? It's me...
          What...?

He studies the SMALL SCRATCH on his finger as he talks.

                    OZ (cont'd)
          Oh, actually, it's healing okay.
          That's pretty much the reason I
          called. I wanted to ask you
          something.
                (here goes)
          Is Jordy a werewolf?

He listens, nodding.

                    OZ (cont'd)
          Uh huh... And how long has that been
          going on...? Uh huh...
                (then)
          No reason... Okay, well, thanks.
          Love to Uncle Ken.

He hangs up. SITS there, taking this in.

                                          CUT TO:

20   INT. SCHOOL HALLWAY - LATER THAT MORNING   20

Oz walks down the hall, distracted. He reaches the library
and PUSHES OPEN the doors.

                                          CUT TO:

21   INT. LIBRARY - CONTINUOUS - DAY   21

Oz walks in to see Buffy RANTING to Giles, Xander and Willow.

                    BUFFY
          I can't believe I let that thing get
          away. Cain was right. I should have
          killed it when I had the chance.

                                          CONTINUED

Oz stops.

                    OZ
          Killed what?

They turn to him.

                    GILES
          The werewolf. It was out last night.

Oz goes over to Willow.

                    OZ
          Is everyone okay? Was anyone
          scratched? Or bitten?

                    WILLOW
          No, we're fine.

                    OZ
          Gladness.

                    BUFFY
          But the werewolf got someone.
          Theresa.

                    OZ
          'Got' as in...

He trails off, leans against a wall.

                    OZ (cont'd)
          Wow. I'm sorry.

                    BUFFY
          And the worst part is, I could have
          stopped it.

                    GILES
          Well, we still have one more night.

                    OZ
               (news to him)
          Another night?

                    BUFFY
          Oh, yeah. And I'm planning on giving
          little wolfie something to howl about.

                    OZ
               (taking this in)
          Hunh...

                                        CONTINUED

                         XANDER
          But while we hang here doing nothing,
          there's a human werewolf walking
          around out there, probably making fun
          of us.

                         WILLOW
          The way werewolves always do.

                         OZ
          But there's really no way to tell who
          it is. Right?

                         XANDER
          Sure there is. Giles knows stuff.
          And I'm practically an expert on this
          subject.

                         WILLOW
          On account of how you were once a
          hyena.

                         OZ
          Xander was...?

                         WILLOW
          Before we knew you.

                         XANDER
                (to Oz)
          I know what it's like to crave the
          taste of freshly killed meat. To be
          taken over by those uncontrollable
          urges--

                         BUFFY
          You said you didn't remember anything
          about that.

                         XANDER
                (oh, yeah)
          I said I didn't remember anything
          about that.
                (then)
          Look, the point is, I have an
          affinity with this thing. I can get
          inside its head.
                (acting it out)
          Okay, I'm a big, bad wolf. I'm on
          the prowl. I'm a sniffing, snarling,
          slobbering predator. I'm...

     Xander stops, looking right at Oz.

                                              CONTINUED

                         XANDER (cont'd)
              Wait a second. It's right in front
              of us. It's obvious who I am!

Oz tenses--

                         XANDER (cont'd)
              I'm Larry.

--then relaxes a bit.

                         XANDER (cont'd)
              He's practically got 'wolf-boy'
              stamped on his forehead. You got the
              dog bite, you got the aggression.
              Not to mention the excessive back-
              hair.

                         BUFFY
              You know, he was a little overly
              gleeful at the thought of tormenting
              Theresa.

                         OZ
              Still, that doesn't necessarily mean--

                         XANDER
                   (starting out)
              I'm going to go talk to him. Force
              a confession out of him.

                         GILES
              Good. Go. In the meantime, let's
              cover our bases. Willow, check the
              student files. See if anyone else
              fits the profile.

He heads for his office.

                         BUFFY
              Where are we going?

                         GILES
              If none of that works, I think I've
              struck upon a way to finally lay this
              problem to rest.

                         BUFFY
              Me and the werewolf, three minutes,
              alone in a cage. That's all I ask.

Buffy follows Giles into his office as Xander goes out.
Willow and Oz are left alone. Willow notices Oz staring off.

                                                        CONTINUED

                         WILLOW
                    Are you okay?

    Oz comes out of his daze.

                         OZ
                    What?

                         WILLOW
                    You kind of knew Theresa.

                         OZ
                    Yeah. I'm trying not to think about
                    it. It's... a lot.

                         WILLOW
                    It is. But we can do stuff to help.
                    Sometimes it feels good to help.

                         OZ
                    Uh-huh.

                         WILLOW
                    Like, looking up names? I'll be
                    doing that most of the night. You
                    could help me help together--

    He cuts her off gently.

                         OZ
                    I can't. I'm... busy.

                         WILLOW
                         (taken aback)
                    Oh. So....

                         OZ
                    I, uh, need to go.

    He WALKS OUT, leaving Willow alone and confused.

    REVEAL Buffy, standing in the office doorway, watching.

                                             CUT TO:

22 INT. LOCKER ROOM - LATER - DAY   22

    The locker room is EMPTY. And CREEPY.

    As we snake our way PAST THE LOCKERS and AROUND SOME CORNERS,
    we begin to HEAR that a FAUCET is RUNNING.

                                             CONTINUED

22 CONTINUED: 22

We TURN the final corner and see Larry as he finishes washing
up. He turns off the faucet, grabs a towel. He dries his
face as he heads into the rows of lockers.

He ROUNDS A CORNER and pulls the towel away from his face.
He is STARTLED when he sees Xander STANDING THERE.

                    LARRY
          Harris. Geez, next time wear a bell.

                    XANDER
          Why so jumpy, Larry?

                    LARRY
          Geeks make me nervous.

                    XANDER
          Is that really it? Or is there
          something you're hiding?

                    LARRY
          I could hide my fist in your face.

Larry opens his locker. PIN-UPS and CUT-OUTS of bikini clad
girls cover every inch inside. Xander SLAMS the door shut.

                    XANDER
          I know your secret, big guy. I know
          what you've been doing at night.

                    LARRY
                (calmly)
          You know, Harris, that nosey-nose of
          yours is going to get you into
          trouble some day. Like today.

Larry grabs Xander and HOLDS him against a locker.

                    XANDER
          Hurting me won't make this go away.
          People are still going to find out.

                    LARRY
          All right, what do you want? Hush
          money? Is that what you're after?

                    XANDER
          I don't want anything. I just want
          to help.

                                              CONTINUED

Larry releases Xander.

                    LARRY
               (skeptically)
          You want to help. What do you think
          you have a cure?

                    XANDER
          No, it's just... I know what you're
          going through. Because I've been
          there. And that's why I know you
          should talk about it.

                    LARRY
               (incredulous)
          Sure, that's easy for you to say.
          You're nobody. But I've got a
          reputation.

                    XANDER
          Larry, please. Before someone else
          gets hurt.

                    LARRY
          If this gets out, it's over for me.
          Forget about playing football;
          they'll run me out of town. I mean,
          come on. How do you think people are
          going to look at me once they find
          out I'm gay?

Xander stands there, frozen. Larry goes on, surprised at
himself.

                    LARRY (cont'd)
          Wow. I said it. And it felt... okay.
               (with more confidence)
          I'm gay. I am gay.

                    XANDER
               (smiles painfully)
          Heard you the first time.

                    LARRY
          I can't believe it. I mean, that was
          almost easy. I... I never felt like
          I could tell anyone. And then you,
          of all people, bring it out in me.

                    XANDER
          It probably would have just slipped
          out even if I wasn't here.

                                             CONTINUED

> LARRY
> No. Because knowing you went through
> the same thing made it easier for me
> to admit it.

> XANDER
> The same thing?

> LARRY
> It's ironic. All those times I beat
> the crap out of you, it must have
> been because I recognized something
> in you that I didn't want to believe
> about myself.

> XANDER
> What? No, Larry, I'm not--

> LARRY
> Oh, of course. Don't worry. I
> wouldn't do that to you.
> (leans in; sincerely)
> Your secret's safe with me.

Larry goes off, leaving Xander there alone.

                                        CUT TO:

23 INT. LIBRARY - LATER THAT DAY   23

Willow is at the computer. Buffy comes over to her.

> BUFFY
> So, what's the scuttle-butt? Anybody
> besides Larry fit the werewolf
> profile?

> WILLOW
> There is one name that keeps getting
> spit out. Aggressive behavior, run-
> ins with authorities, about a
> screenful of violent incidents...

Willow types a bit, hits enter. Buffy looks at the screen
and reacts.

> BUFFY
> Okay, most of those weren't my fault.
> The other guy started it. I was just
> standing up for myself.

                                                        CONTINUED

                       WILLOW
They say it's a good idea to count to
ten when you're angry...

Buffy glares at Willow.

                       BUFFY
One, two, three...

                       WILLOW
I'll keep looking.

                       BUFFY
I noticed you're looking solo.

                       WILLOW
Yeah. Oz wanted to be somewhere that
was away. From me.

                       BUFFY
I'm sorry.

                       WILLOW
I can't figure him out. He's so hot
and cold. Or, lukewarm and cold.

                       BUFFY
Welcome to the mystery that is men.
I think what happens is they grow
body hair, they lose the ability to
talk about what they really want.

                       WILLOW
That doesn't sound like a good trade.

The BELL RINGS. They gather their things.

                       BUFFY
Seems to me you and Oz have some kind
of synapse problem. So if you want
to get anywhere with him, you've got
to make the first move.

                       WILLOW
That doesn't make me a slut?

                       BUFFY
I think your reputation'll remain
intact.

They head out the doors...

                              CUT TO:

...and start down the hall.

                    WILLOW
          It used to be so much easier to tell
          if a boy liked you. He'd punch you
          on the arm, then run back to his
          friends.

                    BUFFY
          Yeah, those were the days.

Xander comes over to them; PUNCHES Buffy on the arm.

                    XANDER
          Hey...

Willow starts away.

                    WILLOW
          I'll see you guys later. Cordelia
          asked me to look over her history
          homework before class. I think that
          means I might have to do it.

She goes off. Xander watches her.

                    XANDER
          Wow. Those two gals have been
          hanging out together a lot.
                    (then)
          This would be a good time to panic.

Buffy and Xander walk together.

                    BUFFY
          How'd it go with Larry?

                    XANDER
                    (defensive)
          What's that supposed to mean?

                    BUFFY
          I think it's supposed to mean, 'How'd
          it go with Larry?'

                    XANDER
          He's not the werewolf. Can't you
          leave it at that? Must you continue
          to push and push?

                    BUFFY
          Sorry. I was just wondering--

                                        CONTINUED

24 CONTINUED: 24

                              XANDER
                    Well he's not!

                              BUFFY
                    Okay.

                              XANDER
                    Okay.

                              BUFFY
                    So there goes our lead suspect.

          She slumps against a locker, exasperated.

                              BUFFY (cont'd)
                    Which puts us right back at square
                    boned.

                              XANDER
                    You're not boned. You're Buffy.
                    Eradicator of evil. Defender of...
                    things that need defending.

                              BUFFY
                    Tell that to Theresa. She could have
                    used some defending before she was
                    ripped apart by that...

          Buffy goes silent.

                              XANDER
                         (trying to be helpful)
                    Werewolf.

                              BUFFY
                    None of the reports said anything
                    about Theresa being mauled. But it
                    was linked to the animal attacks from
                    the other night, so we just assumed
                    werewolf.

                              XANDER
                    What else should we have assumed?

                                             CUT TO:

25 INT. FUNERAL PARLOR VIEWING ROOM - THAT EVENING   25

          CLOSE-ON: TWO PUNCTURE WOUNDS ON A NECK

                              BUFFY (O.C.)
                    Vampire.

                                                      CONTINUED

Buffy and Xander are looking down at the BODY OF THERESA, who lies in an open casket. Buffy has pulled Theresa's collar down to reveal the vampire bite.

                    XANDER
          So that's good, right? I mean, in
          the sense of, the werewolf didn't get
          her and...
                    (then)
          No. There is no good here.

                    BUFFY
          Yeah. Instead of not protecting
          Theresa from a werewolf I was able to
          not protect her from something just
          as bad.

They move to a SIGN-IN BOOK, which sit on a THREE-LEGGED wooden EASEL (conveniently for later, the sharp, pointy-legged kind). Buffy notices the list of names in the book.

                    BUFFY (cont'd)
          She had a lot of friends...

                    XANDER
          Buffy, you can't blame yourself for
          every death in Sunnydale.

Behind them, Theresa RISES out of her casket: she's a VAMPIRE.

                    XANDER (cont'd)
          If it weren't for you, people would
          be lining up five deep needing to get
          themselves buried. Willow would be
          Robbie the Robot's love slave, I
          wouldn't even have a head, and
          Theresa's a vampire!

Buffy is TACKLED FROM BEHIND by Vampire Theresa. They roll around. Buffy SNAPS a leg off of the easel, raises the stake, and is about to thrust it down.

Theresa STARES into Buffy's eyes.

                    VAMPIRE THERESA
          Angel sends his love.

Buffy FREEZES, stunned -- giving Vampire Theresa the opportunity to KNOCK THE STAKE out of Buffy's hand. The stake SLIDES across the floor and UNDER a piece of furniture.

Buffy and Vampire Theresa WRESTLE until Vampire Theresa gets Buffy pinned on her back.

                                                CONTINUED

BUFFY'S POV:

THREE STAKES (the two-and-a-half remaining legs of the easel)
BURST through Vampire Theresa's heart from behind.

Vampire Theresa goes POOF--

--REVEALING Xander standing there with the collapsed easel.

                    XANDER
          Are you okay?

Buffy sits up, severely shaken.

                    BUFFY
          This isn't happening....

Xander drops the easel; kneels down to Buffy.

                    XANDER
          Buffy--

He touches her on the shoulder. She immediately folds
herself into his arms.

                    BUFFY
          He's going to keep coming after me.
          Until...

                    XANDER
          Don't let him get to you.

It's clear that he already has.

                    XANDER (cont'd)
          He's not the same guy you knew.

They continue to HUG. A little too long. They pull apart a
bit and look at each other.

                    BUFFY
          Xander--

Uh-oh.

                    BUFFY (cont'd)
          Thanks.

Xander smiles. Finally, they break. Buffy composes herself.

                    BUFFY (cont'd)
          Well. I've got a lot to do tonight.

                                                      CONTINUED

25 CONTINUED: (3)   25

                         XANDER
          Yeah.

                         BUFFY
          I should probably go do it.

She heads out. Xander watches after her, then follows,
MUMBLING and SHAKING HIS HEAD.

                         XANDER
          Oh, no. My life's not too
          complicated...

OVER THIS: MUSIC STARTS TO PLAY

The opening notes to (what else?) Grateful Dead's 'New Potato
Caboose.'

                                        CUT TO:

26 EXT. WOODS - DUSK   26   *

Establishing, as the MUSIC CONTINUES.

                                        CUT TO:

27 INT. VAN - SAME TIME   27

CLOSE ON: LIQUID SILVER

being poured into a small mold.

REVEAL Cain in his van, going through his pre-hunt ritual.
He HUMS along to the music from a TAPE PLAYER.

The van is CRAMMED with the tools of his trade: RIFLES, BOWS,
ARROWS, NETS, TRAPS, etc.

Cain places the mold on a COOLING RACK. He removes another
mold from the rack and OPENS IT to reveal:

A freshly minted SILVER BULLET.

He sets the bullet aside with a number of OTHER BULLETS.

He reaches over to a SMALL REFRIGERATOR and pulls out a
large, GOOEY SLAB OF MEAT. He PLOPS it onto a counter, takes
a HUNTING KNIFE and SLICES off a few hunks, tossing them into
his BACKPACK.

                                        CONTINUED

27 CONTINUED: 27

    The MUSIC FADES as we:

                                                    DISSOLVE TO:

28 EXT. SUNNYDALE - THAT EVENING (STOCK)   28   *

    The FULL MOON (well, actually it's the waning moon, but it's
    still big and bright) PEEKS over the trees.

                                                    CUT TO:

29 INT. OZ'S HOUSE - NIGHT   29

    Oz pulls some SHACKLES and CHAINS out of a box. He closes a
    metal shackle around his wrist, reaches for a PADLOCK, when:

    There is a KNOCK at the door. Oz looks over. The KNOCKING
    continues, sounding somewhat IMPATIENT.

    Oz leaves the shackles on a table and goes to the door. He
    OPENS it a crack.

                          OZ
                Willow, what are you doing--?

    Willow BARGES RIGHT IN.

                          WILLOW
                Okay, I had this whole thing worked
                out and I had written it down, but
                then it didn't make any sense when I
                was reading it back.

                          OZ
                This really isn't a good time.

    She plows ahead.

                          WILLOW
                I mean, what am I supposed to think?
                First you buy me popcorn, then you
                put the tag in my shirt, and then
                you're all glad I didn't get bit.
                But I guess none of that means
                anything, because instead of looking
                up names with me, here you are all
                alone in your house doing nothing by
                yourself.

                                               CONTINUED

                         OZ
          Willow, we will talk about this
          tomorrow. I promise.

                         WILLOW
          No, darn it, we will talk about this
          now! Buffy told me that sometimes
          what the girl makes has to be the
          first move and now that I'm saying
          this I'm starting to think that the
          written version sounded pretty good
          but you know what I mean!

Oz delicately tries to escort her out.

                         OZ
          I know. It's me. I'm going through
          some... changes.

She breaks his grasp and moves further into the house.

                         WILLOW
          Well, welcome to the world! Things
          happen. You don't think I'm going
          through a lot?

                         OZ
          Not like I am.

                         WILLOW
          Oh, so now you're special! You're
          special boy--

Willow notices the chains and shackles on the table.

                         WILLOW (cont'd)
          --with chains and stuff.
                    (then, confused)
          Why do you have chains and stuff?

                         OZ
          Willow, please--

He doubles over in pain.

                         OZ (cont'd)
                    (shouting)
          Get out!

                         WILLOW
          Oz?

She moves towards him to see if he's okay.

                                                    CONTINUED

29 CONTINUED: (2)   29

                         WILLOW (cont'd)
               Oz, what is it? What's wrong?

When Oz looks back up at Willow, she sees what's wrong: HE'S
THE WEREWOLF.

The werewolf BARES its teeth and GROWLS at Willow.

Willow tries to scream. And then does.

                         WILLOW (cont'd)
               Dyaaeehhhhh!

                                             BLACK OUT.

               END OF ACT THREE

ACT FOUR

30   INT. OZ'S HOUSE - A MOMENT LATER - NIGHT   30

There's a werewolf SNARLING at Willow, remember?

Willow tries to get to the door, but the werewolf LEAPS into
her path. She looks around for an escape and HEADS FOR:

                                        CUT TO:

31   INT. ANOTHER PART OF THE HOUSE - CONTINUOUS - NIGHT   31

Willow runs in, the werewolf close behind. She SCRAMBLES
over a couch, just as the werewolf SWIPES at her legs. It's
a near miss -- the werewolf's claws TEAR THROUGH the cushions
on the couch.

Willow ROLLS AWAY on the ground and gets to her feet. She
tries to RUN out, but the werewolf GRABS her from behind.
Willow BENDS forward and FLIPS the werewolf over.

It CRASHES hard to the floor.

                         WILLOW
              Wow. It worked.

Maybe too well. The werewolf isn't moving. Willow moves to
it, concerned.

                         WILLOW (cont'd)
                    Oz?

The werewolf LEAPS up and SNAPS at her. Willow SCREAMS and
RUNS FOR HER LIFE, pushing a COAT RACK, CHAIRS and anything
else she can find into the werewolf's path.

She's gone.

                                        CUT TO:

32   EXT. SUNNYDALE - NIGHT   32

Willow RUNS FOR HER LIFE, down the street and through the
neighborhood.

The WEREWOLF is on her heels.

                                        CUT TO:

33 EXT. PARK - NIGHT   33

Willow SPRINTS across the grass, hurtles over a BENCH, and
gets to a STONE WALL (much like the one bordering our
cemetery set, only... okay, it's the same wall).

She looks behind her. The werewolf keeps coming.

She JUMPS UP, grabs on to the wall, and with GREAT EFFORT
manages to get to the top.

As she STRADDLES the wall, the werewolf LEAPS...

...and SLAMS near the top of the wall just as Willow PULLS
HER LEG OVER and DROPS TO THE GROUND.

The werewolf FALLS on the other side.

Willow gets to her feet and TAKES OFF AGAIN.

                                        CUT TO:

34 EXT. ANOTHER PART OF SUNNYDALE - SAME TIME (NIGHT)   34

Cain is on the PROWL, a backpack on his back, rifle as his
side.

He hears a LOUD HOWL -- the werewolf is nearby.

                    CAIN
              There you are...

He heads in that direction.

                                        CUT TO:

35 INT. LIBRARY - SAME TIME - NIGHT   35

Giles DROPS a STEEL CASE onto the library table. He UNSNAPS
the latches and OPENS THE CASE.

Inside is an unassembled HIGH-TECH RIFLE. He takes a couple
of the parts and begins PIECING them together.

Buffy comes in, all business.

                    BUFFY
              Sorry I'm late. Had to do some
              unscheduled slaying in the form of
              Theresa.

                    GILES
              She's a vampire?

                                        CONTINUED

35   CONTINUED: 35

                         BUFFY
               Was. Angel sent her to me. A little
               token of his affection.

Giles moves to her.

                         GILES
               Buffy, I'm so sorry--

Buffy puts up her hand; tries to hold it together.

                         BUFFY
               Not now, Giles. We'll all have
               ourselves a good cry after we've
               bagged us a werewolf.

                                             CUT TO:

36   EXT. WOODS - NIGHT   36   *

Willow, nearly out of breath, RUNS FOR ALL SHE'S WORTH.

She STUMBLES; falls to the ground.

She looks back -- the werewolf is there, ADVANCING, only a
few yards away.

A terrified Willow SCAMPERS AWAY on her back. The werewolf
keeps coming. It's practically on top of her.

Willow is frozen with fear.

Suddenly, the werewolf TURNS its head and lifts its nose.
It's caught a SCENT. It moves off, heading into the woods.

Willow waits a moment, then FLEES.

                                             CUT TO:

37   INT. LIBRARY - A MOMENT LATER - NIGHT   37

Giles finishes assembling the rifle by SCREWING ON the SCOPE.

                         GILES
               All set. Let's go find this thing.

They start for the door.

                         BUFFY
               One question: how exactly do we find
               this thing?

                                             CONTINUED

Willow BURSTS through the doors.

                    WILLOW
          It's Oz! It's Oz!

                    BUFFY
          What's Oz?

                    WILLOW
          The werewolf!

                    GILES
          Are you certain?

                    WILLOW
          Can't you just trust me on this?!
               (distraught)
          He... he said he was going through
          all these changes, and then he went
          through all these... changes.

                    BUFFY
          Where is he now?

                    WILLOW
          He chased me here, then he stopped
          and ran off into the woods.

                    BUFFY
          Willow, it'll be okay. We're going
          to take care of everything.

Giles brings the rifle into view and gives it a PUMP.

                    GILES
          Let's go.   *

                    WILLOW
          Go where? You're not going to kill   *
          Oz?! I mean, sure, he's a werewolf.
          But I bet he doesn't mean to be!

                    BUFFY
          Don't worry. We won't hurt him.

Giles reveals a TRANQUILIZER DART.

                    GILES
          I loaded this with enough
          phenobarbital to put down a small
          elephant. It should be enough for a
          large werewolf.

                                             CONTINUED

37 CONTINUED: (2)   37

They head out the doors.

                                                    CUT TO:

38 EXT. SUNNYDALE WOODED AREA - NIGHT (A FEW MOMENTS LATER) 38

The werewolf is following a scent.

It makes its way THROUGH THE WOODS and comes to a clearing.
There, BATHED IN THE MOONLIGHT, sits a pile of MEAT. The
werewolf HOWLS.

REVEAL CAIN

as he steps out from behind a TREE several yards away. He
RAISES HIS RIFLE; PEERS through the scope.

                    CAIN
                (to himself)
          That's it. Let me see you...

POV: THROUGH CAIN'S SCOPE

The werewolf MOVES into the clearing, SNIFFS the meat, and
starts to EAT.

                    CAIN (O.C.)
          Good doggie...

CLOSE-UP: CAIN'S FINGER ON THE TRIGGER

                    CAIN
          Now play dead.

He FIRES--

--and is BLINDSIDED by Buffy.

The shot GOES WIDE.

The werewolf LOOKS UP from his meal. What's this?

Buffy and Cain STRUGGLE for the rifle.

The werewolf HEADS DIRECTLY FOR the two of them.

Buffy wrests the rifle from Cain's hands and BUTTS him in the
gut with it. He's down.

And so is Buffy, as the werewolf LEAPS onto her. Buffy uses
the rifle as a club while she tries to fight it off.

                                                    CONTINUED

38 CONTINUED: 38

Buffy and the werewolf continue to do battle.

Willow stands with Giles, who RAISES HIS TRANQUILIZER GUN and
tries to get a bead on the werewolf without harming Buffy.

                    WILLOW
               Careful!

Giles has a shot, but then Buffy is SPUN in front.

                    GILES
               Damn...

Buffy and the werewolf FALL to the ground with Buffy on top.
The werewolf THRUSTS its legs out--

--sending Buffy FLYING through the air and into Willow and
Giles, who DROPS his gun. The three of them fall in a HEAP
to the ground.

The werewolf gets to its feet and LOCKS EYES with Willow.

Then starts towards her.

A terrified Willow SCRAMBLES for Giles' tranquilizer gun as
the werewolf comes at her. Willow grabs the gun, RAISES it,
closes her eyes...

...and FIRES.

The tranquilizer dart FLIES through the air and lands in the
werewolf's chest. It REELS back in pain, then COLLAPSES just
inches from Willow.

Willow remains frozen, the gun still raised.

                    WILLOW
                 (disbelieving)
               I shot Oz...

                    GILES
               You saved us.

He gently takes the gun from her hands and helps her up as
Cain comes over to them, making no effort to hide his disgust.

                    CAIN
               No wonder this town is overrun with
               monsters. No one here's man enough
               to kill 'em.

                    BUFFY (O.C.)
               I wouldn't be so sure about that.

                                                        CONTINUED

38 CONTINUED: (2)   38

        REVEAL Buffy is holding Cain's rifle. She GLARES at Cain as
        they stand off for a beat.

                        BUFFY
                You know, Mr. Cain, I've been sick of
                you since the moment before I met
                you. And I've been waiting for just
                the right opportunity to take you on.
                But then I realized : a big, strong
                man versus a girl like me?

        Buffy uses all of her strength to BEND the rifle barrel very
        slightly.

                        BUFFY (cont'd)
                Wouldn't be a fair fight.

        She TOSSES the now useless rifle at Cain.

                        BUFFY (cont'd)
                How about you let the door hit you in
                the ass on the way out of town.

        Cain regards her for a beat, sizing her up. He starts to say
        something, then thinks better of it. Instead, he shakes his
        head and WALKS OFF.

        And he's GONE.

        Buffy sees that Willow has knelt down to the werewolf.

                        BUFFY (cont'd)
                Willow?

                        WILLOW
                    (to Giles)
                Is he going to be all right?

                        GILES
                He'll be a little sore in the
                morning, but he'll be Oz.

        Willow smiles, unsure.

                                        DISSOLVE TO:

39 INT. SCHOOL HALL/LOUNGE - THE NEXT MORNING   39   *

        Buffy and Xander walk together, mid-conversation.

                                                CONTINUED

                              XANDER
              This is all so weird. I mean, how
              are we supposed to act when we see
              him?

                              BUFFY
              I'm sure it's weird for him, too, now
              that we know so much.

                              XANDER
              I know I'll never be able to look at
              him the same way again.

                              BUFFY
              Hey, he's still a human being. Most
              of the time.

Xander stops.

                              XANDER
              Who are we talking about?

                              BUFFY
              Oz. Who are you talking about?

Xander sees Larry walking towards them.

                              XANDER
              No one.

Larry passes a couple of Larryettes, who KNOCK some books out
of a GIRL'S arms. They leer at her as she bends to get them.
Larry stops--

                              LARRY
              Let me get those.

--and picks them up for her. He hands the books to the girl
and moves over to Xander and Buffy.

                              LARRY (cont'd)
              Hey, Xander, about what you did? I
              owe you.

                              BUFFY
                   (to Xander)
              What did you do?

                              XANDER
              It really was nothing. That we
              should be talking about. Ever.

                                                    CONTINUED

> LARRY
> I know. It's just, well...

Larry put his hands on Xander's shoulder. Xander reacts uncomfortably.

> LARRY (cont'd)
> Thanks.

He moves off. Buffy watches him go.

> BUFFY
> That was weird.

> XANDER
> What? It's not okay for one guy to like another guy just because he happened to be in the locker room when absolutely nothing happened and I thought I told you not to push!

> BUFFY
> All I meant was he didn't try to look up my dress.

> XANDER
> (covering)
> Oh, yeah. That was the weirdness.

> BUFFY
> Weirdness abounds lately. Maybe it's the moon. It does stuff to people.

> XANDER
> I've heard that.

They looks across the courtyard to see Willow.

> BUFFY
> And it's sure going to put a strain on Willow and Oz's relationship.

> XANDER
> What relationship? What kind of life could they possibly have? You're talking obedience school, paper training. Oz would be burying all their stuff in the backyard. And that kind of breed can turn on its owner.

CONTINUED

39 CONTINUED: (3)   39

                         BUFFY
               I don't know. I see Oz as the loyal
               type.

                         XANDER
               I'm just saying, she's not safe with
               him. If it was up to me--

                         BUFFY
               Xander?

A40 EXT. SCHOOL - DAY   A40   *

     ANGLE: WILLOW

     as she reaches Oz, who is sitting on a bench.

                         BUFFY (O.C.)
               It's not up to you.

     Willow stands in front of Oz for a moment.

                         WILLOW
               Hey.

                         OZ
               Hey.

     An awkward beat. Then:

                         WILLOW
               Did you want to go first?

                         OZ
               I spoke to Giles. He said I'll be
               okay, I'll just have to lock myself
               up around the full moon. Only he
               used more words than that. And a
               globe.

     Oz gets up and they start to walk together.

                         WILLOW
               I'm sorry about how all this ended
               up. With me shooting you, and all.

                         OZ
               That's okay. I'm sorry I almost ate
               you.

                         WILLOW
               That's okay.

                                                        CONTINUED

A40 CONTINUED: A40

    A beat as they walk on.

                                                          CONTINUED

> WILLOW (cont'd)
> I kind of expected you would have
> told me.

> OZ
> I didn't know what to say. It's not
> every day you find out you're a
> werewolf. That's fairly freaksome.
> May take a couple of days getting
> used to.

> WILLOW
> Yeah. It's a complication.

> OZ
> So I guess, maybe, it'd be best if I
> just sort of...

> WILLOW
> What?

> OZ
> You know, stayed out of your way for
> a while.

> WILLOW
> I don't know. I'm kind of okay with
> you being in my way.

> OZ
>   (taking this in)
> You mean... you'd still...

> WILLOW
> Well, I like you. You're nice, and
> you're funny and you don't smoke, and
> okay, werewolf but that's not all the
> time. I mean, three days out of the
> month I'm not much fun to be around,
> either.

A beat, as he smiles at her.

> OZ
> You are quite the human.

> WILLOW
> So, I'd still if you'd still.

> OZ
> I'd still. I'd very still.

CONTINUED

A40   CONTINUED: (3)   A40

                         WILLOW
              Okay.

Willow moves in front of Oz. He stops.

                         WILLOW (cont'd)
              No biting, though.

                         OZ
              Agreed.

She moves off, leaving Oz to consider this.

Willow comes back. KISSES him. Then goes off without a
word. Oz watches her go, stunned.

                         OZ (cont'd)
                    (to himself)
              A werewolf in love...

                                        BLACK OUT.

                    END OF SHOW

BUFFY THE VAMPIRE SLAYER

"Bewitched, Bothered & Bewildered"

Written By

Marti Noxon

Directed By

James A. Contner

SHOOTING SCRIPT

January 12, 1998 (WHITE)

BUFFY THE VAMPIRE SLAYER

"Bewitched, Bothered & Bewildered"

CAST LIST

BUFFY SUMMERS........................ Sarah Michelle Gellar
XANDER HARRIS........................ Nicholas Brendon
RUPERT GILES......................... Anthony S. Head
WILLOW ROSENBERG..................... Alyson Hannigan
CORDELIA CHASE....................... Charisma Carpenter
ANGEL................................ David Boreanaz

JOYCE SUMMERS........................ Kristine Sutherland
JENNY CALENDAR....................... Robia La Morte
SPIKE................................ James Marsters
DRUSILLA.............................*Juliet Landau
OZ..................................*Seth Green
HARMONY.............................. Mercedes McNab
AMY.................................. Elizabeth Anne Allen
MISS BEAKMAN........................*Lorna Scott
CORDETTE #1.........................*Kristen Winnicki
FRENZIED GIRL.......................*Tamara Braun
JOCK................................
KATIE...............................*Jennie Chester
THE BAND............................. Dingoes Ate My Baby

BUFFY THE VAMPIRE SLAYER

"Bewitched, Bothered & Bewildered"

SET LIST

INTERIORS

SUNNYDALE HIGH SCHOOL
     CLASSROOM
     HALLWAY
     LIBRARY
     EMPTY CLASSROOM
     SCIENCE LAB
     LOUNGE
     HALLWAY - ANOTHER AREA
     BOILER ROOM
     ANOTHER HALLWAY
     HALLWAY OUTSIDE LIBRARY

XANDER'S ROOM

FACTORY

THE BRONZE

BUFFY'S HOUSE
     LIVING ROOM
     HALLWAY
     KITCHEN
     BUFFY'S BEDROOM
     FOYER
     BASEMENT

EXTERIORS

CEMETERY

SUNNYDALE HIGH SCHOOL
     COURTYARD
     WALKWAY

BUFFY'S HOUSE
     PORCH
     ROOF
     NEAR BUFFY'S HOUSE

BUFFY THE VAMPIRE SLAYER

"Bewitched, Bothered & Bewildered"

TEASER

CLOSE ON A SMALL SILVER HEART

that dangles from a chain.

1   EXT. CEMETERY - NIGHT   1

   - XANDER, pacing, holding the trinket - contemplating it.
   BUFFY'S sitting on a headstone nearby.

                    XANDER
          What do you think?

                    BUFFY
          It's nice.

                    XANDER
          But do you think Cordelia will like
          it?

                    BUFFY
          I don't know...
                    (points to her heart)
          Does she know what one of these is?

                    XANDER
          Okay, big yuks. When are you guys
          gonna stop making fun of me for
          dating Cordelia?

                    BUFFY
          I'm sorry. But, never.
                    (off his look)
          I just think you could find someone
          more... better.

                    XANDER
          Parallel universe, maybe. Here the
          only other person I'm interested in
          is unavailable.

                    BUFFY
                    (gets the point)
          Oh.

                                                   CONTINUED

                         XANDER
              Besides, Cordy and I have really been
              getting along. We don't fight as
              much. Yesterday we just sat
              together, not even speaking, you
              know, just enjoying comfortable
              silence.
                         (beat)
              Man, that was dull.

                         BUFFY
              I'm glad you guys are getting along.
              Almost really. And you shouldn't
              stress about the gift.

                         XANDER
              This is new territory for me. My
              valentines are usually met with
              heartfelt restraining orders.

                         BUFFY
              She'll love it.

                         XANDER
              I wish dating was like slaying --
              simple. Direct. Stake to the heart,
              no muss no fuss --

He's cut off when A VAMP RISES FROM THE GRAVE HE'S STANDING
ON - RIGHT IN FRONT OF HIM. Xander YELLS. Falls back.
Buffy leaps from her perch - grabs a stake from her coat.

A VICIOUS BATTLE ensues. This vamp is STRONG and Buffy's
almost overcome but finally manages to DUST THE DUDE.

A beat as Buffy recovers. Then she helps Xander to his feet.
They start to move off. As they disappear into the
distance...

                         BUFFY
              Sorry, Xand. Have to say slaying is
              a tad more perilous than dating.

                         XANDER
              You're obviously not dating Cordelia.

                                        BLACK OUT.

                    END OF TEASER

ACT ONE

2 EXT. SCHOOL - DAY   2

School is about to start and kids rush everywhere. CORDY
sees HARMONY and the CORDETTES. They see her too, but keep
going. Their heads bowed as they whisper.

                    CORDELIA
              Hey... Wait up!

Cordy rushes to catch up with them - peeved.

                    CORDELIA (cont'd)
              Excuse me? Where's the fire sale?

                    HARMONY
                  (cool)
              Oh, sorry. Didn't see you.

                    CORDELIA
              Why didn't you guys call me back last
              night? We need to talk about our
              outfits for the dance -- I'm going to   *
              wear red and black so you'd better   *
              switch --

                    CORDETTE #1
              Red and black? Is that what Xander   *
              likes?

                    CORDELIA
              Xander? What's he got to do with it?

                    HARMONY
              Well, a girl wants to look good for
              her geek.

The Cordettes titter.

                    CORDELIA
              Xander is just --

                    HARMONY
              When are you two gonna start wearing
              cute little matching outfits? 'Cause
              I'm planning to vomit.

Harmony starts off. The Cordettes follow. Cordelia can't
believe it.

3 INT. CLASSROOM - DAY   3

XANDER, WILLOW AND BUFFY are all in English class with MISS
BEAKMAN, a tough old dame. The bell rings and students start
to rise.

                    MISS BEAKMAN
          Papers on my desk. Anybody tries to
          leave without giving me a paper is
          looking at a failing grade.

Xander sits with Buffy and Willow, clutching his paper.

                    XANDER
          Hah! This time I am ready for you.
          No "F" for Xander today. This baby's
          my ticket to a sweet "D minus".

The bunch comes up by AMY, daughter of the cheerleading
trophy.

                    WILLOW
          Hey, Amy.

                    AMY
          Hey. Are you guys going to the
          Valentine's Dance at the Bronze? I
          think it's gonna be fun.

Buffy and Willow exchange looks, Willow bursting to say
something.

                    BUFFY
          Go ahead, you know you want to say it.

                    WILLOW
               (to Amy)
          My boyfriend's in the band.

                    AMY
          Cool.

                    BUFFY
          I think you've now told everybody.

                    WILLOW
          Only in this hemisphere.

                    AMY
               (to Buffy)
          What about you?

                                        CONTINUED

3 CONTINUED: 3

                          BUFFY
             Valentine's Day is just a gimmick to
             sell cards.

                          AMY
             Bad break up?

                          BUFFY
             Believe me when I say "Uh huh".

She hands her paper to Miss Beakman --

                          MISS BEAKMAN
             Thank you...

As does Willow.

                          MISS BEAKMAN (cont'd)
             Thank you...

Miss Beakman looks at Amy expectantly. But Amy just stares
deeply into the teacher's eyes. Suddenly, Miss Beakman
SMILES and reaches out for a paper that ISN'T THERE. Miss
Beakman "puts" the phantom paper on the top of her stack.

                          MISS BEAKMAN (cont'd)
             Thank you...

Amy smiles coolly, moves off. Revealing XANDER, who has seen
this whole exchange. He looks after Amy, intrigued. Hands
his paper in, starts after Amy. But getting no response from
Miss Beakman, stops to say crankily:

                          XANDER
             You're welcome.

4 INT. SCHOOL HALLWAY - DAY   4

Buffy and Willow peel off from Amy with goodbye's, walk down
the hall.

                          WILLOW
             I just hate to think of you solo on
             Valentine's Day.

                          BUFFY
             I'll be fine. Mom and I are gonna
             have a pig-out and vidfest. It's a
             time honored tradition among the
             loveless.

CONTINUED

Xander comes abreast of them.

                    XANDER
          Did you guys see that?

                    BUFFY
          What?

                    XANDER
          In class. I thought I just saw Amy
          working some magic on Miss Beakman.

                    BUFFY
          You mean like Witchraft?

                    WILLOW
          Well, her mom was a witch...

                    BUFFY
          And an amateur psycho. Amy's the
          last person should be messing with
          that stuff.

                    XANDER
          Maybe I should talk to --

Now GILES approaches. Xander hushes, gives the others a
look.

                    GILES
          Buffy. Might I have a word with you?

                    BUFFY
          Have a sentence, even.

                    GILES
          Good, well-

Giles is unable to finish because, just as they are passing
her door, MISS CALENDAR emerges from her classroom. Everyone
stops - awkward. It's evident that there is a lot of bad
feeling here. Buffy can't even look at her.

                    CALENDAR
               (takes the leap)
          Rupert.

                    GILES
          Miss Calendar.

                                              CONTINUED

4 CONTINUED: (2)   4

Calendar reacts to the use of her last name. Still - she
forges ahead.

                    CALENDAR
          I - I'm glad we ran into each other,
          actually. I was hoping we could...
          Do you have a moment?

                    GILES
          Oh - well... Not just now. I have
          a matter I must discuss with Buffy.

He turns to Buffy - who finally glances at Calendar. Cold.

                    BUFFY
          Right. Let's go.

Giles nods to Calendar - a hint of sorrow evident in his
eyes. He and Buffy walk off. A beat as Calendar watches
them go, Willow and Xander looking from them to her.

5 INT. LIBRARY - DAY   5

Buffy's at the table, watching Giles pace - clearly agitated
by his encounter with Calendar.

                    BUFFY
          Are you okay?

                    GILES
          Me? I'll be fine. I'm more
          concerned about you, actually.
                    (then)
          Ever since Angel... turned - I've
          been reading up on his earlier
          activities. Learning more about his
          habits, feeding patterns, the like...

                    BUFFY
          And?

                    GILES
          There's a disturbing trend. Around
          Valentine's Day he's prone to rather
          brutal displays of... what he would
          think of as affection, I suppose.

                    BUFFY
          Like what?

CONTINUED

5 CONTINUED: 5

> GILES
> No - no need to go into detail.

> BUFFY
> That bad.

> GILES
> Suffice to say it would be best if
> you stayed off the streets for a few
> nights. I can patrol. Keep my eye
> on things. Better safe than sorry.

> BUFFY
> It's a little late for both.

Off Buffy and Giles - anything but happy Valentine's puppies.

6 INT. FACTORY - NIGHT   6

CLOSE ON A VELVET BOX

Which is opened to reveal an INCREDIBLE ANTIQUE RUBY NECKLACE.

WIDEN TO REVEAL DRUSILLA AND SPIKE AT THE TABLE

Dru has just opened the box and smiles happily over at Spike,
who is still chair-bound.

> SPIKE
> Fancy it, pet?

> DRUSILLA
> It's beautiful. Sparkly...

> SPIKE
> Nothing but the best for my-

He's cut off as a BLOODY HUMAN HEART falls on the table
before DRU with a sickening, wet plop. Drusilla's eyes widen
with absolute delight and we see ANGEL standing at her side,
grinning.

> ANGEL
> Happy Valentine's Day, Dru.

> DRUSILLA
> Ooooh! Angel... It's still warm.

CONTINUED

6 CONTINUED: 6

                              ANGEL
              I knew you'd like it. I found it in
              a quaint little shop-girl.

    Angel grabs the necklace Spike got Dru from the box.

                              ANGEL (cont'd)
              Cute.

    He leans over to Dru with the necklace in hand. Looks to
    Spike.

                              ANGEL (cont'd)
              Here. I'll just...

    He starts to fasten the necklace around Dru's neck. Spike
    rolls closer.

                              SPIKE
              Leave it. I'll get it.

                              ANGEL
              Done.
                   (to Spike)
              I know Dru gives you pity access -
              but you have to admit, it's so much
              easier when I do things for her.

    Spike seethes. Snaps at Angel-

                              SPIKE
              You'd do well to worry less about Dru
              and more about that slayer you
              tramped around with.

                              ANGEL
                   (smiles fondly)
              Dear Buffy. I'm still trying to
              decide the best way to send my
              regards...

                              SPIKE
              You could rip her lungs out. That
              might make an impression.

                              ANGEL
              It lacks poetry.

                                                        CONTINUED

6 CONTINUED: (2)   6

> SPIKE
> It doesn't have to.
> (to Dru)
> What rhymes with lungs?

> DRUSILLA
> Don't worry, Spike. Angel will find
> his way...
> (looks at the heart)
> In time Angel always finds what
> speaks to a girl.

7 INT. THE BRONZE - NIGHT   7

The Bronze is DECKED OUT for a VALENTINE'S DAY DANCE.

DINGOES ATE MY BABIES play on stage, OZ up front.

XANDER AND WILLOW sit at a table. Xander elegantly dressed
and groomed, fidgets nervously with a SMALL GIFT BOX.

Willow watches the band enraptured. OZ sees her. Smiles.
Willow smiles back - gets that "googley" feeling.

> WILLOW
> (to Xander)
> I think I'm a groupie...

Xander smiles at her, then goes back to being nervous.

ON CORDELIA

Who enters, looking drop-dead. She sees HARMONY and the
CORDETTES. Starts to approach. But they all turn their
backs on her. Cordy stops, hurt. At a loss.

8 INT. BUFFY'S LIVING ROOM - NIGHT   8

Buffy and her mother are splayed out in front of the tube.
A prodigious pile of junk food surrounds them. They are
nearly comatose with fullness.

> JOYCE
> Pass me the Malomars.

> BUFFY
> (doesn't move)
> I can't.

CONTINUED

8 CONTINUED: 8

                         JOYCE
                   (doesn't move)
             Good.

The doorbell rings. Buffy pulls herself off the couch with
great effort.

9 EXT. BUFFY'S PORCH - NIGHT   9

Buffy opens the door. Nothing but the chilly night breeze.
She looks around, suddenly alert.

10 INT. BUFFY'S HALLWAY\LIVING ROOM - CONT.   10

Buffy closes the door. Sees that the television now chatters
to an EMPTY ROOM. Her mom is nowhere to be seen.

                         BUFFY
             Mom?

Silence.

11 INT. BUFFY'S KITCHEN - CONT.   11

Buffy moves through the kitchen cautiously. A noise SPINS
her around - but it's just a tree branch scratching the
window.

She takes a few steps back. We can see behind her, but she
can not, that the back door is OPENING. She walks smack into-

JOYCE

Buffy SHOUTS. SPINS - ready to FIGHT.

                         JOYCE
             Buffy! It's me.

                         BUFFY
                   (letting down)
             Sorry... You startled me.

                         JOYCE
             I - I went to check the back door.

She lifts a LONG BLACK FLOWER BOX. Hands it to Buffy.

                                                          CONTINUED

11 CONTINUED: 11

> JOYCE (cont'd)
> Somebody left these for you.

Buffy takes the box - cautiously opens it.

CLOSE ON THE BOX

A dozen beautiful, blood red roses. And a card - "SOON."

OFF BUFFY

Dread creeping over her features.

12 INT. THE BRONZE - NIGHT   12

Xander spots Cordelia. Takes a deep breath and approaches.

> XANDER
> Hey.

> CORDELIA
> Your clothes. You look so nice.

> XANDER
> I let Buffy dress me.
> (off her look)
> Well, not physically...

> CORDELIA
> Perfect. You just had to make this
> harder, didn't you?

A beat. Xander is perplexed.

> XANDER
> Okay. Clearly the fact that I please
> you visually got us off on the wrong
> foot here.

> CORDELIA
> Xander-

> XANDER
> Let me finish. I've been thinking a
> lot about us. The why and the
> wherefore. And, you know - once,
> twice. A kissy here. A kissy there.
> You can chalk it up to hormones. But
> hormones only take you so far.
> (more)

12 CONTINUED: 12

                          XANDER (cont'd)
                    (then)
          Okay. Really far. And maybe that's
          all we have here. Tawdry teen lust.
                    (sincere)
          But maybe - not. Maybe something in
          you sees something... special in me.
          And vice versa. I mean, I think I
          do. See something. So-

He thrusts the gift box into her hands. Struck dumb,
Cordelia opens it. Pulls the silver heart fro mit.

                          CORDELIA
                    (pained)
          Xander. Thank you. It's beautiful.
          I want to break up.

                          XANDER
                    (stunned/re: necklace)
          Not really the reaction I was going
          for.

                          CORDELIA
          I'm sorry. I really am. It's
          just - who are we kidding? I mean,
          even if parts of us do see
          specialness... We just don't fit.

                          XANDER
                    (anger growing)
          Yeah, okay -- you know what's a good
          day to break up with someone? **Any
          day besides Valentine's Day**. Were
          you just running low on dramatic
          irony?

                          CORDELIA
          I know. I didn't mean to do it like
          this-

Xander reacts. Tries hard to maintain.

                          XANDER
          Well you did.

He walks off. Cordelia looks down at the heart.

13 INT. SCHOOL HALLWAY - DAY   13

Xander walks the hall, a picture of misery. A few girls who
were at the Bronze the night before pass, giggle. A JOCK
that he passes slaps him on the back and says with
incongruous bonhomie:

                    JOCK
          Dude! Way to get dumped!

Xander sucks it up. Walks on. Then he sees BUFFY, who is
power-freaked after her visit from Angel.

                    XANDER
          Buffy. My bud. You would not
          believe the kind of day --

                    BUFFY
               (cutting him off)
          I can't talk right now. It's Angel.

                    XANDER
          Well, do you need help?

                    BUFFY
          It's all right.

She leaves him in the dust. Then Xander sees CORDELIA,
HARMONY and the Cordettes standing near by. Harmony smirks.

                    HARMONY
          Gee, Xander, maybe you should learn
          a second language so that **more** girls
          can reject you.

Cordelia looks away, ashamed, as Harmony and the Cordettes
crack up.

That's it. Xander turns and goes through the doors to the
hall.

14 INT. ANOTHER HALLWAY - DAY   14

As soon as he is in he passes AMY. He stops her, grabbing
her arm. Sudden purpose in his eyes.

                    AMY
          What are you doing!

Xander backs her slightly against the wall.

                                              CONTINUED

14 CONTINUED: 14

                    XANDER
          Amy! Good to see you! You're a
          witch.

                    AMY
          No, I'm not! That was my mom,
          remember?

                    XANDER
          I'm thinking it runs in the family.
          I saw you working that mojo on Miss
          Beakman. Maybe I should tell someone
          about that.

                    AMY
          That's not even -- I never -- that's
          so mean!

                    XANDER
          Blackmail is such an ugly word...

                    AMY
          I didn't say blackmail.

                    XANDER
          Yeah, well I'm about to blackmail you
          so I thought I'd bring it up.

                    AMY
          What do you want?

                    XANDER
          What do I want? I want a little
          respect around here. I want -- for
          once -- to come out ahead. I want
          the hellmouth working for me.

He looks at Cordy through the glass in the doors.

                    XANDER (cont'd)
          You and me, Amy... We're gonna cast
          a little spell.

                                        BLACK OUT.

                    END OF ACT ONE

ACT TWO

15 INT. EMPTY CLASSROOM - DAY

Amy is looking at Xander, perplexed.

                    AMY
          A love spell?

                    XANDER
          Just the basic. You know - can't
          eat, can't sleep, can't breathe
          anything but little old moi.

                    AMY
          That kind of thing is the hardest.
          I mean, to make someone love you for
          all eternity-

                    XANDER
          Whoa. Back up. Who said anything
          about eternity? A man can only talk
          self-tanning lotion for so long
          before his head explodes.

                    AMY
          Then - I don't get it. If you don't
          want to be with her forever - what's
          the point?

                    XANDER
          The point is - I want her to want me.
          Desperately. Then I can break up
          with her and subject her to the same
          hell she's putting me through.

                    AMY
          I don't know, Xander. Intent has to
          be pure with love spells.

                    XANDER
          Right. I intend revenge. Pure as
          the driven snow. Now are you going
          to play or do we need to chat some
          more about invisible homework?

Amy knows she's beat.

                    AMY
          I'll need something of hers. A
          personal object.

16   INT. LIBRARY - DAY   16

        Buffy enters - drops the card that Angel left for her on the
        book GILES is reading. He picks it up - looks at it.

                        BUFFY
                "Soon?" Soon what, Giles? I mean,
                you never held back on me until the
                big, bad thing in the dark became my
                ex-honey.

                        GILES
                Where did this come from?

                        BUFFY
                He said it with flowers.
                        (off his look)
                This is no time to start being
                protective guy. I can't just hang
                around - and I can't prepare when I
                don't know what's coming.

        Giles finally nods gravely.

                        GILES
                Of course - you're right. Sit down.

17   INT. SCHOOL HALLWAY - DAY   17

        Cordy is walking down the hall when she sees Xander marching
        toward her, purposeful. She starts to go the other
        direction - but Xander cuts her off.

                        XANDER
                Don't flatter yourself. I'm not
                going to make a big scene. I just
                want the necklace back.

                        CORDELIA
                What? I thought it was a gift.

                        XANDER
                Last night it was a gift. Today it's
                scrap metal. I figure I can melt it
                down - sell it for fillings or
                something.

                        CORDELIA
                You're pathetic...

        A beat. Xander taps his foot impatiently.

CONTINUED

                         XANDER
          Come on. I'm not going to add to the
          "Cordelia Chase Cast-Off Collection."

                         CORDELIA
                    (stalling)
          It's in my locker.

                         XANDER
          I can wait.

Cordelia HUFFS over to her locker. Opens it.

CLOSE ON CORDELIA

Who hides behind the locker door. Waits until Xander isn't
looking and then, discretely removes the necklace from around
her neck. She's been wearing it under her blouse.

ON XANDER

Who watches Cordelia SLAM the locker door shut. Move back to
him with the necklace in her outstretched hand.

                         CORDELIA
          Here. Thank God we broke up. Now
          I don't have to pretend to like it.

Xander SNATCHES it from her hand. Moves off.

18 INT. SCIENCE LAB - NIGHT   18

The room is dark - except for the light of one candle. Amy
has drawn a LARGE FEMALE SYMBOL on the ground in red chalk.
Xander, shirtless, kneels in the center of the chalk circle,
holding the aforementioned candle - which has Cordelia's name
written on it. Herbs and such boil in a lab beaker. A
picture of Cordelia sits in front of Xander.

Amy reads from her spell book.

                         AMY
          "Diana, goddess of love and the hunt.
          I pray to thee. Let my cries bind
          the heart of Xander's beloved. May
          she neither rest nor sleep..."

Amy drops the HEART-SHAPED NECKLACE into her brew. The brew
ignites and starts to spew RED SMOKE. Amy starts to tremble.

                                                    CONTINUED

18 CONTINUED: 18

               AMY (cont'd)
    "until she submits to his will only.
    Diana! Bring about this love and
    bless it!

Amy is quaking with cosmic energy as she addresses Xander -
her tongue urgent.

               AMY (cont'd)
    Blow out the candle! Now!

Xander obeys her command. They are plunged into-

BLACK

A long, silent beat. Then - Xander's shaky voice.

               XANDER
    Great. Really. Good spell... Can I
    put my shirt on now?

19 INT. LOUNGE - DAY 19

The next morning. Xander enters, ready for love. Then he
spots Cordy in the lounge with Harmony. Saunters over. He
stands near Cordy for a beat, smiling and preening. Finally:

               CORDELIA
    What?

               XANDER
        (all smiles)
    Morning, ladies.
        (seductively)
    Some weather we've been having.

Cordy is obviously surprised by his approach.

               CORDELIA
    What do you want? You can't be
    sniffing around for more jewelry to
    melt - 'cause all you ever gave me
    was that Walmart-looking thing.

Xander's smile falters - he moves a little closer to her.
Speaks softly.

               XANDER
    Is this love? 'Cause, maybe on you
    it doesn't look that different-

                            CORDELIA
                        (shoves him back)
            What is up? Are you going, like,
            stalker-boy on me?

That's enough testing for Xander.

                            XANDER
            Sorry. My mistake.

                            CORDELIA
            Yeah. I'd say so.

Xander moves off, chagrined. Cordelia turns to Harmony.

                            CORDELIA (cont'd)
            What is his deal?!

                            HARMONY
            I know. Did he cut his hair or
            something? He looked half-way decent
            for a change.

Off Cordy. Confused by Harmony's comment.

20 INT. LIBRARY - DAY   20

        Buffy is with Giles, going over further Watcher diaries.

                            GILES
            Ah, here's another. Valentine's Day,
            yes, Angel nails a puppy to --

                            BUFFY
            Skip it.

                            GILES
            But --

                            BUFFY
            I don't want to know. I don't have
            a puppy. We can skip it.

                            GILES
            Right. Let me get the next batch.

He crosses to his office as Xander enters glumly.

                            XANDER
            I have a plan. We use me as bait.

> BUFFY
> You mean, make Angel come after **you**?

> XANDER
> No I mean chop me into little pieces
> and stick me on hooks for fish to
> nibble at cuz that would be more fun
> than my life.

> BUFFY
> I heard about you and Cordy. It's
> her loss.

> XANDER
> Not the popular theory...

Buffy runs her hand through his hair, looking into his eyes.

> BUFFY
> You know what I'd like? Why don't
> you and I go do something tonight.
> Just us.

> XANDER
> Really?

> BUFFY
> Yeah, we can comfort each other.

> XANDER
> Would lap dancing enter into this
> scenario at all? 'Cause I find that
> very comforting.

> BUFFY
> Play your cards right...

> XANDER
> Okay. You do know that I'm Xander,
> right?

> BUFFY
> I don't know... I heard you and Cordy
> broke up, I was surprised how glad I
> was.

She's very close to him now, and since you ask, yes there's
heat. Yet her advances are mroe than sexkittenish -- they're
sincere.

CONTINUED

20 CONTINUED: (2)   20

                        BUFFY (cont'd)
            It's funny how you can see a person
            every day and not really **see** them,
            you know?

                        XANDER
                    (enraptured)
            It's funny. And it's just getting
            funnier.

                        BUFFY
            When you think about it, we make a
            lot of sense --

Amy enters, somewhat timidly.

                        AMY
            Xander, can I talk to you for a
            minute?

                        XANDER
                    (to Amy)
            Yeah. Okay.
                    (to Buffy)
            Hold that thought. Tightly.

He goes off with Amy.

21 INT. HALL OUTSIDE LIBRARY - CONTINUOUS   21

They stop right by the doors, Xander looking in anxiously at
his newly affectionate Buffy.

                        AMY
            Xander, I don't think the spell
            worked out right.

                        XANDER
            Yeah, we bombed. No biggie.

                        AMY
            Well, we could try again. I'm still
            pretty new at this.

                        XANDER
            It's okay. You know what? It was
            wrong to meddle with the forces of
            darkness and I see that now. I think
            we've all grown. I gotta go.

                                                      CONTINUED

21 CONTINUED: 21

                         AMY
              Well, we don't have to cast any
              spells -- we could just hang out.

                         XANDER
              Sure... what?

                         AMY
              Well, I really liked spending time
              with you. You're so sweet... It's
              funny how you can see a person every
              day and --

                         XANDER
                    (his expression
                     drains)
              -- not really see them?

                         AMY
              Exactly!

The wind goes right out of Xander's sails. In fact, his
sails fall down. He looks in to see

ANGLE: BUFFY THROUGH THE WINDOW

Who smiles seductively at him as Giles reads something to her
that she doesn't hear.

                         AMY (cont'd)
              So anyway, I thought it might be fun
              to--

                         KATIE
              Hi, Xander?

KATIE'S quite attractive, and clearly smitten.

                         XANDER
              What?

                         KATIE
              You're in Mr. Baird's history class,
              right? I thought maybe we could
              study together tonight.

                         AMY
              Do you mind? We were talking.

                         XANDER
              I really have to leave right now.

CONTINUED

21 CONTINUED: (2)   21

                          KATIE
                Well, here's my number if you want
                to --

She holds up a little slip of paper, but he takes off. A
beat later and he appears in the frame, takes the paper and
leaves again.

22 INT. XANDER'S ROOM - NIGHT   22

Xander races in and locks the door, exhausted and shaken. He
moves to his bed and starts to lie down. But YELPS and JUMPS
UP when he realizes that he is NOT ALONE. WILLOW sits up,
smiles. Xander, wary, starts to inch for the door.

                          WILLOW
                Sorry. I wanted to surprise you.

                          XANDER
                Good job. High marks.

                          WILLOW
                Don't be so jumpy. I've been in your
                bed before.

                          XANDER
                Yeah, Will, but we were in footie
                pajamas.

Willow's manner becomes more and more sweetly predatory.
This is a new Willow. Sexual, mature.

                          WILLOW
                Xand. I've been thinking.

                          XANDER
                Will, I think I know what you were
                thinking, but this is all my fault,
                I cast a spell and it sort of
                backfired --

                          WILLOW
                     (cutting him off)
                How long have we been friends?

                          XANDER
                A long, long time. Too long to do
                anything that might change it now.

CONTINUED

>   WILLOW
>   But friendships always change.
>   People grow apart.   They grow <u>closer</u>.

>   XANDER
>   This is good.   How close are we now?
>   I feel very comfortable with this
>   amount of closeness.   In fact, I
>   could even back up a few paces and
>   still be happy...   See?

>   WILLOW
>   I want you, Xander.   To be my first-

>   XANDER
>   (weakly hopeful)
>   Baseman?   Please tell me we're
>   talking softball.

Now she gets out of bed.   We see now that she's WEARING HIS
BUTTON DOWN SHIRT.   She moves toward him.

>   XANDER (cont'd)
>   That's... dry clean only.

>   WILLOW
>   Shhhhh.   We both know it's right.

She pins him against the door.   Tries to kiss him.   But he
turns away.

>   XANDER
>   It's not that I don't find you sexy-

>   WILLOW
>   Is it Oz?   Don't worry about him.
>   He's sweet - but he's not you.

>   XANDER
>   Yes he is!   And you should go to him.
>   'Cause he's me.

She nibbles his ear.

>   XANDER (cont'd)
>   Willow, don't make me use force...

>   WILLOW
>   Force is okay...

He pushes her away.

22 CONTINUED: (2)   22

                    XANDER
          That's it. This has all gotta stop.
          It's time for me to act like a man.
          And hide.

He flees, leaving Willow in his room.

23 INT. SCHOOL HALLWAY - DAY   23

     A new day. Cordelia approaches Harmony and the others - but
     they give her the cold shoulder.

                    CORDELIA
          Ha. Very funny. What did I do
          now - wear red and purple together?

                    HARMONY
                (cold as ice)
          You know what you did. Xander is
          wounded because of you.

They start to walk away.

                    CORDELIA
          Are you tripping? I thought you
          wanted me to break up with him-

                    HARMONY
          You'd better look at yourself,
          Cordelia. Only a sick pup would let
          Xander get away - no matter what her
          friends said.

Harmony and the others leave Cordelia stunned. Finally she
calls after them:

                    CORDELIA
          **What does it take to make you people
          happy?**

24 INT. SCHOOL HALLWAY - ANOTHER AREA - DAY   24

CLOSE ON

SLO MO - a pair of feet move down the hall. COOL GUY music
plays over. But shen we WIDEN we see that the feet belong to
a terrified XANDER instead of a hip love God.

                                                      CONTINUED

24 CONTINUED: 24

    Every person in the hallway is STARING at him. The woman all
    GAPE adoringly and the men all GLARE - enraged. Xander ducks
    into the library.

25 INT. LIBRARY - DAY   25

    Giles sees Xander enter - reacts to his obvious agitation.

                        GILES
              Xander. What is it?

                        XANDER
              It's me. Throwing myself at your
              mercy.

                        GILES
              What? Why?

                        XANDER
              I made a mess, Giles. See, I found
              out that Amy's into witchcraft? And
              I was hurt, I guess, so I made her
              put the love whammy on Cordy. But it
              backfired. And now every woman in
              Sunnydale wants to make me her cuddle-
              monkey. Which may sound swell on
              paper but-

    Calendar enters - marches up to GILES.

                        CALENDAR
              Rupert. We need to talk.
                   (notices Xander)
              Hey, Xander. Nice shirt.

    Calendar tries vigilantly to stay focused. But is drawn all
    the while like a magnet to XANDER. As she speaks, she rests
    her hand casually on Xander's arm.

                        CALENDAR (cont'd)
              Rupert, I know you're angry at me and
              I don't blame you. But I'm not going
              away. I care too much about you to --
                   (to Xander, feeling
                    his arm)
              Have you been working out?

    Giles grabs Calendar. Moves her away from Xander, livid.

                                                        CONTINUED

                        GILES
                     (to Xander)
          I can't believe you'd be fool enough
          to do something like this.

                        XANDER
          Oh no. I'm twice the fool it takes
          to do something like this.

                        GILES
          Has Amy tried to reverse the spell?

                        XANDER
          I get near Amy and all she wants to
          talk is honeymoon plans.

                        CALENDAR
          Rupert, maybe I should talk to Xander
          alone.

                        GILES
          Do you have any idea how serious this
          is? People under the influence of
          love spells are deadly, Xander. They
          lose all capacity to reason. And if
          what you say is true, and the whole
          female population is affected...
                     (then)
          Don't leave this library. I'll find
          Amy. See if we can stop this thing.

Giles begins to go - but remembers Calendar, who stares at
Xander longingly. Giles grabs her.

And he takes off with Calendar in tow. A beat. Then Xander
drags the card catalog in front of the library doors.

He steps back -- and the door opens anyway, since they open
out. Buffy steps around the card catalog.

                        BUFFY
          Alone at last.

Xander looks up to see BUFFY ENTER, WEARING NOTHING BUT A
RAINCOAT AND HEELS. The raincoat is tied with a belt.

                        XANDER
          Buff! Give me a heart attack-

She looks him in the eye. Deadly.

CONTINUED

25 CONTINUED: (2)   25

                    BUFFY
          I'm going to give you a lot more than
          that.

Xander scrambles away from her. But Buffy's right on top of
him. Moving in.

                    XANDER
          Buffy. For the love of God, don't
          open that rain coat.

                    BUFFY
          Come on, it's a party.
                    (plays with belt)
          Aren't you gonna open your present?

                    XANDER
          Not that I don't want to... Sometimes
          the remote, impossible possibility
          that you might like me was all that
          sustained me...
                    (frustration mounting)
          But not now. Not like this. This
          isn't real to you. You're only here
          because of a spell. I mean, if I
          thought you had one clue what it
          would mean to me... But you don't, so
          I can't -

Buffy's expression shifts. A flash of DEADLY ANGER crosses
her features. Fatal Attraction time.

                    BUFFY
          So - this is all a game to you.

                    XANDER
          A game? I - no...

Buffy's ire rises. She advances on him - menacing.

                    BUFFY
          You make me feel this way and then
          reject me. What am I - a toy?

                    XANDER
          Buffy, please. Calm down-

                    BUFFY
          I'll calm down when you explain
          yourself!

CONTINUED

25 CONTINUED: (3)   25

          Buffy looks like she's about to inflict bodily harm - but
          then the doors open and AMY enters. Furious.

                              AMY
                    Get away from him. He's mine.

          BUFFY turns on Amy. Seething.

                              BUFFY
                    I don't think so. Xander? Tell her.

                              XANDER
                    What? I - I-

                              AMY
                    He doesn't have to say. I know what
                    his heart wants.

          Amy starts to move toward Xander. Buffy blocks her.

                              BUFFY
                    Funny. I know what your face wants-

          And BUFFY DECKS AMY. Amy flies back and hits the floor,
          bloodied. Buffy turns to Xander - wild eyed.

                              BUFFY (cont'd)
                    What is this? You're two-timing me?

          Amy starts to incant. Angry eyes boring into Buffy.

                              AMY
                    "Goddess Hecate, work thy will..."   *

          Amy raises her arms to Buffy. Her eyes GO BLACK.

                              XANDER
                    Uh oh.

                              AMY
                    "Before thee let the unclean thing   *
                    crawl!"   *

          A ball of energy flies from AMY'S HANDS.

                              XANDER
                    Buffy!

          The ENERGY EXPLODES as it HITS Buffy - engulfing her until IT
          AND BUFFY seem to VAPORIZE. A beat as Xander and Amy recover.

                                                            CONTINUED

25 CONTINUED: (4)   25

Xander moves to where Buffy disappeared. Looks to the floor.

CLOSE ON XANDER

Horrified.

                    XANDER (cont'd)
          Oh my God.

                              BLACK OUT.

               END OF ACT TWO

ACT THREE

26 INT. LIBRARY - DAY   26

GILES ENTERS with CALENDAR IN TOW.

                    GILES
          Good Lord, what was that-

                    XANDER
          Buffy.

                    GILES
          Where is she?

CLOSE ON THE FLOOR

Where a LARGE RAT, AKA BUFFY, emerges from the crumpled up
raincoat. It darts this way and that, freaked.

                    GILES (cont'd)
          Oh my God.

                    AMY
               (glaring at Calendar)
          Why is she here?

                    XANDER
          Do you think we could focus for one
          minute? You turned Buffy into a rat!

Amy moves to Xander - takes him by the arm.

                    AMY
          Buffy can take care of herself.
          Let's go someplace private.

Xander tries to shake her off.

                    XANDER
          Can you..? I'm not going anywhere
          until you change her back!

Now CALENDAR takes Xander's OTHER arm. Speaks to Amy.

                    CALENDAR
          You heard him. Undo your magic trick
          and get lost.

                                                    CONTINUED

26 CONTINUED: 26

                    AMY
          Who made you Queen of the world? I
          mean, you're old enough-

                    CALENDAR
          What can I say? Xander's too much
          man for the pimple squad-

Amy fumes. Her eyes go black.

                    AMY
          "Goddess Hectate, to you I pray-"

SLAP. A hand goes around her mouth. Xander.

                    XANDER
          Would you quit with the Hectate!?

Still covering her mouth, Xander moves with Amy to Giles and
hands her off to him.

                    XANDER (cont'd)
          No more talky from this one.

27 INT. SCHOOL HALLWAY - DAY   27

Cordelia closes her locker. Is surprised to see HARMONY, the
Cordettes and a BUNCH OF OTHER WOMEN - of all ages and
sizes - staring daggers at her. Harmony approaches, the
others staying back.

                    CORDELIA
          Okay. What now? You don't like my
          locker combo?

                    HARMONY
          It's not right. You never loved him.
          You just USED him. You make me sick.

                    CORDELIA
          Harmony, if you need to borrow my
          Midol, just **ask**.

Harmony slaps Cordelia in the face. Cordy stops, shocked.
She turns to go and Katie is there, **slams** her back into the
lockers.

28 INT. LIBRARY - DAY   28

CLOSE ON BUFFY RAT

Darting toward a safe corner.

ON GILES, XANDER, ET AL.

                    GILES
          We have to trap the Buffy-rat.

Xander spots her. Follows her into the corner.

                    XANDER
          Good, Buffy. Just...

He's about to pick her up when the library doors SLAM open
and OZ strides in. He moves to Xander and PUNCHES HIM.

Buffy Rat, freaked, RUNS OUT THE SWINGING LIBRARY DOORS.

                    OZ
              (looking at his hand)
          That - kinda hurt.

                    XANDER
          Kinda?! What was that for?

                    OZ
          I was on the phone all night,
          listening to Willow cry about you.
          I don't know exactly what happened,
          but I was left with the very strong
          urge to hit you.

                    XANDER
          I didn't touch her. I swear-

Giles interrupts, coldly furious. Looking at the ground.

                    GILES
          Xander. Where did Buffy go?

Xander and Giles both get down and look at the ground. Amy   *
and Calendar don't move -- they are too busy glaring at each   *
other. Xander notices Oz's puzzled look.   *

                    XANDER
          Amy turned Buffy into a rat.

                    OZ
              (nods)
          Oh.

                                                    CONTINUED

28 CONTINUED: 28

                         GILES
          I don't see her.
                  (to Xander)
          If anything happens to her, I'll...
          Just - go home. Lock yourself away.
          You're only going to cause more
          problems here. Amy, Jenny and I will
          work on breaking the spells.
                  (to Oz)
          Oz - if you could aid us in finding
          Buffy...

                         OZ
          Sure. Absolutely.

Xander is about to speak. But Giles cuts him off.

                         GILES
          Go. Get out of my sight.

Xander takes off - hurt and ashamed.

29 INT. SCHOOL HALLWAY - DAY   29

Xander checks the hall. Sees the GANG of WOMEN, involved in
some kind of ANGRY commotion. He heads in the OTHER
DIRECTION, but stops as he realizes that the sounds are
VIOLENT.

ON THE WOMAN

Gathered around CORNELIA. Now they are HITTING HER, PULLING
HER HAIR...

                         HARMONY
          You thought you could do better? Is
          that it?

                         CORDELIA
          No! I, no....!

                         FRENZIED GIRL
          We'll knock that snotty attitude
          right out of you!

A SHOWER OF BLOWS rains down on Cordelia. She SCREAMS.

ON XANDER

Who now sees that it's CORDELIA in trouble. He runs toward-

                                                    CONTINUED

29 CONTINUED: 29

THE MOB

Sees Xander coming their way. SHRIEK with joy.

                    KATIE
          It's him! It's him!

The mob RUNS toward Xander.

XANDER sees Cordelia KNOCKED to the ground. She's getting
trampled... He has no choice but to go forward.

CORDELIA tries to regain her footing. Somebody KICKS her.

XANDER fights through the MANIC WOMEN, who tear his clothes,
scratch and grab at him...

                    HARMONY
          Stop! Xander! I love you!

Xander finally manages to get to Cordelia. He lifts her into
his arms. She buries her head in his shoulder, crying.

Xander turns and encounters an ENORMOUS FEMALE CAFETERIA
WORKER. She blocks his way. Smiles. A beat. Xander RUNS
with Cordelia in the OTHER DIRECTION.

30 INT. LIBRARY - DAY   30

Giles and Amy sit at the table, with Amy's spell book open
before them. Calendar hovers nearby. Giles is reading
intently - but both AMY and Calendar are distracted.

                    GILES
          You must have botched the ritual so
          that Cordelia's necklace **protected**
          her from the spell. That one should
          be reversible. But where did you
          learn animal transformation?

                    AMY
          Why did you send Xander away? He
          needs me.

                    CALENDAR
          That's a laugh.

                    AMY
          He loves me. We look into each
          other's souls.

                                                    CONTINUED

30 CONTINUED: 30

                              CALENDAR
                    No one can love two people at once.
                    What we have is real.

                              GILES
                    Instead of making me ill why doesn't
                    one of you try to help?

                              AMY
                    You don't know what I'm going through!

                              GILES
                    I know it isn't love. It's
                    obsession -- selfish, banal
                    obsession. Xander has put himself in
                    danger and if you really cared about
                    him you'd help me save him instead of
                    nattering on about your feelings.
                    Now let's get to work. Jenny --

But she's gone.

                              GILES (cont'd)
                    Damn...

31 EXT. SCHOOL WALKWAY - DAY   31

Xander and Cordelia, back on her feet now, round a corner.
Xander checks behind him.

                              XANDER
                    I think we-

They both stop dead in their tracks when they see-

AN EVEN LARGER MOB OF WOMEN

And this group is HOSTILE. ARMED. Led by none other than
WILLOW - who carries an AXE.

                              XANDER (cont'd)
                    -lost them...

A moment as they face off with the mob. Willow steps
forward. She has been crying.

                              WILLOW
                    I should have known I'd find you with
                    her.

CONTINUED

31 CONTINUED: 31

                         XANDER
              Will. Come on. You don't want to
              hurt me.

                         WILLOW
              Oh no? You have no idea what this is
              like for me. I love you so much.
              I'd rather see you dead than with
              that bitch!

She MOVES TOWARD XANDER WITH THE AXE - but is KNOCKED OVER by
HARMONY, who tries to get the axe away from her. Xander and
Cordelia seize the moment and take off.

32 INT. SCHOOL BOILER ROOM - DAY   32

BUFFY RAT runs down the stairs and into the boiler room. A
moment later, OZ follows, holding a FLASHLIGHT.

Buffy Rat disappears behind a furnace pipe. Oz moves slowly
around the room, his flashlight searching dark corners.

                         OZ
                    Hey. Buffy?

CLOSE ON BUFFY RAT (AND/OR RAT CAM)

Oblivious - she runs along the baseboard. Sniffing. Doing
rat things.

Then she turns a corner and runs SMACK into a GIGANTIC (to
her, anyway) TOM CAT. The cat HISSES, bares his horrible
teeth. Buffy rat backs off and the cat moves off, disappears
up the stairs and into the school.

Buffy Rat darts into a dark corner, terrified.

33 EXT. NEAR BUFFY'S HOUSE - NIGHT   33

Xander and Cordelia race down the street. He looks over his
shoulder, slows.

                         XANDER
              Now I really think we lost them.

                         CORDELIA
                    (genuinely scared)
              Dammit, Xander, what is going on?
              Who died and made you Elvis?

                                                      CONTINUED

33 CONTINUED: 33

Xander sees Buffy's house ahead.

                    XANDER
          There's Buffy's place. Let's get
          inside. Then I'll explain.

34 EXT. BUFFY'S PORCH - NIGHT   34

    JOYCE, surprised, opens the door for Xander and Cordelia.

                    JOYCE
          Xander! Cordelia?

35 INT. BUFFY'S KITCHEN - NIGHT   35

    Joyce follows them into the kitchen.

                    JOYCE
          What happened? Why are you all
          scratched up? Where's Buffy?

                    XANDER
          She's... around.

                    JOYCE
          Well. Sit down and tell me about it.
               (to Cordy)
          Why don't you run upstairs and grab
          some bandages out of the bathroom?

A beat after Cordy takes off. Xander smiles weakly. Joyce
sighs and smiles back. And keeps smiling. Uh oh.

                    JOYCE (cont'd)
               (brightly)
          Let me get you something to drink.
          Are you in the mood for cold or hot?

                    XANDER
          I - uh -

Joyce stands, moves to the counter behind him. Then she
turns, puts her hands on his shoulders.

                    JOYCE
          I think it's more of a... <u>hot</u> night.
          Don't you?

                                              CONTINUED

35   CONTINUED: 35

Xander drops his head on the table with a thud. Totally
defeated.

                    XANDER
          Whatever.

                    JOYCE
          Goodness. You are so tense.

She starts to kneed his shoulders. She's bending down to
KISS his neck when-

                    CORDELIA (O.C.)
          What are you doing?! Make me yak!

Joyce snaps her head up. Looks at Cordelia coolly.

                    JOYCE
          Go back upstairs, Cordelia. This is
          between us.

                    CORDELIA
          Gross. I think not.

Cordy grabs Joyce. They struggle - but Cordy is stronger and
easily throws Joyce OUT THE BACK DOOR. LOCKS IT.

                    CORDELIA (cont'd)
          And keep your mom-aged mitts away
          from my boyfriend... Former!

Now Cordy turns to Xander - pissed.

                    CORDELIA (cont'd)
          Why has everyone gone insane?

                    XANDER
          Insane? It's impossible for you to
          believe that other women find me
          attractive?

                    CORDELIA
          The only way you could get girls to
          want you would be Witchcraft!

                    XANDER
          That is **such a** --well okay yeah, good
          point.

They are silenced when A ROCK FLIES THROUGH THE WINDOW. Then
JOYCE'S HAND appears, feeling for the DOOR LOCK.

                                                      CONTINUED

35 CONTINUED: (2)   35

                         JOYCE
              Xander? Honey? Let Joycie in!

A beat. Then Xander and Cordy BOLT.

36 INT. BUFFY'S ROOM - NIGHT   36

Xander and Cordy SLAM into Buffy's room. Xander runs to the
window. Opens it and leans out.

                         XANDER
              Good. The mob still hasn't found us.
              We should be safer up here --

He's cut off as ANGEL, VAMP FACE AND ALL, appears at the
window, grabbing him and pulling him out.

                         ANGEL
              Works in theory...

                                        BLACK OUT.

                    END OF ACT THREE

42.

ACT FOUR

37 INT. SCHOOL BOILER ROOM - NIGHT   37

RAT CAM (BUFFY RAT P.O.V.)

She creeps along, moves toward a bunch of CARTONS.

Suddenly into view comes A BIG, BAD-ASS RAT TRAP - with a
TASTY-LOOKING HUNK'O CHEESE on it.

Buffy Rat sniffs CLOSER.

38 EXT. BUFFY'S ROOF - NIGHT   38

Angel pulls Xander closer. Gets in his face.

                    ANGEL
          Where's Buffy?

                    XANDER
          Cordy, get out of here!

Impatiently, Angel **throws** Xander off the roof.

39 EXT. BUFFY'S HOUSE - CONT.   39

Xander hits the ground hard. A moment later Angel lands
gracefully next to him. Lifts a dazed Xander with one hand-

                    ANGEL
          Perfect. I wanted to do something
          special for Buffy - actually - to
          Buffy. But this is so much better.

Xander KNEES ANGEL, who falters briefly but then BACKHANDS
him - sending him flying. Angel pins Xander to the ground,
wrenches his head to one side, baring his tender white neck.

                    ANGEL (cont'd)
          If it's any consolation, I feel very
          close to you right now-

Angel opens wide - moves in for the kill. Hands GRAB Angel
and easily pull him off, throw him against a tree.

XANDER looks up - grateful.

                                                      CONTINUED

39 CONTINUED: 39

                              XANDER
              Buffy?! How did you-

But he stops when he sees his rescuer. Dumbfounded.

DRUSILLA

Smiles down at him. Extends a hand.

                              DRUSILLA
              Don't fret, Kitten. Mommy's here.

Xander backs away from her. But she GRABS him, helps him up.

                              ANGEL
                            (furious)
              I don't know what you're up to, Dru,
              but it doesn't amuse.

Dru turns on ANGEL, seething. Petting a horrified Xander all
the while.

                              DRUSILLA
              If you so much as harmed one hair on
              this boy's precious head-

Angel can't believe his ears.

                              ANGEL
              You've got to be kidding? Him?

                              DRUSILLA
              Now, now. Just because I finally
              found a real man...

Angel shakes his head, uncomprehending.

                              ANGEL
              A real man? I guess I really **did**
              drive you crazy.

He fades back as Dru concentrates on her new boytoy. She
gazes at him lovingly. Traces the linens of his eyes, his
lips...

                              DRUSILLA
              Your face is a poem. I can read it...

                              XANDER
              Really? It doesn't say - "spare
              him" - by any chance?

                                                    CONTINUED

                              DRUSILLA
                    Shhhhhh.

She BARES her VAMP TEETH.

                              DRUSILLA (cont'd)
                    How do you feel about eternal life?

                              XANDER
                    Don't you think we could start with
                    coffee? A movie maybe?

Drusilla smiles - bends to his neck. Xander struggles,
desperate - when, suddenly, THE NIGHT IS FILLED WITH HOSTILE
SHOUTS. Drusilla looks up - wide eyed.

THE MOB

Still led by Willow, but even larger than before. It now
includes CALENDAR and HARMONY and KATIE.

                              CALENDAR
                    There he is!

                              WILLOW
                    Get them!

DRU AND XANDER are surrounded. Besieged by crying, violent
women. Xander is YANKED from her arms. He and Dru are
separated in the melee.

                              CALENDAR
                    Mine! He's mine!

Wild women rip at his clothes, tear at his hair. WILLOW
watches - lover's wrath burning in her eyes as she twists her
axe, waiting for her moment.

Now Xander's knocked to the ground and pinned by a LARGE
WOMAN. WILLOW steps forward. Raises her AXE. Looks down at
him, sorrowful.

                              WILLOW
                    All you had to do was love me.

She's about to bring the axe down when Cordelia slams into
her, knocking her to the ground.

40   INT. BUFFY'S FOYER - NIGHT   40

     Cordy and Xander make it into the house, just barely managing
     to close the door against the FRENZIED WOMEN outside.

41   EXT. BUFFY'S HOUSE - CONT.   41

     Drusilla is part of the MOB that lays siege to Buffy's house.
     She pulls the BACK DOOR OFF THE HINGES. Two women run in --
     Dru starts to follow -- but SLAMS into an invisible barrier.

     Now we see Angel, leaning against a tree nearby. Smirking.

                         ANGEL
              Sorry Dru. Guess you're not invited.

     Dru, beyond frustrated, SCREAMS.

42   INT. BUFFY'S FOYER - NIGHT   42

     Xander and Cordelia don't have a chance to catch their breath
     before JOYCE appears in the living room doorway holding a
     LARGE CARVING KNIFE. She is distraught.

                         JOYCE
              It's never gonna work for us, Xander.
              We have to end it.

     The other two women who came in the back run up and join
     Joyce. Freaked, Xander and Cordelia race for-

43   INT. BUFFY'S BASEMENT - NIGHT   43

     -where they lock the door.

                         CORDELIA
              Deja vu much? Here's another good
              reason not to date you. People are
              always trying to kill me when I'm
              with you! So - what do we do now?
              Wait for Buffy to come?

                         XANDER
              I... wouldn't hold my breath.

44   INT. SCHOOL BOILER ROOM - DAY   44

     RAT CAM: the trap looms large. The Buffy Rat approaches.

CONTINUED

44 CONTINUED: 44

     ANGLE: OZ

     Still searching for Buffy Rat, unconsciously sings to himself-

                         OZ
                    (theme from "BEN")
               "...Ben, the two of us need look no
               more... we both found what we were
               looking for-"

45 INT. SCIENCE LAB - NIGHT   45

     Again with the candle light and the red chalk "female"
     symbol. Giles and a sullen AMY stand at the lab table, with
     her spell book. A beaker boils with a new brew.

                         GILES
               Right. You go first.

46 INT. BUFFY'S BASEMENT - NIGHT   46

     Cordelia and Xander are nailing the door shut. We hear
     someone trying it.

                         CALENDAR (O.C.)
               Xander? Xander, it's okay, it's me...
                    (sudden pounding)
               OPEN THE DOOR! XANDER!

                         XANDER
               Give me another nail.

                         CORDELIA
               If we die in here I'm gonna kick your
               ass! I mean it.

                         XANDER
               None of this would have happened if
               you hadn't broken up with me. But
               no, you're so desperate to be popular.

                         CORDELIA
               Me? I'm not the one who embraced the
               black arts just to get girls to like
               me. Well, congratulations, I guess
               it worked.

                                                            CONTINUED

46 CONTINUED: 46

                         XANDER
          It would have worked fine! Except
          your hide's so thick not even magic
          can penetrate it!

                         CORDELIA
                    (quieter)
          You mean, the spell was for me?

A KNIFE comes through the door right between them. Cordy
SCREAMS and they both run down the stairs.

As they reach the cellar floor, glass shatters from the
window, an arm reaching in at them.

47 INT. SCIENCE LAB - NIGHT   47

Giles drops a tuft of RODENT HAIR into the boiling beaker.
Again, a great plume of smoke rises.

                         AMY
          "Diana! Hectate! I hereby license
          three to depart-"

48 INT. SCHOOL BOILER ROOM - NIGHT   48

RAT CAM

Buffy Rat finally GOES FOR THE CHEESE in the trap.

49 INT. SCIENCE LAB - NIGHT   49

                         AMY
          "Goddess of creatures great and
          small - I conjure thee to withdraw!"

50 INT. SCHOOL BOILER ROOM - NIGHT   50

Oz is still looking around when he is flooded by light from
behind a bunch of crates. As it dissipates, he steps forward.

                         OZ
          Buffy?

Buffy is on the ground behind the crates, which hide her
delicate situation from view. (i.e. nekkidness.)

                                                      CONTINUED

50 CONTINUED: 50

                              BUFFY
              Whoah.

51 INT. BUFFY'S BASEMENT - NIGHT   51

    The door FLIES open, the women pouring down.

    Cordelia and Xander back into a corner, Xander wielding a
    heavy wrench.

                              CORDELIA
              Oh god...

                              XANDER
              Get behind me!

52 INT. SCIENCE LAB - NIGHT   52

    Now Giles adds some hers to the brew. MORE SMOKE.

                              GILES
              "Diana, Goddess of love, be gone.
              Hear no more your siren's song!"

53 INT. BUFFY'S BASEMENT - NIGHT   53

    Willow heads the pack that converges on Xander. He is buried
    under their tearing hands.

54 INT. SCIENCE LAB - NIGHT   54

    Giles throws Cordelia's necklace in the pot. All at once
    there is a great CGI rush of light from every window and
    doorway in the place -- all disappearing into the pot.

55 INT. BUFFY'S BASEMENT - NIGHT   55

    Everybody stops, staggers back, slightly dazed. Xander is
    curled up in the fetal position. Meekly he looks around.

56 INT. SCHOOL BOILER ROOM - NIGHT   56

    Oz approaches Buffy.

CONTINUED

56 CONTINUED: 56

> BUFFY
> Uh, hi, Oz. I seem to be having a
> slight case of nudity.

> OZ
> But you're not a rat. Call it an up
> side.

> BUFFY
> Can you grab me some clothes?

> OZ
> Oh, yeah. Don't go anywhere.

> BUFFY
> Really not an issue.

57 INT. SCIENCE LAB - NIGHT   57

Giles and Amy look around them. Everything seems normal.

Giles gives Amy a stern look. Sheepishly, she hands him the
book of spells.

58 INT. BUFFY'S BASEMENT - NIGHT   58

Xander gets up, Cordelia coming out from the corner as the
women look at each other, bewildered. Joyce, in particular,
looks disturbed.

> JOYCE
> What... what did we --

> CORDELIA
> Boy! That was the best scavenger
> hunt ever!

She smiles brightly at the others, hoping they'll buy it.

59 INT. SCHOOL HALLWAY - DAY   59

Buffy and Xander walk.

> BUFFY
> Scavenger hunt?

> XANDER
> Well, your mom seemed to buy it.

CONTINUED

> BUFFY
> So she says. I think she's just so
> wigged at hitting on one of my
> friends that she's repressing. She's
> getting really good at that,
> actually. I should probably worry.

> XANDER
> Well, I'm back to being incredibly
> unpopular.

> BUFFY
> It's better than everyone trying to
> axe murder you, right?

> XANDER
> Mostly. But... Willow. Won't even
> talk to me.

> BUFFY
> Any particular reason she should?

> XANDER
> How much groveling are we talking
> here?

> BUFFY
> A month, at least. This was worse
> for her than anyone. She loved you
> before you invoked the great roofie
> spirit. The rest of us...

> XANDER
> You remember, huh?

> BUFFY
> Oh yeah. I remember coming on to
> you. I remember begging you to
> undress me... And then a sudden need
> for cheese.
>   (beat)
> I also remember that you didn't.

> XANDER
> Need cheese?

> BUFFY
> Undress me. It meant a lot to me,
> what you said.

CONTINUED

59 CONTINUED: (2)   59

                         XANDER
          I would never take advantage of you
          like that. Okay, it was touch and go
          for a minute there, but...

                         BUFFY
          You came through, Xander. There may
          be hope for you yet.

                         XANDER
          Tell that to Cordelia.

                         BUFFY
          You're on your own, there.

He goes off.

60 EXT. COURTYARD - DAY   60

Cordy and Harmony are back in lock step, the other Cordettes
around.

                         HARMONY
          Cody Weinberg called me at home last
          night.

                         CORDELIA
          Cody? The one with the 350 SL?

                         HARMONY
          The very one. Said he's thinking of
          taking me to the pledge dance on
          Thursday.

                         CORDELIA
          That's so huge!

                         HARMONY
          Yeah! There's just two other girls
          he's gonna ask first and if they
          refuse

They (literally) bump into Xander.

                         HARMONY (cont'd)
          Watch it!

                         XANDER
          Sorry.

CONTINUED

60 CONTINUED: 60

A beat as he and Cordy look at each other. She looks down.

                    HARMONY
          Excuse me, who asked you to share our
          oxygen? God.

Xander starts off. Harmony calls after him.

                    HARMONY (cont'd)
          I'm glad your mom stopped working the
          drive thru long enough to dress you.

He just keeps walking, his face grimly set.

                    HARMONY (cont'd)
          That reminds me, did you SEE
          Jennifer's backpack? It's so trying
          to be --

                    CORDELIA
          Harmony, shut up.

Everyone stops -- including Xander, who slowly turns, as:

                    CORDELIA (cont'd)
          You know what you are, Harmony?
          You're a sheep.

                    HARMONY
          I'm not a sheep.

                    CORDELIA
          You're a sheep. Sweaters are made
          from your woolly coat.

She moves toward Xander, turning back to face Harmony.

                    CORDELIA (cont'd)
          All you ever do is what everyone else
          does, so you can say you did it
          first. And here I am scrambling for
          your approval, when I'm way cooler
          than you are because I'm not a sheep!
          I do what I want, I wear what I want,
          and you know what? I'll date whoever
          I want to date, no matter how lame he
          is!

She grabs Xander's hand and they walk off, leaving Harmony
stunned.

                                                    CONTINUED

60 CONTINUED: (2)   60

ANGLE: XANDER AND CORDELIA

She is breathing shallow, terrified at her own display of
independence.

                    CORDELIA (cont'd)
          Oh, god, oh, god...

                    XANDER
          You're gonna be okay. Just keep
          walking.

                    CORDELIA
          Oh god, what have I done? No one's
          ever gonna speak to me again.

                    XANDER
          Sure they will. If it helps, when
          we're around them you and I can fight
          a lot.

                    CORDELIA
          You promise?

                    XANDER
          You can pretty much count on it.

                                   BLACK OUT.

                    THE END

BUFFY THE VAMPIRE SLAYER

"Passion"

Written By

Ty King

Directed By

Michael E. Gershman

SHOOTING SCRIPT

January 21, 1998 (WHITE)

BUFFY THE VAMPIRE SLAYER

"Passion"

CAST LIST

BUFFY SUMMERS......................... Sarah Michelle Gellar
XANDER HARRIS......................... Nicholas Brendon
RUPERT GILES......................... Anthony S. Head
WILLOW ROSENBERG...................... Alyson Hannigan
CORDELIA CHASE....................... Charisma Carpenter
ANGEL................................ David Boreanaz

JOYCE SUMMERS........................*Kristine Sutherland
JENNY CALENDAR.......................*Robia La Morte
SPIKE................................*James Marsters
DRUSILLA.............................*Juliet Landau
JUJU MAN.............................*Richard Assad
POLICEMAN............................
STUDENT..............................

BUFFY THE VAMPIRE SLAYER

"Passion"

SET LIST

INTERIORS

SUNNYDALE HIGH SCHOOL
     LIBRARY
     HALLWAY
     CALENDAR'S CLASSROOM
     HALLWAY OUTSIDE LIBRARY
     WOODSHOP CLASSROOM
     LOUNGE
     HALLWAY/STAIRS/LANDING

THE BRONZE

BUFFY'S HOUSE
     BUFFY'S BEDROOM
   *DINING ROOM/LIVING ROOM

WILLOW'S BEDROOM

THE FACTORY
     ON A RAISED PLATFORM

*"DRAGON'S COVE" MAGIC STORE

GILES' APARTMENT

*OMITTED

*BLACK MAGIC STORE - BACK ROOM

*BUFFY'S HOUSE - KITCHEN

EXTERIORS

SUNNYDALE HIGH SCHOOL
     COURTYARD

THE BRONZE

WILLOW'S BEDROOM

BUFFY'S HOUSE
     YARD OUTSIDE BUFFY'S BEDROOM WINDOW
     STREET IN FRONT OF BUFFY'S HOUSE
     *BUFFY'S FRONT YARD/FOYER

GILES' APARTMENT
     WALKWAY LEADING TO GILES' APARTMENT

INDUSTRIAL PARK OUTSIDE THE FACTORY

CEMETERY

BUFFY THE VAMPIRE SLAYER

"Passion"

TEASER

1   BLACK: 1

Over which, a VOICE...

                    ANGEL (V.O.)
             (softly)
        Passion...

FADE UP ON:

2   INT. THE BRONZE - NIGHT   2

The place is teeming with the hip, young, non-speaking extra crowd. WE HEAR MUSIC, MUMBLED CONVERSATIONS and AMBIENT NOISE, but no specific DIALOG.

On the dance floor, BUFFY shares a "friendly" dance with XANDER as WILLOW and CORDELIA watch from a table.

WE CIRCLE around just outside the perimeter of the crowd, always focusing on the sensuously gyrating Slayer on the floor.

ALL MOTION SLOWS TO A LANGUID CRAWL (SLO-MO) as we recognize ANGEL, a face in the back of the crowd across the room. From the shadows, he watches Buffy with a fierce intensity, his eyes fixed in an unblinking, unsettling stare.

                    ANGEL (V.O.)
        ...it is born...

The rest of the world seems to part as WE BEGIN A SLOW PUSH in on Angel, keeping Buffy in the FOREGROUND.

                  ANGEL (cont'd; V.O.)
        ...and though uninvited, unwelcome,
      unwanted...

SOMEONE walks by FOREGROUND, WIPING THE SHOT, REVEALING that Angel has vanished.

                  ANGEL (cont'd; V.O.)
        ...like a cancer, it takes root.

                         CUT TO:

3 EXT. ENTRANCE TO THE BRONZE - (LATER THAT) NIGHT   3

WE STILL HEAR only AMBIENT NOISE and MUFFLED TALK as Buffy
and pals exit the Bronze, moving past a COUPLE necking
carnally in a dark niche. The couples' passion hides their
faces.

                    ANGEL (V.O.)
          It festers. It bleeds. It scabs...

As our gang passed the couple, the FEMALE slides to the
ground like a spent rag doll, revealing the MALE to be a
"post-suck" Angel in vamp face.

Now, having dropped his human shield, Angel watches Buffy
walk away. We see him MORPH into human form.

                    ANGEL (cont'd; V.O.)
          ...only to rupture, and bleed anew.

                                        DISSOLVE TO:

4 INT. BUFFY'S BEDROOM - (ANGLE IN THROUGH WINDOW) - NIGHT 4

From outside, as Buffy closes the window, locks it, then
turns and begins to remove her dress from the Bronze.

                    ANGEL (V.O.)
          It grows... it thrives...

                            OVERLAPPING DISSOLVE TO:

5 INT. BUFFY'S BEDROOM - (SHORT TIME LATER) NIGHT   5

Buffy, now in nightwear, crosses to her bed, crawls under the
blankets.

She reaches to turn off the bedside lamp. She doesn't notice
Angel, now silhouetted by moonlight, at her window.

                    ANGEL (V.O.)
          ...until it consumes.

                            OVERLAPPING DISSOLVE TO:

6 INT. BUFFY'S BEDROOM - (LATER THAT) NIGHT - WIDE SHOT   6

As Buffy now sleeps soundly. No sign of Angel.

WE START A SLOW PUSH IN ON HER. A beat, then—

                                        CONTINUED

6 CONTINUED: 6

JUMP THE PUSH

To jarringly CUT THE DISTANCE to the sleeping Buffy IN HALF.
Still SLOWLY PUSHING IN. Another beat, then--

JUMP THE PUSH AGAIN:

We're now in close. Buffy's angelic face, eyes closed, lies
atop the pillow. WE'RE STILL MOVING IN SLOWLY.

                    ANGEL (V.O.)
          It lives...

NOW VERY CLOSE, as Buffy shifts only slightly, and a single,
think lock of hair cascades down her face.

                    ANGEL (cont'd; V.O.)
          ...so, it must die...

Suddenly, a HAND SLICES INTO FRAME, reaches for Buffy...

...and gently lifts errant strand of hair back off of her
face.

The hand withdraws from her face.

WE GO WITH IT, pulling back to reveal ANGEL, sitting on her
bed.

                    ANGEL
                  (softly)
          ...in time.

                                        BLACK OUT.

               END OF TEASER

ACT ONE

7   INT. BUFFY'S BEDROOM - MORNING   7

A security blanket of sunshine lights the room as Buffy
wakes. A smile. The promise of a new day.

Buffy rolls onto her side, coming face to face with an
envelope made of parchment paper. The envelope is propped
against the side of her pillow at eye level.

She sits up, heart-beating, picks up the envelope.

CLOSE ON: THE PARCHMENT ENVELOPE

She removes a sheet of parchment paper, unfolds it to reveal
a CHARCOAL SKETCH - skilled, accurate, lovingly rendered - of
Buffy sleeping, her head on her pillow... obviously drawn
while she slept the night before.

                    BUFFY (V.O.)
          He was in my room...

8   INT. LIBRARY - DAY   8

GILES, Xander and Cordelia are here. Buffy has obviously
just arrived as she crosses to join them.

                    GILES
          Who?

                    BUFFY
          Angel. He was in my room last night.

                    GILES
               (concerned)
          You're sure.

                    BUFFY
          Positive. When I woke up, I found a
          picture he'd left under my pillow.

                    XANDER
          A visit from the pointed-tooth fairy.

                    CORDELIA
          Wait, I thought vampires couldn't
          come in unless you invited them in.

                                              CONTINUED

8 CONTINUED: 8

                          GILES
          Yes, but if you invite them in once,
          thereafter, they are always welcome.

                          XANDER
          Ya know, I think there may be a
          valuable lesson for you gals here
          about inviting strange men into your
          bedrooms...

                          CORDELIA
                  (realizes)
          Oh, my god! I invited him into my
          car once! That means he could come
          back into my car whenever he wants!

                          XANDER
          Yep. Now you're doomed to having to
          give him and his vamp pals a lift
          whenever they feel like it. And
          those guys never chip in for gas.

                          BUFFY
          Giles, there has to be some spell to
          reverse the invitation, right? I
          mean, a barrier -- "no shoes, no
          pulse, no service" kind of thing?

                          CORDELIA
          That also works for cars.

                          GILES
          Well, I could certainly check my--

All eyes turn as two STUDENTS step into the library. They
both freeze at the four pairs of eyes fixed on them.

                          XANDER
          Hel-lo... excuse me, but have you
          ever heard of knocking?

                          STUDENT
          We're supposed to get some books. On
          Stalin. For a report.

                          XANDER
          Does this look like a Barnes and
          Noble?

                          GILES
          Xander! This is the school library.

                                              CONTINUED

8 CONTINUED: (2)   8

> XANDER
> (innocently)
> Since when?

> GILES
> (to the student)
> Yes, third row, historical biography.

> STUDENT
> Okay... uh, thanks.

The Students pass them, walk behind the shelves.

Buffy, Giles, Cordelia and Xander look at one another for a beat, frustrated. Silenced.

> XANDER
> So... about-ay ee-thay ampire-vay...
> (off looks)
> Allway-hay?

Giles nods, and the gang crosses to the doorway and exits.

After a beat, one of the students emerges from the stacks.

> STUDENT
> Uh, did you say that was...
> (looks around)
> Hello?

                                        CUT TO:

9 INT. HALLWAY/EXT. COURTYARD -- MOMENTS LATER   9

Xander, Buffy, Cordelia and Giles walk the empty hallway.

> GILES
> So, apparently Angel has decided to
> step us his harassment of you.

> CORDELIA
> By sneaking into her room at night
> and leaving stuff? Why not just
> slash her throat, or strangle her in
> her sleep, or cut out her heart...?
> (off looks)
> What? I'm trying to help.

                                        CONTINUED

>   GILES
> It's a classic battle strategy, to
> throw ones opponent off his game.
> He's <u>trying</u> to provoke you. To taunt
> you... goad you into a misstep of
> some sort.

>   XANDER
> The "nyah, nyah, nyah, nyah" approach
> to battle.

>   GILES
> Yes, Xander, once again you've
> managed to boil a complex thought
> down to its simplest possible form.

>   BUFFY
>   (concerned)
> Giles, Angel once told me, when he
> was obsessed with Drusilla, one of
> the first things he did was to kill
> her family...

>   XANDER
>   (to Buffy)
> Your mom...   *
>   *

>   BUFFY   *
>   (nods)
> I'm going to have to tell her...   *
> something. The truth.   *

>   GILES
> No! You can't do that!

>   XANDER
> Yeah. The more people who know the
> secret, the more it cheapens it for
> the rest of us.

>   BUFFY
> But, I have to do something. Angel
> has an all access pass to my house
> and I'm not always there when my mom
> is. I can't protect her.

>   GILES
> I told you, I'll look for a spell...

>   BUFFY
> What about until you find a spell?

                                              CONTINUED

9 CONTINUED: (2)   9

                         CORDELIA
               Until then, you and your mom are
               welcome to ride around with me in my
               car. You can protect her there.

                         GILES
               Buffy, I understand your concern, but
               it is imperative you remain level-
               headed in this.

                         BUFFY
               Easy for you. You don't have Angel
               lurking in your bedroom at night.

                         GILES
               I know how hard this is for you. But
               as the Slayer, you do not have the
               luxury of being slave to your
               passions. You mustn't let Angel get
               to you, regardless of how provocative
               his behavior may become.

                         XANDER
               There you go. You Zen, you win.

                         BUFFY
               Great, so basically, what you're
               saying is, "Just ignore him and maybe
               he'll go away."

                         GILES
               Precisely.

                         XANDER
               Hey, how come Buffy doesn't get a
               snotty "once again you boil it down
               to its simplest form" thing?
                    (then, to Buffy)
               Watcher's pet.

10 INT. JENNY CALENDAR'S CLASSROOM -- SAME TIME   10

     Willow sits in the front row of JENNY'S computer class.

                         JENNY
               Don't forget I need your sample
               spreadsheets by the end of the week.

     The BELL RINGS. The exodus begins.

                                                          CONTINUED

10 CONTINUED: 10

                         JENNY (cont'd)
                    (calls after them)
          And I want both a paper print-out and
          a copy on disk.
                    (to an exiting Willow)
          Willow...

                         WILLOW
                    (stops, turns)
          Yes?

                         JENNY
          I may be a little late coming in
          tomorrow. Do you think you could
          take over my class until I show?

                         WILLOW
                    (elated)
          Really? Me? Teach the class? Sure!
                    (now, panic)
          Oh, wait... but what if they don't
          recognize my authority? What if they
          try to convince me that you always
          let them leave class early? What if
          there's a fire drill? What if
          there's a fire?

                         JENNY
                    (calming)
          Willow... Willow, you'll be fine.
          I'll try not to be too late, okay.

                         WILLOW
          Okay... good. Earlier is good.
                    (then, a bit of a
                     smile)
          Will I have the power to assign
          detention? Or make 'em run laps?

                         BUFFY (O.C.)
          Willow...

Willow and Jenny turn to see Giles and Buffy standing at the
doorway to the hall. Buffy and Jenny's eyes meet. There's
still a little tension there.

                         JENNY
                    (trying, a greeting)
          Hello, Rupert... Buffy.

                                                        CONTINUED

10 CONTINUED: (2)   10

                         BUFFY
                    (doesn't respond to
                    Jenny)
               Hey, Will. I thought I might take in
               a class. I could sure use someone
               who knows where they are.

Willow looks from Jenny to Buffy, then crosses quickly to
join Buffy at the door.

                         WILLOW
                    (Sotto to Buffy, re:
                    Jenny)
               Sorry. I have to talk to her. She's
               a teacher. And teachers are to be
               respected. Even if they're only
               filling in until the real teacher
               shows up. Otherwise, chaos could
               ensue, and...

Buffy and Willow exit. Giles lingers.

                         JENNY
               How've you been?

                         GILES
               Not very well. Since Angel lost his
               soul, he seems to have regained his
               sense of whimsy.

                         JENNY
               This sounds bad.

                         GILES
               He's been in Buffy's bedroom. I'm
               going to have to drum up a spell to
               keep him out of the house.

                         JENNY
               Here.
                    (hands him a book)
               Might help. I've been... reading up
               since Angel changed. I don't think
               you have that.

                         GILES
               Thank you.

                         JENNY
               How is Buffy doing?

                                                    CONTINUED

10 CONTINUED: (3)   10

                    GILES
          How do you think?

                    JENNY
          Rupert, I know you feel betrayed.

                    GILES
          Yes, that's one of the unpleasant
          side effects of betrayal.

                    JENNY
          I was raised by the people Angel hurt
          the most. My duty to them was the
          first thing I was ever taught. I
          didn't come here to hurt anyone. I
          lied to you because I thought it was
          the right thing to do. I didn't know
          what would happen.
                    (beat: quietly)
          I didn't know I was going to fall in
          love with you.

He's surprised -- moved.

                    GILES
          Jenny...

                    JENNY
          Oh god -- is it too late to take that
          back?

                    GILES
          Do you want to?

                    JENNY
          I want to be right with you. I don't
          expect... more. But I want to make
          all this up to you.

                    GILES
                    (not unkindly)
          I understand. But I'm not the one
          you need to make it up to. Thank you
          for the book.

He goes.

11 INT. BUFFY'S DINING ROOM - THAT NIGHT   11

Buffy and JOYCE sit for dinner. Buffy picks at her food,
preoccupied. Joyce notices.

                    JOYCE
          Okay... what's wrong?

                    BUFFY
          It's... nothing.

                    JOYCE
          Come on, you can tell me anything.
          I've read all the parenting books, so
          you can't surprise me.

                    BUFFY
                (considers, then)
          Do you remember that guy, Angel?

                    JOYCE
          Angel...? The college boy who was
          tutoring you in history?

                    BUFFY
          Right. Well, he's... and I'm...
                (chickens out)
          We're sort of dating. Were dating.
          We're going through kind of a serious
          "off again" phase right now.

                    JOYCE
          Don't tell me. "He's changed. He's
          not the same guy you fell for."

                    BUFFY
          In a nutshell. Anyway, ever since...
          he changed... he's been kind of
          following me around.
                (a little heavier)
          Having a little trouble letting go.

                    JOYCE
          Buffy, has he hurt you... done
          anything to you...?

                    BUFFY
          No, Mom, I just... it's just, maybe
          I'm a little afraid of him.

                    JOYCE
          "Afraid"? He has hurt you!

                                              CONTINUED

11 CONTINUED: 11

                          BUFFY
               No, not... physically. He's just
               been hanging around... a lot. In the
               shadows, leaving me notes...

Joyce crosses to the phone, really worried now. She starts
dialing.

                          JOYCE
               That's it. I'm calling the police.
               What's Angel's last name?

                          BUFFY
                    (thinks)
               It's...

Buffy draws a blank, then quickly crosses to hang up the
phone on Joyce.

                          BUFFY (cont'd)
               No, Mom, trust me. This isn't...
               "police" serious. I just... just
               promise me if you ever see him around
               the house, or... in the house, that
               you'll get me.

                          JOYCE
               What if you're not around?

                          BUFFY
                    (trying to downplay)
               Well, whatever you do... just don't
               invite him in.

12 INT. WILLOW'S BEDROOM -- (LATER THAT) NIGHT   12

Willow is in a night shirt as she moves around the room,
talking on the phone. She shuts her computer screen off.

                          WILLOW
                    (into the phone)
               I agree with Giles, you need to just
               try and not let him get to you.
               Angel's only doing this to try to get
               you to do something stupid.
                    (in disgust)
               I swear, men can be such jerks
               sometimes...
                    (then, adding)
               ...dead or alive.

13 INT. BUFFY'S BEDROOM - SAME TIME - INTERCUT - NIGHT   13

    Buffy sits up in bed, her back against her headboard, as she
    talks on the phone.

                    BUFFY
              (into phone)
         I just hope Giles can find a "keep
         out" spell soon. I know I'll sleep
         easier once I can... sleep easier.

14 BACK TO: WILLOW'S BEDROOM - NIGHT   14

    Willow absentmindedly taps fish food into an aquarium without
    looking as she putters around.

                    WILLOW
              (into phone)
         I'm sure he will. He's, like,
         BookMan. Until then, just try to
         keep happy thoughts and...

    Willow crosses toward her bed, sees a large parchment paper
    envelope on her pillow. She trails off on the phone as she
    picks up the envelope, opens it.

                    BUFFY (V.O.)
              (phone-filtered)
         "And"... what? Willow...?

    THE CAMERA STARTS DRIFTING, keeping Willow in frame as she
    pulls something from the envelope: one end of a long, thin
    gold necklace. So far, so good as the chain unspools.

    THE DRIFTING SHOT moves to where WE SOON SEE WILLOW through
    the glass and water of the AQUARIUM in the FOREGROUND.

    And just as Willow pulls out the last of the necklace, WE
    REALIZE that there are NO FISH IN THE AQUARIUM...

    Because the gold chain is like a 14 karat stringer to her
    HALF DOZEN DEAD TROPICAL FISH AT THE END.

                                        SMASH CUT TO:

15 INT. BUFFY'S BEDROOM - SHORT TIME LATER - NIGHT   15

    Willow and Buffy now sit up side by side, backs against the
    headboard in Buffy's bed. Both are heavily laden with
    crosses and weapons, amazingly alert and wide-eyed.

                                        CONTINUED

15 CONTINUED: 15

                         WILLOW
              Thanks for having me over, Buffy.
              Especially on a school night and all.

                         BUFFY
              Hey, no problem. Sorry about your
              fish.

                         WILLOW
              It's okay, we hadn't really had time
              to bond yet. I just got them for
              Hanukkah. Although, for the first
              time, I'm glad my parents didn't let
              me have a puppy.

                         BUFFY
              It's so weird... Every time something
              like that happens my first instinct
              is to run to tell Angel. I can't
              believe it's the same person. He's
              the complet opposite of what he was.

                         WILLOW
              Well... Sort of, except...

                         BUFFY
              Except what?

                         WILLOW
              You're still the only thing he thinks
              about.

There is a beat of SILENCE. Then...

                         WILLOW (cont'd)
              So...
                   (pointing to crossbow
                    by Buffy's feet)
              ...are you using that?

16 EXT. YARD OUTSIDE BUFFY'S BEDROOM WINDOW - SAME TIME   16

     As Angel smiles from the shadows, turns and leaves.

17 INT. THE FACTORY - JUST BEFORE SUNRISE   17

     SPIKE is chairbound, brooding, as DRUSILLA enters from the
     shadows, her hands held behind her.

                                                    CONTINUED

17 CONTINUED: 17

> DRUSILLA
> Spike... Love... I've brought
> something for you...

Drusilla produces a cute, tiny PUPPY from behind her back,
holds it out as she approaches Spike.

> DRUSILLA (cont'd)
> Poor thing. She's an orphan. Her
> owner died... without a fight. Do
> you like her, Spike? I brought her
> especially for you, to cheer you up.
>   (kneels in front of
>   Spike)
> I've named her "Sunshine."
>   (to Spike, as if to
>   a child)
> ...open wide...

Spike rurns his head away defiantly.

> DRUSILLA (cont'd)
> Come on, Love. You need to eat
> something to keep your strength up.
> Now, open for Mommy...

> SPIKE
>   (roars)
> I won't have you feeding me like a
> child, Dru!

> ANGEL (O.C.)
> Why not? She already bathes you,
> carries you around and changes you
> like a child.

Drusilla lights up as she turns to see Angel entering.

> DRUSILLA
> My Angel! Where have you been? The
> sun is almost up, and it can be so
> hurtful. We were worried.

> SPIKE
> No, we weren't.

> DRUSILLA
> You must forgive Spike. He's just a
> bit testy tonight. Doesn't get out
> much anymore.

                                          CONTINUED

17 CONTINUED: (2)   17

                              ANGEL
                    Well, maybe next time I'll bring you
                    with me, Spike. Might be handy to
                    have you along if I ever need a
                    really good parking space.

                              SPIKE
                         (roars)
                    Have you forgotten that you're a
                    bloody guest in my bloody home!?

                              ANGEL
                    And as a guest, if there's anything
                    I can do for you... Any...
                    responsibility I can assume while you
                    spin your wheels...
                         (purposeful leer
                          toward Dru)
                    ...anything I'm not already doing,
                    that is...

                              SPIKE
                         (roars)
                    That's enough!

                              DRUSILLA
                    Awww, you two boys... fighting over
                    me... makes a girl feel--

Dru trails off, her words giving way to a frightened, child-
like cry. She closes her eyes, holds out her hands.

                              SPIKE
                    Dru! Pet? What is it?!

                              DRUSILLA
                         (cryptically)
                    The air... it worries. Someone... an
                    old enemy is seeking help to destroy
                    our happy home.

                                                  CUT TO:

18 INT. "DRAGON'S COVE" MAGIC STORE - EARLY MORNING   18   *

    A dimly lit, creepy looking storefront. Odd, wrinkled forms
    suspended in murky liquid in jars, things woven from hair,
    and totems carved from bone fill the dank, decaying shelves.
    Black paraffin candles flicker in every crevice.

                                                  CONTINUED

18 CONTINUED: 18

    A shriveled, dark-featured JUJU MAN in a dakhi robe takes a
    glass jar containing something that looks like an animal
    fetus from a shelf, looks it over... then slaps a price tag
    on it with a yellow, plastic price tagging gun. He turns as
    the DOOR CREAKS OPEN behind and Jenny enters.

                    JUJU MAN
                  (creepy voice)
          Welcome. How many I serve you today?
          Love potion? Perhaps a voodoo doll
          for that unfaithful...

                    JENNY
          I need an orb of Thesulah.

                    JUJU MAN
                  (drops the creepy
                   voice)
          Oh, you're in the trade. Follow me.
                  (turns, crosses)
          Sorry about the spiel, but around
          Valentine's Day, I get a lot of
          tourists shopping for love potions
          and mystical revenge on old lovers.
          Sad fact is, Ouija boards and
          Rabbits' feet are what pay the rent
          here.

    He ducks through a curtain. Jenny follows him.   *

19 OMITTED   19   *

    It is near, well-lit, uncluttered, modern... unlike the "show
    room" outside.

                    JUJU MAN
          So... how'd you hear about us?

                    JENNY
          My uncle, Enyos, told me about you.

                    JUJU MAN
          Ah, you must be Janna, then. Sorry
          to hear about your uncle. He was a
          good customer.

    JuJu pulls a box from a shelf. There is a crystal globe
    inside.

                                                      CONTINUED

18 CONTINUED: (2)   18

                         JUJU MAN (cont'd)
              Here ya go, one Thesulan orb. Spirit
              vault used in Rituals for the Undead.
                   (shakes his head)
              Nasty folk, the Undead... Love to
              shoplift. Insist on haggling...

Jenny takes the box, handing over her credit card (the
transaction continues over the following).

                         JUJU MAN (cont'd)
              Don't get much call for those lately.
              Sold a couple as "new age"
              paperweights last year. I do love
              the "new agers." They paid for my
              youngest to go to college.
                   (remembers)
              By the way, you do know that the
              transliteration annals for the
              Rituals for the Undead were lost.
              Without the annals, the surviving
              text of Rituals is gibberish.

                         JENNY
              And without a translated text, the
              orbs of Thesulah are pretty much
              useless. I know.

                         JUJU MAN
              I only bring it up because I have a
              strict policy of no refunds.

                         JENNY
              It's okay. I've been working on a
              computer program for rendering the
              Romanian liturgy to English, based on
              random sampling of the text.

                         JUJU MAN
                   (shakes his head)
              Ahhhn, I don't like computers,
              myself. They give me the willies.

                         JENNY
                   (smiles)
              Well, thanks.

                                                    CONTINUED

18 CONTINUED: (3)   18

                    JUJU MAN
          By the way... none of my business,
          really, but what are you planning to
          conjure up if you can decipher the
          text?

                    JENNY
          A present for a friend of mine...

                    JUJU MAN
          Oh, yeah. What are you gonna give
          him?

She holds the orb up. In her hand, it begins to glow.

                    JENNY
                (at the orb)
          His soul.

                                        BLACK OUT.

                    END OF ACT ONE

ACT TWO

20 EXT. HIGH SCHOOL CAMPUS - MORNING   20

Buffy and Willow walk toward the school.

Xander joins them.

>   XANDER
> Well, good morning, ladies. And what
> did you two do last night?

>   WILLOW
> Oh, we had kind of a pajama-party-
> sleepover-with-weapons thing.

>   XANDER
> Ah, and I don't suppose either of you
> had the presence of mind to locate a
> camera to capture the moment?

>   WILLOW
> I have to go. I have a class to
> teach in about five minutes and I
> need to get there early to glare
> disapprovingly at the stragglers.
>   (then, disappointed)
> Oh, darn. She's here...

Buffy turns to look where Willow is looking.

ANGLE ON: JENNY - BUFFY'S POV

As she also walks toward the entrance.

PAN TO: GILES

Giles watches Jenny from a distance. His sense of longing is
almost palpable.

>   WILLOW (O.C.)
> Five hours of drawing up lesson plans
> yesterday down the drain.

Giles sees Buffy seeing him, guiltily crosses inside.

BACK WITH: BUFFY, XANDER AND WILLOW

As Buffy registers Giles' reaction.

CONTINUED

20 CONTINUED: 20

                    BUFFY
          I'll see you guys in class.

     Buffy angles away to intercept Jenny on her way inside.

                    BUFFY (cont'd)
          Hey.

                    JENNY
          Hi. Is there something -- did you
          want something?

                    BUFFY
               (trying to start)
          Look, I know you're feeling bad about
          what happened and I want to say...
          good. Keep it up.

                    JENNY
          Don't worry, I will.

     She turns to go -- Buffy stops her with:

                    BUFFY
          Wait. I, uh --
               (one more try)
          He misses you.

     This is not what Jenny expected. Buffy continues:

                    BUFFY (cont'd)
          He doesn't say anything to me, but I
          know he does. I don't want him to be
          lonely.
               (avoiding her eye)
          I don't want anyone to.

                    JENNY
          Buffy, if I have a chance to make it
          up to you --

                    BUFFY
          We're good here. Let's leave it.

     A moment, and she goes.

21 INT. SCHOOL HALLWAY - DAY   21

     Buffy finds Giles. Cordelia sees them and crosses.

                                                        CONTINUED

21 CONTINUED: 21

                         GILES
            Buffy... so, how was your night?

                         BUFFY
            Sleepless... but no fatalities.

                         GILES
            I found a ritual to revoke the
            invitation to vampires.

                         CORDELIA
            Oh, thank goodness. I actually had
            to talk my grandmother into switching
            cars with me last night.

Giles gives Cordy an incredulous look, then back to Buffy.

                         GILES
            The ritual itself is fairly basic,
            actually: recitation of a few simple
            rhyming couplets, burning of moss
            herbs, hanging of crosses, sprinkling
            of holy water...

                         BUFFY
            Great. All stuff I just happen to
            have lying around the house.

Giles and Buffy start away, leaving Cordelia behind.

                         CORDELIA
            Holy water?! But... my car has
            leather upholstery!

                                        CUT TO:

22 EXT. WILLOW'S BEDROOM - NIGHT   22

CLOSE ON: WILLOW AND BUFFY

WE'RE LOOKING IN THROUGH A WINDOW IN WILLOW'S BEDROOM, with
Willow and Buffy inside, facing outside.

                         WILLOW
            I'm going to have a hard time
            explaining this to my dad.

Willow produces a wooden cross, holds it up TOWARD CAMERA,
and starts nailing on it with a hammer.

23 INT. WILLOW'S BEDROOM - NIGHT   23

Buffy looks on as Willow nails the last of four wooden
crosses to the frame around her French windows. Behind them,
Cordelia pokes around Willow's room, bored.

                    BUFFY
          You really think this'll bother him?

                    WILLOW
          Ira Rosenberg's only daughter nailing
          crucifixes to her bedroom wall? I
          have to go to Xander's house just to
          watch "A Charlie Brown Christmas"
          every year.

                    BUFFY
          Yeah, I see your point.

                    WILLOW
             (smiles)
          Although, it is worthwhile just to
          see Xander do the Snoopy dance.

                    CORDELIA
             (re: aquarium)
          Uh, Willow, are you aware that there
          are no fish in your aquarium?

Willow reacts, a hint of sadness wells up.

                    BUFFY
          You know, Cordelia, we've already
          done your car. You can call it a
          night if you want.

Like a shot, Cordelia crosses to her coat on Willow's bed.

                    CORDELIA
          Sure, two's company, three's... not.
          And you know I'd do the same for you
          if either of you had a social life.

Cordelia picks up her coat from Willow's bed, revealing a
parchment paper envelope on the pillow.

                    CORDELIA (cont'd)
          Oh, hey... this must be for you.

Willow and Buffy exchange a concerned look. Willow takes the
envelope, removes the paper inside, glances at it.

She reacts with concern, then holds the page out to Buffy.

                                              CONTINUED

23 CONTINUED: 23

>   WILLOW
>   (to Buffy)
>   It's for you...

Buffy takes the paper from Willow.

CLOSE ON: THE PAGE

With a charcoal sketch of a sleeping Joyce Summers.

>   BUFFY (V.O.)
>   Mom...

>   CUT TO:

24 EXT. STREET IN FRONT OF BUFFY'S HOUSE - NIGHT   24

As Joyce turns her car into her driveway, the headlights
sweep across Angel, who seems to appear in front of the car
from out of nowhere. Joyce SLAMS ON HER BRAKES.

>   JOYCE
>   Oh, my God...!

Angel crosses to open the door for Joyce.

>   ANGEL
>   Mrs. Summers, I have to talk to you.

>   JOYCE
>   (discomfited)
>   You're... Angel.

>   ANGEL
>   Did Buffy tell you about us?

Joyce steps tentatively from the car with a grocery bag.

>   JOYCE
>   She told me she wants you to leave
>   her alone.

Angel goes with Joyce as she starts toward the house. He
hovers close, making her cross difficult.

>   ANGEL
>   (distraught)
>   I can't... I can't do that.

>   CONTINUED

24   CONTINUED: 24

                         JOYCE
              You're scaring her.

                         ANGEL
                    (pleading)
              You have to help me. Joyce, I need
              to be with her. You can convince
              her. You have to convince her.

Joyce fumbles for her keys on the fly. She's starting to wig.

                         JOYCE
              I'm telling you to leave her alone...

                         ANGEL
              You have to talk to her for me,
              Joyce. Tell her I need her. She'll
              listen to you.

                         JOYCE
                    (increasing
                    discomfort)
              Please, I just want to get inside...

Joyce finally gets her keys out, but drops the grocery bag in
the process. She bends down to gather up the contents.

Angel bends down, almost nose to nose with Joyce.

                         ANGEL
              You don't understand, Joyce. I'll
              die without Buffy... She'll die
              without me.

                         JOYCE
              Are you threatening her?

                         ANGEL
              Please! Why is she doing this to me?

Joyce abandons the spilled bag and calmly moves to her front
door now, Angel right with her.

                         JOYCE
              I'm calling the police, now.

Joyce reaches the front door, jams the key into the lock.

                                                    CONTINUED

24 CONTINUED: (2)   24

                         ANGEL
               I haven't been able to sleep since
               the night we made love. I <u>need</u> her,
               I know you understand.

Joyce, floored by Angels' statement, finally gets the door
open, stumbles inside. She turns back toward Angel, her eyes
wide in fear as he is right there.

But, as Angel hits the doorway, he is stopped short. It's as
if an invisible shield covers the opening.

A NOISE BEHIND JOYCE. She turns, and Angel looks up as Buffy   *
descends the stairs in the house, holding burning sage.   *
Willow stands at the tops of the stairs behind her, reciting   *
from Jenny's book.   *

                         WILLOW   *
                    (in Latin)
               "...his verbes, consenus rescissus   *
               est."   *
                    (...by these words, consent repealed.)   *

Buffy breezes past Joyce to just inside the open doorway,
face to face with Angel, who is unable to move any closer.

                         BUFFY
                    (flatly)
               Sorry, Angel. I've changed the
               locks.

Buffy slowly, coolly closes the front door in Angel's face,
leaving him stranded on the porch.

And revealing Joyce, standing behind the door, fixing Buffy
with an odd expression.

25 INT. JENNY CALENDAR'S CLASSROOM - NIGHT   25

Jenny is at her terminal, intently working at her computer.
The orb of Thesulah sits next to her on the desk.

She glances up to see Giles in the doorway, hovering. She
turns off her monitor guiltily.

                         JENNY
               Oh, hi.

                         GILES
               You're working late.

                                                        CONTINUED

25   CONTINUED: 25

                         JENNY
               Special project.
                    (beat)
               I spoke to Buffy today.

                         GILES
               Yes?

                         JENNY
               She said you missed me.

                         GILES
               She is a meddlesome girl.

          But the truth of it is on his face.

                         JENNY
               Rupert, I don't want to say anything
               if I'm wrong, but I may have some
               news... I have to finish up -- can I
               see you later.

                         GILES
               Yes. You could stop by the house.

                         JENNY
               Okay.

                         GILES
               Good.

          There's heat here, but no kiss. He goes, both of them in
          better moods than before. She turns back to the monitor
          concentrating again.

26   INT. "DRAGON'S COVE" MAGIC SHOP - NIGHT   26   *

          The neon "OPEN" sign is turned off as the JuJu man makes
          preparations to close for the night.

          THE SILHOUETTE OF A WOMAN in a long gown falls across the
          glass door. After a beat, the woman steps into the shop.

                         JUJU MAN
               Can't you read the sign?

          Drusilla approaches him, holding the PUPPY from before.   *

                                                            CONTINUED

26 CONTINUED: 26

> JUJU MAN (cont'd)
> (cowed)
> Wh-what do you want?

> DRUSILLA
> Miss Sunshine here tells me you had
> a visit today... But she worries.
> She wants to know what you and the
> mean teacher talked about?

                                             CUT TO:

27 INT. JENNY CALENDAR'S CLASSROOM - NIGHT   27

CLOSE ON: JENNY

Her face lit by the glow of the computer monitor. She scans
the screen intently as it scrolls by.

> JENNY
> Come on... come on...

Suddenly, something on screen catches her eye. A wave of
incredible joy washes over her face.

> JENNY (cont'd)
> (exhilarated)
> That's it! This will work.
> (a small laugh)
> This will work.

WIDER ANGLE

Jenny uses the mouse to initiate the print command. A nearby
printer begins spitting out pages as Jenny ejects a 3.5 inch
disk from the disk drive, takes it out, putting it on the
edge of her desk by the wall.

She rises, REVEALING ANGEL, who was obscured by the monitor.
She GASPS.

> JENNY (cont'd)
> Angel! How did you get in here?!

> ANGEL
> I was invited...
> (off her puzzled look)
> The sign in front of the school:
> "Formatia trans sicere educatorum."

                                                    CONTINUED

27 CONTINUED: 27

                         JENNY
              "Enter, all ye who seek knowledge."

                         ANGEL
              What can I say? I'm a knowledge
              seeker.

Jenny back away, terrified, as Angel comes nearer.

                         JENNY
              Angel... I have good news.

                         ANGEL
              I heard. You went shopping at the
              local boogedy boogedy store.

Angel reaches her desk. He picks up the orb. It glows again
briefly in his grasp.

                         ANGEL (cont'd)
              The orb of Thesulah. If memory
              serves, this is supposed to summon a
              person's soul from the ether, store
              it until it can be transferred.
                     (stares into the orb)
              You know what I hate most about these
              things...?

Angel hurls the orb against the wall with tremendous force,
shattering it into a hundred pieces.

                         ANGEL (cont'd)
              They're so damned fragile. Must be
              that shoddy Gypsy craftsmanship.

As Jenny backs away, Angel crosses to in front of the
monitor. He stares down at it, shakes his head.

                         ANGEL (cont'd)
              I never cease to be amazed by how
              much the world has changed in just
              two and a half centuries. It's a
              miracle to me. You put the secret to
              restoring my soul in here...

Angel swipes the computer and monitor the floor, where   *
they crash, then begin to spark and smoke.

He turns back to the printer, which holds the pages.

                                                  CONTINUED

27 CONTINUED: (2)   27

                    ANGEL (cont'd)
          ...and it comes out here.

He takes the pages from the printer, scans them and smiles.

                    ANGEL (cont'd)
          The Ritual of Restoration. Wow, this
          brings back memories.

He starts to tear the pages.

                    JENNY
          Angel, wait...! That's your--

                    ANGEL
          My what? My "cure." No thanks. Been
          there, done that. And deja vu just
          isn't what it used to be.

Then, he looks down, sees the computer and monitor on the
ground. They are smoking, and a small flame licks up now.

                    ANGEL (cont'd)
          Well, isn't this my lucky day. The
          computer and the pages. Looks like
          I get to kill two birds with one
          stone.

Angel tosses the pages onto the computer fire, which quickly
begins to consume them.

He then turns his attention back to Jenny, who watches in
horror, backed into a nearby corner. He is now in vamp face.   *

                    ANGEL (cont'd)
          And teacher makes three.

Angel leaps across the room, slamming Jenny against the wall.

Jenny rises, dazed and bleeding from a gash on her forehead.

Jenny looks around, bolts for the door and out into the
hallway outside. Angel smiles after her.

                    ANGEL (cont'd)
          Oh, good... I need to work up an
          appetite first.

28 INT. SCHOOL HALLWAY/LOUNGE - SAME TIME   28

    Jenny flees in panic. She reaches the lounge, runs outside,
    Angel not far behind.

29 EXT. COURTYARD - CONTINUOUS - NIGHT   29

    Jenny runs out in the darkness, Angel close behind. Up
    ahead -- a door. It's locked, but after a few tries, Jenny
    slams it open with her shoulder. Angel is right behind
    her -- but she slams the door, literally, in his face.

30 INT. HALLWAY/STAIRS/LANDING - CONTINUOUS - NIGHT   30

    She enters the hall. Angel is almost on her when she reaches
    a cleaning cart, pushes it in his way. He tumbles as she
    runs up a flight of stairs. She just reaches the landing
    when Angel comes up the opposite side, charging and grabbing
    her.

    She screams. He clamps his hand over her mouth.

                    ANGEL
          Sorry, Jenny. This is where you get
          off.

    He snaps her neck. She falls, dead.

                    ANGEL (cont'd)
    I never get tired of doing that...

                                        BLACK OUT.

                    END OF ACT TWO

ACT THREE

31   EXT. BUFFY'S FRONT YARD/FOYER - NIGHT   31   *

Giles knocks on Buffy's door. It opens to reveal Willow.

               GILES
          Willow? Hi.

               WILLOW
               (upbeat)   *
          Hi. Come on in. Here's the book.   *

She hands him Jenny's book.   *

               GILES
               (a beat, then)   *
          Yes, I should do my apartment   *
          tonight. Did the ritual work out all   *
          right?   *

               WILLOW
          Oh, yeah. It went fine.   *
               (then)
          Well, it went fine up until the part   *
          where Angel showed up and told
          Buffy's mom that he and Buffy had...
          well, you know, that they had... they
          had... you know...
               (dawns on her)
          Uh, you do know, right?

               GILES
          Oh, yes, sorry.

               WILLOW
               (relieved)
          Oh, good. Because I just realized,
          that being a librarian and all, maybe
          you really didn't know--

               GILES
          No... thank you, I got it.

               WILLOW
          You would have been proud of her,
          though. She totally kept her cool.
               (chipper)
          Okay. Well, I'll tell Buffy you
          dropped by...

                                                       CONTINUED

31 CONTINUED: 31

Willow starts to close the door.

> GILES
> Wait! Do you think I should
> perhaps... intervene on Buffy's
> behalf with her mother? Maybe say
> something.

> WILLOW
> Sure! Like what would you say?

> GILES
> Well, like... for instance, I could
> say... that is...
> (gives up)
> So, you will tell Buffy I dropped by,
> then?

> WILLOW
> You bet. As soon as she comes back
> down from talking with her mom.

32 INT. BUFFY'S BEDROOM - SAME TIME   32

The two of them sit in uncomfortable silence.

> BUFFY
> That stuff with the herbs and the
> Latin, that's, um... He's just real
> superstitious.

> JOYCE
> Oh.

Some more silence.

> BUFFY
> I figure if we're careful not to --

> JOYCE
> Was he the first?

Buffy looks at her, busted.

> JOYCE (cont'd)
> No. Wait. I don't want to know.
> Or, I don't think I want to --

CONTINUED

32 CONTINUED: 32

                         BUFFY
          Yes. He was the first. I mean, the
          only.

                         JOYCE
          He's older than you.

                         BUFFY
          I know.

                         JOYCE
          Too old, Buffy. And he's obviously
          not very stable. I really wish... I
          thought you would show more judgement.

                         BUFFY
          Mom, I -- he wasn't like this before.

                         JOYCE
          Are you in love with him?

                         BUFFY
          I was...

                         JOYCE
          Were you careful?

                         BUFFY
          Mom --

                         JOYCE
          Don't 'Mom' me, Buffy -- you don't
          get to get out of this. You had sex
          with a boy you didn't even see fit to
          tell me you were dating.

                         BUFFY
                (by rote)
          I made a mistake.

                         JOYCE
          Don't just say that to shut me up
          because I think you really did.

                         BUFFY
          I know that! Mom, my life is so...
          I can't tell you everything.

                                              CONTINUED

32 CONTINUED: (2)   32

                         JOYCE
             How about anything? Buffy, you can
             shut me out of your life, I'm pretty
             much used to that, but don't expect
             me to stop caring about you 'cause
             it's never gonna happen. I love you
             more than anything in the world.

Buffy says nothing. Joyce waits a moment, somewhat spent.

                         JOYCE (cont'd)
             That would be your cue to roll your
             eyes and tell me I'm grossing you out.

                         BUFFY
             You're not. I'm glad.

The silence warms between them.

                         JOYCE
             Well, I guess that was the talk.

                         BUFFY
             How did it go?

                         JOYCE
             I don't know, it's my first.

                         BUFFY
             Well, what did you tell Grandma when
             you...

                         JOYCE
             Nothing!
                   (thinks)
             I don't think she knows...

33 EXT. WALKWAY LEADING UP TO GILES' APARTMENT - NIGHT   33

Giles crosses up the walk toward his front door. Note: Opera
music plays over this scene.

Giles reaches his front door, where he finds a single red
rose angled between the knob and the jamb. The corners of
his mouth twitch slightly upward in a bit of a grin.

He lifts the rose to his face, sniffs it. The bit of a grin
becomes a full-bore smile of anticipation.

34 INT. GILES' APARTMENT - CONTINUOUS   34

As the door opens, and Giles pokes his head in.

                    GILES
                (calls out)
          Hello? Jenny...?

Giles hears MUSIC - SOMETHING SOFT AND ROMANTIC - coming from
an album on his TURNTABLE.

                    GILES (cont'd)
                (calls again)
          It's me...

Then, he sees the wine chilling in the bucket on his desk,
next to a pair of crystal stemware wine glasses.

A note on a piece of PARCHMENT PAPER attached to the ice
bucket reads simply, "UPSTAIRS."

A flustered smile wrinkles Giles' face as he takes the wine
bottle and glasses, crosses toward the steps.

Giles starts tentatively up the stairs leading to his
bedroom, through the votive candles that line the stairway on
either side, and over the roses strewn over the steps.

As he takes the last few steps to the loft, his bed comes
into view. WE SEE that there is a woman in his bed. We
recognize the hair as being Jenny's.

ON: GILES

As he smiles, a sort of overwhelming happiness. A gleam
twinkles in his eye. He is about to say something, when...

The happiness fades from his smile. The smile fades from his
lips. The gleam fades from his eyes. And all color drains
from his face.

What he sees is horrific.

NEW ANGLE: FROM BEHIND GILES, AT ANKLE LEVEL

With the bed in the distance. Giles' feet are on the top
step. They don't move.

Neither does Jenny Calendar.

                                            CONTINUED

34 CONTINUED: 34

THE WINE GLASSES AND BOTTLE FALL FROM HIS HAND, CRASH to the
floor, spreading glass and vino across the loft.

                                                       CUT TO:

35 EXT. OUTSIDE GILES' APARTMENT - LATER - NIGHT   35

CLOSE ON: GILES

Looking weary, distraught. The red and blue lights of
emergency vehicles wash across his sallow, drawn face.

WIDER ANGLE

Giles looks down as a sheet covered body is wheeled out past
him by the PEOPLE FROM THE CORONER'S OFFICE.

Giles is in shock, showing no emotion, mostly because...
well, because he's in shock.

                    POLICEMAN
              Mr. Giles, we're going to have to ask
              you to come with us, just to answer
              a few questions.

                    GILES
              Of course... yes... procedure.
                    (a flicker of life)
              I need to make a telephone call
              first... if that's alright.

                                                   DISSOLVE TO:

36 EXT. BUFFY'S FRONT YARD - LOOKING IN THROUGH THE FRONT   36
    WINDOW INTO THE LIVING ROOM/DINING ROOM - MOMENTS LATER   *

WE'RE TRACKING BACK VERY SLOWLY, as WE WATCH Buffy and Willow
through the window.   *

Buffy is reliving the "sex talk" she just endured with her   *
mother.

                    WILLOW
                (unheard dialog)
              So, was it horrible?

                    ANGEL (V.O.)
              Passion... it drives some to
              distraction...

                                                       CONTINUED

36 CONTINUED: 36

                         BUFFY
                    (unheard dialog)
               It wasn't too horrible...

Then. Buffy reacts to the (UNHEARD) RINGING TELEPHONE.

                         ANGEL (cont'd, V.O.)
               ...some to despair...

She lifts the receiver with her usual upbeat mood, and turns
to lean with her back against the wall.

                         BUFFY
                    (unheard dialog, over
                     the phone)
               Hello...?

                         GILES
                    (unheard dialog, over
                     the phone)
               Buffy?

                         BUFFY
                    (unheard dialog, into
                     the phone)
               Giles! Hey, we finished the sp-

                         GILES
                    (unheard dialog, over
                     the phone)
               Jenny... Ms. Calendar... she's been
               killed...

On the phone, Buffy's face goes slack and she starts to slide
down the wall until she's sitting on the floor.

                         BUFFY
                    (unheard dialog, into
                     the phone)
               What...?

                         ANGEL (cont'd, V.O.)
               ...some to vengeance...

                         GILES
                    (unheard dialog, over
                     the phone)
               It was Angel...

                                                    CONTINUED

36 CONTINUED: (2)   36

Willow notices, crosses quickly to Buffy, kneels down in
front of her, as Buffy lets the phone receiver fall to the
floor.--

                    WILLOW
               (unheard dialog)
          Buffy...?

--Willow picks up the phone.--

                    WILLOW (cont'd)
               (unheard dialog, into
                the phone)
          Giles?

                    GILES
               (unheard dialog, over
                the phone)
          Willow. Angel's killed Jenny.

--After a moment, the shock of the conversation begins to
register on her face.--

Willow CRIES OUT,--

                    WILLOW
               (unheard dialog,
                anguished cry)
          What? No.: Oh, no...

--the first sound WE CAN ACTUALLY HEAR OUTSIDE, as the faint,
MUFFLED PAIN leaks out through the window, into the night air.

Joyce enters, sees Willow crying, goes to her, holds her.

                    JOYCE
               (unheard dialog)
          Willow! My god, Buffy, what's wrong?
          Has something happened?

ANGLE: ANGEL

Watching. Loving it.

                    ANGEL (V.O.)
          It drives some to murder... and
          others to madness.

37 EXT. BUFFY'S FRONT YARD - MOMENTS LATER   37

Buffy and Willow run from the house as Cordelia's car pulls   *
up to the curb.

Garlic strings and about a dozen crosses dangle from the
rearview mirror like bulky Christian air fresheners. Xander
is in the passenger seat, Cordelia behind the wheel. They
both look shaken.

The girls go to the car as Xander and Cordelia come out and
meet them at the curb.

                    BUFFY
          Well? Where's Giles?

                    XANDER
          No luck. By the time we go to the
          station, the cops said he'd already
          left. I guess they just wanted to
          ask him some questions.

                    CORDELIA
          I still don't get it. Why Ms.
          Calendar? She was so... harmless.

                    XANDER
                    (harsh)
          Because Angel's a blood-sucking
          coward. They pick on the harmless.

                    CORDELIA
          And we're sure it was Angel?

                    BUFFY
                    (hard)
          It was Angel, alright.

                    CORDELIA
          Did Giles say... is Ms. Calendar
          going to... you know, be a vampire?

                    WILLOW
          No.

                    BUFFY
          Cordelia, will you drive us to Giles'
          house?

                    CORDELIA
          Of course.

                                        CONTINUED

37 CONTINUED: 37

> WILLOW
> But do you think maybe he wants to be
> alone?
>
> BUFFY
> (as they get in)
> I'm not worried about what he wants.
> I'm worried about what he's going to
> do.

                                                CUT TO:

38 INT. GILES' APARTMENT - SAME TIME   38

NOTE: This scene should, ideally, be filmed in one,
continuous Steadi-Cam ® shot.

WE START ON GILES' BED. The sheets and bedding have been
stripped away by the Coroner.   *

From OFFSCREEN, a SOFT "POP, POP, POP", almost like the sound
of dripping water, plays in an endless loop under.

Then, a CLANG of METAL ON METAL rings out, followed by the
SOUND OF SHUFFLING FOOTSTEPS.

WE MOVE OFF THE BED now, TRACKING ACROSS THE FLOOR TOWARD THE
STAIRWAY.

WE MOVE PAST THE BROKEN GLASS and spilled wine and begin down
the stairs. The remains of the roses still litter the
stairs, although now they have been trampled flat by the
shoes of long-gone E.M.S. and Police personnel.

Most of the votive candles have burned down to nothing,
although a few are flickering out their last moments.

Another CLANG OF METAL ON METAL, as WE REACH the bottom of
the stairs and PAN ACROSS the source of the constant FAINT
POPPING SOUND - the needle of the turntable POPS, POPS, POPS
as it searches in vain for more music at the end of the still
revolving romantic album from before.

WE MOVE OFF THE TURNTABLE NOW, and PAN ACROSS to an open
sling bag on Giles' desk. The bag contains a potpourri of
weapons, from a crossbow to a mace to an old dueling pistol
to wooden stakes.

A GASOLINE CAN is tossed on top of the other weapons, and the
bag is lifted by Giles.

                                                    CONTINUED

38 CONTINUED: 38

WE MOVE UP TO GILES' FACE. His eyes are almost impassive,
filled with scary cool rage as he hefts the bag to his front
door and, with a grim determination, slips out into the
night. He's a man on a suicide mission.

WE STAY BEHIND, still inside the apartment, as we TILT DOWN
to an entry table just inside the door.

ON THE TABLE: a PARCHMENT PAPER ENVELOPE and the SHEET OF
PAPER that was inside it: a CHARCOAL SKETCH of a deceased
JENNY, her head lying on Giles' pillow, her eyes open.

                                        BLACK OUT.

                    END OF ACT THREE

ACT FOUR

39   INT. GILES' APARTMENT - (FIVE MINUTES LATER) NIGHT   39

Just as we last left it. The already slightly ajar door
cracks open wider and Xander pokes his head in.

                    XANDER
          Hello...? Giles...?

Xander ducks under the yellow CRIME SCENE tape to enter the
room, followed by Buffy, Willow and Cordelia.

The group fans out, starts poking around.

Xander crosses to the empty wine bucket, sees the single rose
on the desk, and the album cover propped up next to the still
revolving turntable.

                    XANDER (cont'd)
               (re: album cover)
          Looks like Giles had big plans for
          the night.

                    BUFFY
               (flatly)
          Giles didn't set all this up...

Buffy is at the entry table by the front door. She has
Angel's sketch of Jenny in her hand.

Buffy puts the picture down, crosses to the stairs and up.

                    BUFFY (cont'd)
          ...Angel did. All this is like the
          pretty gift wrap he wrapped Ms.
          Calendar's body in.

                    XANDER
          Oh, man. Poor Giles.

ANGLE ON: WILLOW

By an open and very stripped-bare trunk.   *

                    WILLOW
          Look, all his weapons are gone.

                    CORDELIA
          But, I though he kept his weapons at
          the library.

                                                  CONTINUED

                    XANDER
          Those are his everyday weapons. These
          were his "good" weapons. The ones he
          only breaks out when company comes to
          visit.

                    WILLOW
          So, it is what we were afraid of.
          Giles isn't here.

                    CORDELIA
          Well, then, where is her?

ANGLE ON: BUFFY

As she comes back down the stairs. She has a distant,
unfocused look in her eyes.

                    BUFFY
                (shaken)
          He'll go to wherever Angel is.

                    WILLOW
          That mean the Factory, right?

                    CORDELIA
          So, Giles is going to try to kill
          Angel, then.

                    XANDER
                (bitter)
          Well, it's about time somebody did.

                    WILLOW
                (shocked)
          Xander!

                    XANDER
                (with attitude)
          I'm sorry. But let's not forget that
          I hated Angel long before all of you
          guys jumped on the bandwagon. So, I
          think I deserve something for not
          saying "I told you so" long before
          now. And, if Giles wants to go after
          the...
          fiend who murdered his girlfriend, I
          say "Faster, Pussycat. Kill. Kill."

                                              CONTINUED

39   CONTINUED: (2)   39

                         BUFFY
                    (flatly)
               You're right.

                         WILLOW
               What?!

                         XANDER
               Thank you.

                         BUFFY
               There's only one thing wrong with
               Giles' little revenge scenario.

                         XANDER
               And, what's that?

                         BUFFY
                    (ominous)
               It's gonna get him killed.

40   INT. THE FACTORY - SAME TIME   40   *

     Spike rolls around, livid, as Angel stands to the side and
     Drusilla plays with the puppy.   *

                         SPIKE
                    (bellows at Angel)
               Are you insane?! We're supposed to
               kill the bitch, not leave gag gifts
               in her friends' beds.

                         DRUSILLA
               But, Spike... the bad teacher was
               going to restore Angel's soul.

                         SPIKE
               And what if she did? If you ask me,
               I find myself preferring the old,
               Buffy-whipped Angelus. Because this
               new, improved one is definitely not
               playing with a full sack.

     Drusilla WHIMPERS like a hurt puppy.

                         SPIKE (cont'd)
               Hey, I love a good slaughter as much
               as the next bloke, but his hijinks
               will only serve to leave us with one
               incredibly brassed-off Slayer...

                                                      CONTINUED

40 CONTINUED: 40

                         ANGEL
               Don't worry, roller boy. We don't
               have anything to worry about. I've
               got everything under control.

Almost before the words are out of his mouth, a Molotov
cocktail hits the table, igniting it in a ROAR OF FLAME.

All three move away from the table, looking around.

ANGLE: ANGEL

An arrow hits him square in the shoulder. He stumbles back
in pain, struggling to take out the arrow and looks up to see

ANGLE: GILES

striding calmly toward him.

As he approaches, Giles pulls from his shoulder bag a
Louisville Slugger. In the same motion he swings the bat
into the flame, catching the end on fire.

Angel is just pulling the arrow out of his shoulder as Giles
hits him square in the face with the flaming baseball bat.

Angel falls back. He looks up at Giles, blood on his face,
smiling ruefully.

                         ANGEL (cont'd)
               Geez, what ever happened to wooden
               stakes?

Giles hits him over the shoulder, bringing him to his knees.

                         GILES
               They don't hurt enough.

He hits Angel again and again, the bat making flaming arcs as
Angel is driven further to the ground.

ANGLE ON: SPIKE AND DRUISILLA

Drusilla takes a step toward the fight, but Spike puts a hand   *
on her arm to stop her.

                         SPIKE
               Ahn-ahhh... no fair going into the
               ring unless he tags you first.

ANGLE: GILES AND ANGEL

                                                     CONTINUED

40 CONTINUED: (2)   40

Giles swings again, but Angel knocks the bat away. Comes up
at Giles, punches him hard, then grabs him in a choke hold.

                    ANGEL
          All right, you've had your fun. But
          you know what it's time for now?

Buffy comes up from behind Angel, staggers him with a kidney
punch. He lets go of Giles, gasping for breath, as Giles
drops to the ground unconscious.

                    BUFFY
          My fun.

She hits Angel, kicks him, drives him back.

ANGLE: SPIKE AND DRUSILLA

as they fade into the shadows, escaping.

ANGLE: THE FLAMES

as they spread to the chairs and nearby boxes.

Angel decks Buffy and takes off, scrambling up to the
gangway. Buffy runs after, jumps onto a box, thence to
another, thence to the gangway where she tackles Angel.

Buffy gains the upperhand as they spar, leaning Angel against
the railing, the fire raging below them.

                    ANGEL
          You know, even when I feed off other
          girls, the name I call out... is
          yours.

Suddenly Buffy sees

ANGLE: GILES

on the ground, out cold, the fire reaching closer to him.

Angel takes her moment of distraction to knock her down. He
takes off.

Buffy is momentarily torn but then she jumps down and drags
Giles to safety as he begins to regain consciousness.

They head out the door.

41   EXT. INDUSTRIAL PARK OUTSIDE THE FACTORY - CONTINUOUS   41

As Buffy and Giles are met by Willow, Xander and Cordelia.

                    WILLOW
          Buffy!

                    CORDELIA
          Are you okay?

Giles turns on Buffy.

                    GILES
               (not happy)
          Why did you come here? This was not
          your figh--

WHAP! Buffy decks Giles with a single, wicked, angry punch
to the face. He falls back, gets to his knees.

                    BUFFY
          You bastard!

                    GILES
               (weakly)
          You don't understand...

She is fighting back tears as she advances on him. He is
still on his knees, practically shaking.

                    BUFFY
          How could you do that? You're trying
          to get yourself killed? You can't!
          You can't leave me alone... not
          now... I can't do this by myself!

There's a lost girl in that last sentence. Giles stares at
her, despair draining out of him.

                    GILES
          Jenny...

Buffy goes to him, drops to her knees, holds him tightly. He
hangs limp in her arms, looking at nothing.

                    GILES (cont'd)
          Jenny...

The others stand, watch, as she holds him.

                    ANGEL (V.O.)
          Passion... is the source of hope...

42   EXT. GILES APARTMENT - NIGHT   42

As Giles approaches his front door, hesitates, then pulls
down the remnants of the yellow POLICE CRIME SCENE tape.

                    ANGEL (V.O.)
          ...and the cause of despair...

                                        DISSOLVE TO:

43   EXT. CEMETERY - DAY   43

CLOSE ON: A BUNCH OF FLOWERS

As they are carefully laid on the ground.

                    ANGEL (V.O.)

It is the source of life...

TILT UP: TO A TOMBSTONE - "JENNIFER CALENDAR"

                    ANGEL (V.O., cont'd)
          ...and the cause of death.

WIDER ANGLE

Giles and Buffy stand next to Jenny's grave.

                    GILES
          In my years as a Watcher, I've
          buried... too many people. Some I
          knew... most I didn't. Jenny is the
          first one that I've loved.

                    BUFFY
          Sometimes, I wonder if any good ever
          comes of it.

                    GILES
          Comes of what?

                    BUFFY
          Falling in love. Letting your
          emotions call the shots for you.
          Because if there is an upside, I sure
          haven't come across it.
                    (sighs)
          You're right about that rule of
          yours. You're the Watcher, I'm the
          Slayer...
                    (more)

                                             CONTINUED

43   CONTINUED: 43

                    BUFFY (cont'd)
          we don't have the luxury of passion.
          It just gets in the way. Life's
          easier without it.

                    GILES
          Yes. It's just not... life.

                    BUFFY
          I'm sorry I couldn't kill him for
          you... for her... when I had the
          chance.

44   INT. JENNY CALENDAR'S CLASSROOM - DAY   44

      Willow stands at the front of the classroom, a lesson plan
      notebook clutched in front of her. She is running the class
      for a day, but she gets no joy from the assignment.

                    BUFFY (V.O.)
          ...but I think I'm finally ready...

                    WILLOW
                  (muted)
          Principal Snyder has asked me to fill
          in for Ms. Calendar, until the new
          computer science teacher arrives...
          so, I'm just going to stick to the
          lesson plan that she left...

      Willow sets the lesson plan notebook on Jenny's desk,
      inadvertently knocking the 3.5 inch disk with the copy of
      Thesulah's translated Restoration Ritual over the edge.

      WE FOLLOW THE DISK, as it drops, getting wedged in the small
      space between the desk and the baseboard...

      Just out of sight.

                    BUFFY (V.O., cont'd)
          ...because I know now that there's
          nothing that's he's ever going to
          change him back to the Angel I fell
          in love with.

                                                      CONTINUED

44 CONTINUED: 44

As WE MOVE IN CLOSE ON JENNY'S HIDDEN COMPUTER DISK behind
the desk, we--

                                        BLACK OUT.

                      END OF SHOW

Giles (to Buffy): "What did you sing about?"

Buffy: "I, uh . . . don't remember. But it seemed perfectly normal."

Xander: "But disturbing. And not the natural order of things and do you think it'll happen again? 'Cause I'm for the natural order of things."

Only in Sunnydale could a breakaway pop hit be a portent of doom. When someone magically summons a musical demon named Sweet, the Scoobies are involuntarily singing and dancing to the tune of their innermost secrets. The truths that are uncovered are raw and painful, prompting the question, "where do we go from here?"

Now, in one complete volume, find the final shooting script of the acclaimed musical episode "Once More, With Feeling." Complete with color photos, production notes, and sheet music!

The Script Book: Once More, With Feeling

Available now from Simon Pulse
Published by Simon & Schuster

A magical incantation invokes in the three Halliwell sisters powers they've never dreamed of. As the Charmed Ones, they are witches charged with protecting innocents.But when Prue is killed at the hands of the Source, Piper and Phoebe believe the Power of Three to be broken.

That is, until their half-sister, Paige Matthews, arrives at the Manor, with a few tricks—and a few questions—of her own....

Look for a new title every other month! Original novels based on the hit television series created by Constance M. Burge.

Published by Simon Pulse

. . . A GIRL BORN
WITHOUT THE FEAR GENE

FEARLESS™

A SERIES BY
FRANCINE PASCAL

PUBLISHED BY SIMON & SCHUSTER

3029-01

Aaron Corbet isn't a bad kid—he's just a little different.

On the eve of his eighteenth birthday, Aaron is dreaming of a darkly violent and landscape. He can hear the sounds of weapons clanging, the screams of the stricken, and another sound that he cannot quite decipher. But as he gazes upward to the sky, he suddenly understands. It is the sound of great wings beating the air unmercifully as hundreds of armored warriors descend on the battlefield.

The flapping of angels' wings.

Orphaned since birth, Aaron is suddenly discovering newfound—and sometimes supernatural—talents. But not until he is approached by two men does he learn the truth about his destiny—and his own role as a liason between angels, mortals, and Powers both good and evil—some of whom are bent on his own destruction....

the

fallen

a new series by Thomas E. Snigoski

Book One available March 2003

From Simon Pulse

Published by Simon & Schuster

Once upon a time

is timely once again as fresh, quirky heroines breathe life into classic and much-loved characters.

Reknowned heroines master newfound destinies, uncovering a unique and original happily ever after. . . .

Historical romance and magic unite in modern retellings of well-loved tales.

✦✦✦✦✦

THE STORYTELLER'S DAUGHTER
by Cameron Dokey

BEAUTY SLEEP
by Cameron Dokey

SNOW
by Tracy Lynn